The Darcys of New Orleans

Maggie Mooha

PRAISE FOR *ELIZABETH IN THE NEW WORLD*

"JANE AUSTEN FANS! THIS IS FOR YOU!!!!! This is an extremely well written "sequel" to Jane Austen's Pride and Prejudice. The author skillfully takes the reader on a new journey when Elizabeth Bennett ventures to the New World, after her beloved Darcy dies in a duel involving his nemesis Wickham. But is Darcy really gone? Or has his aunt, Lady Catherine concocted a ruse to keep her nephew from the socially unworthy clutches of Elizabeth Bennett? A tale of romance, intrigue, passion, exotic locations, heroism, and one of the greatest love stories for the ages!" ~dandelackland

"A breathtakingly original twist and continuation on a cherished Austen classic, Elizabeth in the New World opens doors to "what-ifs" and imaginative, well thought out scenarios that will leave fans of the original book enthralled and satisfied. A well written, exciting novel that is both daring and unique. I look forward to more from this author!" ~Sebastian Moran

"This book is a fantastic continuation of the Elizabeth and Darcy story. I'd read before bed and tell myself, "just finish this chapter, then go to sleep." But it was hard, because I couldn't wait to read what would happen next! The characters were very well-developed, and the story compelling. Great ending, too. I can't wait for a sequel so I can continue on their journey." ~Amy Pippins

"I consider this among the outstanding Austen variations that I have read and give it my highest recommendation. This book has it all, an enduring love story amidst historical references to slavery, other social and class changes, and characters who grew in character while loving each other. The depth of emotion is wonderful. This is quite a masterpiece for a first book." ~Donna D. Krug

"All I expected was a light romance. This is a romance, all right, but it is also so much more. It's an exposé on the whole class system. I was immediately drawn into the adventure story, and the further I read, the more engrossing the story got. Mooha writes the characters in such a way that you really care about them. At the conclusion I was literally in tears." ~Madelyn

www.BOROUGHSPUBLISHINGGROUP.com

ISBN 978-1-951055-40-0

To family: those we are born to and those we choose

ACKNOWLEDGMENTS

This book took a lot of research, which was fun because I got to go to New Orleans. More about that later. The books I used the most were:

Creole – A History and Legacy of Louisiana's Free People of Color - edited by Sybil Kein
The Free People of Color in New Orleans, An Introduction by Mary Gehman
Jane Austen's England by Roy and Lesley Adkins

And, of course, *Pride and Prejudice* by Jane Austen

Another source that I used in portraying Elizabeth's troubles at the beginning of the book was a course I took on-line through the Beau Monde Group's Regency Academe concerning sex and childbirth. It was extremely helpful. They offer many such classes to both members and non-members. You will find them on Facebook.

A few notes on the characters: I had Philippe be an engineer because many free people of color sent their sons to France to study engineering. His invention to separate the sugar from the cane (triple pan evaporating system) was an actual invention by an African-American inventor, Norbert Rilleaux that he patented in 1843. You can find out more about it at this website https://blackinventor.com/norbert-rillieux. As for a mechanical device to harvest sugar cane, that would not be invented until 1958.

Also, I incorporated a woman who is still known in New Orleans as The Voodoo Queen, Marie Laveau. Some have her birth year as 1794, some as 1801. She would have been too young for my story if she had been born in 1801, so 1794 it was. She was known far and wide as a healer and practitioner of voodoo, but early in her life she made her living as a hairdresser after she was widowed. Many referred to her in those years as The Widow Paris. She was a free woman of color. Since she was a hairdresser for master and servant alike, she gathered much intel about wealthier households from their servants. This created an impression that she could "read minds" since she was privy to the secrets of many households through listening to the staff. If you are interested in finding out more, this website is one of many that I utilized https://allthatsinteresting.com/marie-laveau

You might also have noticed that all the women of color, even though they could move freely through New Orleans society, were required to cover their hair with a *tignon*, which was a decorated turban of sorts. It was rumored at the time that white women of high society were instrumental in getting that law passed since they were in competition for white men with the free women of color in town. Many of these free women were extremely beautiful and alluring, as many of them were of Senegalese descent and had come from Haiti as refugees during the revolution there.

I took great pains to make sure that the story was true to the dates in history when various events took place. This was true of the burning of Barataria by the Americans only a few months before the Battle of New Orleans. Why Jean Lafitte and his brother and their pirates threw in with the American cause is a mystery, since the British attempted to bribe them handsomely to join their side, and the American's destroyed their headquarters. Lafitte and his men were instrumental in the American victory at the Battle of Chalmette.

This brings us to the matter of the quadroon balls. I had never heard of them before my trip to New Orleans, but every book I read about the period and my guide on the Hidden History Tour (https://www.hiddenhistory.us) mentioned them. These gatherings were primarily for well-to-do young white men and young women of color These free women of color usually had one grandparent who was of African descent, therefore they were one-quarter African, hence the name quadroon. The purpose of these balls was to introduce these young men to free women of color who would be their wives in "left-handed marriages," or unofficial relationships. The system was called *plaçage*. These women were given property, they and their children inherited money and property due to these relationships, but their marriages were not recognized as legal. The girls' mothers would take care of all the contractual arrangements between her daughter and the young man.

At first, I was going to incorporate one of those balls into the story, but the more I read about them, I realized that none of the characters, save Poppy and her two youngest daughters, could attend. Then, I came upon an article that debunked the entire notion that quadroon balls ever took place. If you are interested, here is where I found it https://afropunk.com/2016/10/know-your-black-history-deconstructing-the-quadroon-ball. You can make up your own mind about what happened. In any case, the Darcys needed to be there, so a tweaked the system a bit. Also, Elizabeth Ann had half African blood, not a quarter… Artistic license.

As for the two sisters joining the Ursalines together, that was pure fiction. There were no orders of free women of color at that time, and no order that would accept free women of color into their ranks. Later in the century however, Henriette Delille, a free woman of color, founded the Sisters of the Holy Family in 1842. It was the first black order of sisters in the city and they did much good work caring for orphans, tending the sick during the yellow fever epidemic, and conducting catechism classes for their community. The Sisters of the Holy Family still exists today.

Also, the scene in which Emma pricks her finger and Philippe's and mixes their blood is based on a true story of a man who so wanted to marry the love of his life who was a woman of color, that he mixed their blood in a similar way and then claimed the "one drop of Negro blood" rule that permeated the south. Their love story did not end well.

General Jackson did enlist the help of many free men and women of color during the Battle of New Orleans. There are some that claim that the commander of the British forces, General Packenham, was felled from his horse and killed by a shot fired by a free man of color. The free women of color volunteered to nurse the wounded and provide other supportive roles during the battle. Jackson's speech that I quoted was, in fact his, but the promises he made to the freemen who volunteered to fight were never kept. The legislature would not honor them.

You may also wonder at the Darcys' seemingly *laissez faire* attitude in raising their children. I think we all pressume that the Victorian "spare the rod and spoil the child" was always the attitude in childrearing in England, but it was not. The Georgians, especially those with wealth, were quite lenient with their children up to a certain age, usually seven, considered the age of reason. If you would like to find out more, I found my information here: www.historyextra.com – *The Georgian Guide to Perfect Parenting*

There are numerous websites and articles that I used to help verify facts that I use in the story. Here are a few of them:

- jeanlafitte.net
- Jstor – The Patterson and Ross Raid on Barataria
- reddit.com – Ask An Historian
- Black Voice News – Slave Names in the Americas
- Free People of Color in Louisiana – LSU Libraries
- blackinventor.com/norbert-rilleaux/
- William Willberforce and His Circle of Friends by Richard Gathro
- www.mylearning.org

I hope you enjoy reading the story as much as I enjoyed writing it.

THE DARCYS OF NEW ORLEANS

It is right it should be so
Man was made for Joy & Woe
And when this we rightly know
Thro the World we safely go

–William Blake

Chapter 1

Darcy rushed into his house in town and slammed the door. "How is she? Where is she?" He nearly threw his hat and coat at John, his waiting butler.

"Your wife is upstairs in her chamber, sir, with the surgeon."

"Oh, good lord." His heart leapt to his throat. Quickly, he lunged for the stairs. He knew if the surgeon had been called, he should expect the worst.

Emma came rushing from the drawing room. "At last, Father." She grasped his arm, her expression agitated. "We sent for you hours ago."

"What do you mean, 'hours ago'?" He led his daughter toward the stairway. "I came as soon as I received your message." *Hours ago? Blast.* He realized what had happened. They needed his vote today and his cohorts in Parliament had kept the message from him. He could feel his anger rising. He would deal with them later. Now, all that mattered was Elizabeth.

As they climbed the stairs to the upper floor, Emma told him, "They will not let me in her bedchamber… Something went wrong with the baby." She looked away. He knew it was embarrassing for his daughter to mention, much less discuss, such things with him. "It is too soon."

When she turned back to him, he read her worry. "I know."

He began to pull his arm from her grasp, but she held on tightly. "Benji is there in front of her door like a little temple dog. I told him to go to the nursery, but he would not listen to me."

Darcy shook his head. "I will deal with your brother." He kissed Emma on the forehead and bounded up the rest of the stairs, taking them two at a time. From the end of the long hallway, he could see his son sitting on the floor in front of the French doors of his wife's room. As he approached, the boy jumped to his feet and held out his hand.

"You cannot go in there, Papa." He stood firm. "The surgeon said."

"The surgeon be damned," Darcy stated. Benji would not waver. Darcy could see he was breathing hard and had a frightened but determined look in his eye. As Darcy made a move to physically remove him from the doorway, Benji asked, "Is Mama going to die, Papa?" His eyes were filling.

"Let us see what the surgeon says, all right?" Darcy asked rather more softly than before, stroking the boy's head. "I will knock and see if he can come out and tell us about Mama." The boy visibly relaxed. Before Darcy could knock on the doors, they opened, and the surgeon stepped out.

"My wife?"

"Is resting. I gave her a sleeping draught. Let the *accoucheur* and the women do their work. She will sleep for several hours now."

"When can I see her?" His voice broke slightly.

"Soon. Let us talk first." He looked gravely into Darcy's face and took him by the arm and led him down the hallway. Benji followed. Darcy turned to look at his son. That boy was nothing if not determined. "Go stand by the door and keep watch. There's a good lad."

"All right, Papa." Darcy watched as his son resumed his place by the bedchamber door.

Darcy ran his fingers through his hair as he and the surgeon walked out of earshot. He was so agitated he could barely stand still. "Tell me… Will she live?" Darcy's stomach was churning.

"If there is no fever, I believe she has a chance at life. But…" The surgeon paused. "There will be no baby."

Darcy swallowed and nodded his head. "I presumed as much. Still, after a while…" The surgeon held up his hand. Darcy left off speaking.

"There will be no more children, Mr. Darcy. No more children."

"Are you quite sure?"

"Quite sure, sir. I am afraid that in the interests of staunching the bleeding, there were… things that had to be done. I hope you will forgive me for taking such measures and for disregarding the rules of modesty."

Whatever the surgeon had done was done, and there was no purpose in questioning it now. He was fairly sure the man dispensed with the sheet that covered Elizabeth and did his work without it. Modesty? What did Darcy care of modesty if there was a chance that Elizabeth would survive?

The surgeon took advantage of the pause and continued, "The *accoucheur* you hired is a follower of that William Hunter fellow. The man had the sheets of the bed freshened before your wife was well into her labour. He even washed the birthing chair, and had the audacity to ask me to wash my hands and face. How ridiculous."

The surgeon continued on in this vein, but Darcy had long ceased listening. He finally interrupted the diatribe. "Does she know? Does my wife know there will be no more children?"

"Yes. I told her. She was quite beside herself, hence the sleeping draught."

Darcy knew how much Elizabeth wanted this baby. There had been so many disappointments between the arrival of Emma and the birth of Bennet Fitzwilliam Darcy, or Benji as everyone called him save himself and his grandfather. Now, finally, another possibility to expand their little family, and it again ended in tragedy. Darcy was lost in these thoughts as the surgeon's voice interrupted them.

"Once she recovers..." He stopped mid-sentence. Darcy knew what that meant. The surgeon was saying *if* she recovered. "She can live a normal life. After a time, she can resume all her normal activities." He looked up into Darcy's face. "All her normal, marital duties, if you understand me, sir." Darcy nodded his head, unable to discuss such a thing with this man. "Husbands in this sort of situation are concerned about such matters, and rightly so." Darcy swallowed and nodded again. The surgeon turned and began walking back to Elizabeth's bedchamber. "I will gather my things and be off then. Call if you have any further need of me, but I think rest, good food, and patience are all that she will need now. If we are lucky." He opened the door and looked inside. "You will be able to see her in a few minutes, but she will not wake for some time." The surgeon disappeared into Elizabeth's room and Darcy was left standing outside with a fretful six-year-old looking up at him.

Now, with the hope of Elizabeth's return to health, and knowing he would see her in a few minutes, he turned his attention to his son. "Why did you not return to the nursery when Emma told you to do so?" His tone was stern and instantly he regretted it.

"I wanted to see if Mama was all right," Benji squeaked. Darcy took a breath and pulled his wits about him. Of course. The boy was as fearful for his mother as Darcy had been for his beloved wife.

"I will not be having a new brother or sister, will I?"

Darcy looked down at his son. Obviously, he heard everything the surgeon said. It always amazed him how children could not hear anything when one was shouting for them, but they could hear a whisper that they were not supposed to hear. The poor child was learning cruel lessons too early because of his loyalty and his obstinance. Darcy could see the boy's eyes brimming with tears. It was all Darcy could do not to break down himself. He crouched down so that his head was even with his son's.

"No, son. No brother or sister." The boy swallowed hard and would not look his father in the face. He said nothing. Darcy knew that stance.

"Is Mama going to die too, like the baby?" He was still not looking into his father's face and blinking back tears. Darcy could stand it no longer. He took the boy in his arms. Bennet threw his arms around his father's neck and began sobbing in earnest.

"It is all right, Bennet. It will be all right." He said these words to comfort the child, even though he did not believe them himself. After a few minutes, Benji let go of his father's embrace. Darcy took out a handkerchief and wiped the boy's eyes. "Blow your nose, Bennet," Darcy said softly. The boy did as he was told.

One of the French doors opened softly, and the surgeon emerged, closing the door quietly behind him. He looked at Darcy. "I will take my leave now."

"Yes, of course." Darcy shook himself free from his own thoughts. "I will walk you down."

"No need. I know the way." As the surgeon walked away, Bennet took his father by the hand. "Papa, why don't you call me 'Benji' like everyone else? Mama does."

"I named you Bennet to honor your grandfather, your mother's father. That is what your friends and intimates will call you once you are older."

"I like Benji better."

"It makes people think your name is Benjamin."

"Oh, I don't mind."

"I mind." Darcy opened the door to Elizabeth's room. "Now be quiet. Mama is sleeping."

***

Elizabeth's eyes fluttered and she felt a small, cool hand on her forehead. She turned and peered into her son's worried face. "Are you awake, Mama?"

"Oh, Benji," she whispered. "What are you doing here? Where's Papa?"

"I am right here, Lizzy." Darcy was across the room, turning away from the window. Elizabeth knew that he was opening the windows to her room to let in the fresh air. Ever since his own accidental wounding in that duel with Wickham, he would always open the windows in a sick room despite the common belief that fresh air would cause one to catch cold. Stubborn man. Still, the cool air did make her feel better.

"You slept a long time. Papa and I were worried."

"Oh, I am sorry you were worried, dear heart," she said, looking into his face, and then, without any ability to stop them, the tears began to flow. Elizabeth could not control her weeping, and watched helplessly as Darcy bundled his son out of the room.

"Your mother will see you later, Bennet. Now go and find your sister, there's a good lad."

"But Mama—"

"I will see to your mother. Now, go. Find Emma." Elizabeth could hear her son still protesting as the door closed.

Darcy returned to Elizabeth, knelt by the bed, and cradled her against him. By this time, she was sobbing as if her heart would break. It was broken, and the more she thought of the loss she had suffered, the less control she had over herself. Darcy, bless him, said nothing comforting. She did not want words at this moment, only his presence.

He produced one of her kerchiefs that stood at the ready on her night table and touched each eye as her weeping began to subside. She took it from him and covered her nose and mouth. Taking a few deep breaths, she finally croaked out, "My goodness. What a display." Darcy kissed her on the forehead.

"Are you in much pain, Lizzy?"

16

Yes, she was in pain, but while the laudanum had dulled the ache in her body, nothing could relieve her heartache. When she looked up at his sympathetic expression, she nodded slightly, and her eyes began to fill once again. He seemed to sense what she needed.

"Shall I leave you to rest, my love? Or shall I stay?"

Elizabeth wanted him near, but knew that she would weep until she was drained if she had to look at his sympathetic expression again. "Perhaps you could send in Marie?"

He kissed her again. "I am at your service," he said gently, and rang for her maid. Elizabeth closed her eyes again and heard him exchange a few words with Marie before sleep engulfed her again.

***

The next few days were spent watching and waiting for signs of puerperal fever, which took the lives of so many women after they had given birth. Being at home seemed to be a talisman against such infections, although no one had any idea why. The poorer women who gave birth at the lying-in hospitals fared much worse. Darcy hoped that his wealth was a shield strong enough to protect his family. He prayed that it might be so.

Darcy ceased his attendance at Parliament during this time and instead fretted at home while mounds of documents were delivered each day. He tried mightily not to spend every free moment in Elizabeth's room, but failed most miserably. She slept a great deal, which he hoped was a sign that her body was mending.

Retreating daily to his library, Darcy forced himself to read through the masses of documents that had accrued during this last session of Parliament. His mind was not on his work, but on the woman upstairs who had come so close to death. As he looked down at the papers scattered over his desk, he rubbed his forehead and began again. Nothing he was reading was penetrating his apprehensive brain. What if the surgeon was incorrect? What if he told him Elizabeth would recover only to extricate himself from Darcy's grasp?

Darcy knew he was completely unreasonable where Elizabeth and his children were concerned. He also knew the surgeon would do no such thing, but his mind went, as it usually did, from one catastrophe to another. This was exactly the thinking that drove him on to throw over the very essence of who he was and sign on as a lowly deckhand on a merchant ship to follow Elizabeth to Grenada all those years ago. No, that was not quite right. He did not throw over who he was: only the trappings of who he was. If he had learnt anything from that experience, it was that his social position and his estate were superficial paraphernalia and had nothing to do the essence of a gentleman: duty, sacrifice, faithfulness, and honor.

And what of love? Oh, he did love her then. When he sat to think of it as he was doing now, he admitted to himself that perhaps he loved her even more now. Why did everyone seek love with such single-mindedness? To do so produced this constant aching in the heart, especially at times like this when the spectre of unthinkable loss stole into their lives.

On the evening of the fourth day, there was no sign of fever and Elizabeth began to take some solid food for the first time. Darcy could feel himself inhale the first easy breath since this entire episode began. He still had not spoken to Elizabeth about the surgeon's pronouncement. She seemed fragile, and he resolved to speak to her when she was stronger. Bennet was as bothersome as a gadfly and had to be shooed from his mother's room often. Nearly every time Darcy entered her bedchamber, he was sitting with her reading or conversing. Elizabeth, for her part, had a far-off look, and only glanced at her son if he spoke directly to her. Darcy observed her in this state and his heart sank. Even as her body recovered, her spirit remained terribly wounded.

Nearly a week passed, and Darcy was again in his library attempting to keep himself abreast of what was happening in Parliament in his absence. It was evening and the house was quiet.

Emma entered the library. "I am sorry to disturb you, Father." She was dressed to go out. It took Darcy a moment to return from his thoughts and direct his attention to his daughter.

"You are dressed well." Darcy could not keep the disapproval from his tone. What was that girl thinking? Her mother had been on death's door only a few days ago.

"Have you forgotten, Father? With all that has happened, I believe you have. I am to dine with the Gordon-Smythes this evening. Charlie Bingley is calling for me in a few minutes." He watched as she caught sight of a mirror in the corner of the room and began ministrations to her hair.

Darcy could scarcely believe his ears. Surely Emma would cancel her engagement and stay at home with her mother. He was greatly vexed, but he would not let her know it. She knew her own mind, and much like her mother, he knew his anger would only inflame his daughter's will.

"How can you think of going to a gathering with your cousin when your mother is in such a state?" He tried mightily to mask his irritation.

She turned to look at him. He was already standing. "What am I do to for her?" The imperiousness of her attitude was quite evident. "You told me yourself that the danger has passed. My presence at home is neither here nor there."

He should not have named her after his Aunt Catherine's mother. He could hear his aunt's haughty tone in her voice. A vein was beating in his temple. Rather than leaping over the desk to take hold of her and shake her, which crossed his mind, he took a deep breath and sat down again, leaning his elbows on the surface and weaving his fingers together. He pressed them against his mouth. He took another breath and closed his eyes. What to do with such a daughter? Then it dawned on him. "Is that Montjoy fellow to be there tonight?" He looked up at her. She would not meet his gaze but twirled about to face the mirror again and began fussing with her hair.

"Perhaps."

He knew her well enough to know that she was attempting to lie to him without actually lying. It infuriated him. "You know I do not approve of him. He is a rake and a reprobate." He then rose from the desk and crossed the room to her.

She turned to look at him. "Oh, Father. There is not a young man alive on this earth of whom you would approve. Edmund Montjoy is amusing, and," she hesitated a moment and stepped back from her father, "and he likes me. And I like him."

"You are blind to his character," Darcy said sternly.

Emma shook her curls and turned a steady gaze on her father. "I think he may ask me to marry him."

Darcy was quite taken aback by this news. Apparently, circumstances between his daughter and this Montjoy character had proceeded apace right under his nose. How many times, at some social gathering or other, had Elizabeth laid her hand on his arm to prevent him from crossing the room and interrupting an exchange between his daughter and that... that... profligate?

"I forbid you to go," Darcy said sternly. With that, there was a knock on the door, and John's voice could be heard.

"Sir?"

"Come in, John." He did not take his eyes off his daughter.

"Sir, Mr. Charles Bingley the Younger is here for Miss Emma." Darcy looked over at his daughter. To her credit, she did not move, but waited for her father to speak. He turned his attention to the butler. "Have him wait in the drawing room."

"Very good, sir." The door to the library closed. The two stood apart in the stance of two adversaries.

"How can you leave your mother?" he asked again. Her expression seemed to soften for a moment. Her face then took on that cross aspect he had observed in her since she was tiny child.

"Why does she keep trying to have all these babies? It is mortifying." She turned away from her father.

She could not have wounded him more if she had struck him. "It is not for you to judge your mother." Darcy tried to elicit a coolness he did not feel. It was all he could do to contain himself.

She turned upon him. "Is it her or is it you who wants another heir in case something happens to Benji?" He could hear her voice breaking slightly. She had gone too far, and she knew it. Not able to look at her another moment, he turned from her and strode across the room.

He stood with his back to her for a long moment, and finally turned to look at her. "Such things are not of your concern, but since you brought it up, I will tell you." He could see her shifting and clenching and unclenching her hands. She would not look at him directly.

"No, Father, I am sorry, you need not..."

"No. No. You asked and I will tell you. I do not care if your mother and I have any more children. To be frank with you, when we first married, I was hoping for children, but would have loved your mother no less if there were to be none at all. When you were born, it was one of the happiest days of my life, and so it was with your brother Bennet." He stopped for a moment to gather himself. Emotional outbursts of this sort were exceedingly unnerving. He turned away from her for a moment. There was no sound in the room. When he directed his gaze to her again, he hoped that at this distance, she could not see that his eyes were wet with unshed tears. Swallowing hard, he continued, "Our family is perfection itself to me." He paused again, and then more to himself than to her he said, "Perhaps I should say all of this to your mother." He ran his hands through his hair again.

At that, Emma ran to him and threw her arms around him as he stood unmoving. She leaned her head against his chest. "I am sorry, Father. So sorry." He disengaged his arm and patted her lightly on the back but said nothing. There was another knock at the door.

"Sir?"

"A moment, John."

"Oh, I forgot all about Charlie. I will tell him to leave."

Darcy sighed. "No, now that I think of it, perhaps you should go." She looked up at him incredulously. "It will avoid explanations. I believe your mother will tell her sister and the rest of her family what happened in her own time. Your Aunt Jane need not hear it from Charlie." Emma nodded. She pulled a kerchief from her sleeve and dabbed her eyes.

"Now, go smile and greet your cousin."

She walked to the door, and as she reached it, he said, "And stay away from that Montjoy fellow." She turned again, and he saw that arch look he had seen so many times on the face of his beloved Elizabeth. She raised her eyebrow, turned, and was gone.

***

With the encounter with her father almost entirely forgotten, Emma was enjoying herself exceedingly. The Gordon-Smythes fancied themselves matchmakers of sorts and had Edmund Montjoy escort Emma into dinner and he seated himself next to her. Edmund was amusing, and seemingly doted on her every word.

"Shall you join our shooting party next month?" he asked Charlie Bingley when he tore his gaze away from Emma.

"I expect not. I have one more year at Oxford."

"Oh, how dull," Edmund retorted and smiled his glittering smile at Emma. "I tried Oxford, but found all that Latin tiresome." He swiveled his head around at the other guests.

Lady Gordon-Smythe laughed. "You were ousted, Edmund, and everyone knows it."

"I was ousted because I could not bring myself to...conjugate," he said with a wink. This was what Emma found so charming about him. His ability to play with words. How clever.

"I heard that you spent almost *all* your time at Oxford 'conjugating,'" Thomas Bellum said pointedly. This sent the whole table into gales of laughter. Only Charlie Bingley did not seem amused. Emma sent him a pointed look across the table. How odd. The elder Charles Bingley, her father's friend, was so affable and charming while his son was so irritatingly serious. Emma found herself pitying the girl who would get such a bad-tempered husband.

The conversation drifted into calmer waters and Lord Gordon-Smythe suggested that everyone, not only the ladies, adjourn to the drawing room for piquet. As Emma rose from the table, her host caught her eye and winked. Yes, the Gordon-Smythes did consider themselves matchmakers.

Edmund was always at Emma's side and was her partner at cards. She did notice Charlie glaring at her from time to time when she could wrest her attention from Edmund, and he could catch her eye. He always behaved like an older brother, even though they were scarcely two years apart. No doubt he would spend the carriage ride home scolding her for her frivolous behavior. No matter. She was a woman of eighteen and knew what she wanted, and she wanted Edmund Montjoy. And she was sure that he wanted her. It would be a task, however, to gain her father's approval. She would enlist her mother's help once she recovered. Her father always acquiesced to her mother's wishes. Well, nearly always.

Edmund took advantage of a lull in the festivities to invite her out to look at the garden. Emma's heart began to flutter. She must not seem too eager. She adopted an expression that was as bored as she could muster and consented to being escorted out on the balcony. Edmund had not yet kissed her. Perhaps that was his plan. She had already decided to allow it. After that, she was sure of a proposal.

She leaned against the balustrade and gazed out at the garden. Edmund, rather than standing next to her, walked up behind her and ran his hands down her arms. Oh, this was unexpected. She felt a shiver run through her entire body. A most pleasurable shiver. "Emma," he whispered into her hair. She could feel the heat of his body, which he pressed close to her back. He should not be doing what he was doing. She should not be allowing it. She did not care.

"Oh, Edmund," she cried softly, and turned to embrace him. At that, the balcony doors swung open and Charlie was upon them. Edmund disengaged himself immediately and nearly jumped back.

"It is time to go home," Charlie said sternly, while looking squarely at Edmund. Then turning to his cousin, he said, "I promised your father we would return before midnight and it is nearly that now."

Stupid Charlie, Emma thought to herself. *He has ruined everything.* She looked between the two men. Before she could say a word, Lady Gordon-Smythe trounced onto the terrace. "Oh, there you are, my dears. Coffee?"

"I would love some, thank you." Edmund made a charming bow to Emma and brushed past Charlie without a look.

"No thank you, my lady." Charlie took Emma's hand. "We need to be going now." Emma did not object although she was annoyed with her cousin. She knew her manners well enough not to make a scene. Charlie had probably saved her from being the subject of gossiping tongues. She would be patient. Edmund Montjoy would come to her. She was sure of it.

***

Nearly seven weeks had passed, and Elizabeth had long since left her bed and rejoined the household. The Season was nearly over and the Darcys had accomplished what they had set out to do. Emma Darcy was out in society. Elizabeth's sister, Jane, and her husband, Charles, and even their son Charlie helped immensely in that regard, escorting Emma to various balls and dinners and a myriad of social engagements. She knew her husband was not much interested in social gatherings and was adamant that he would not attend any assemblies without her. It was a cause for much whispering and conjecture among their fashionable set, but now that Emma was launched, Elizabeth was as unconcerned with such things as her husband usually was.

The next few weeks were a blur. She wanted to return to her life as she had known it before, but she seemed drained. Drained of hope. This had been her tenth pregnancy, but she had produced only two children. Most had ended before she even felt the quickening of the life within her. Her sister Jane seemed to have a child every other year, and she and Charles could boast of a fine family of seven children. Of course, Jane had her sorrows as well. Two of her children died before they reached the age of reason. One was stillborn, and the other died of scarlet fever when he was only three.

Elizabeth tried to think her way out of her mood by reminding herself of all her blessings. She had two healthy children, one who would be an heiress in her own right and one who would inherit Pemberley. She had a husband who loved her and was the soul of patience. She lived much of the year at Pemberley, which was a grand and beautiful house. She had a house in town, and everyone in their rarified circle treated her and her family with the utmost deference.

Even though all these thoughts coursed through her brain, even as she recognized the logic of them, she felt alone and desolate. Why could the heart not follow the mind? Why did it want what it could not have? In the midst of her unhappiness, she berated herself, for as she saw it: there was no reason for such despair.

***

With Parliament adjourning in a few weeks, Darcy decided to end their stay in London early. He watched as Elizabeth organized the household for their move back to Pemberley while Emma made it plain that they were leaving town much too early, not even staying for Ascot. But Darcy was impatient for home. It also crossed his mind that her mood might improve if Elizabeth left this house and all its sorrows.

On the last night in the Mayfair house, Darcy dismissed his man and continued his undressing himself. He sat at the end of the bed, removing his pantaloons, congratulating himself that his figure could still support such a close-fitting garment. He attributed his strong physique to his insistence on walking from Mayfair to Parliament each day. It created quite a scandal among the members at first, but as time wore on, they found many other things to gossip about, and his habits were relegated to eccentricity.

As he pulled the last leg free and stood shirtless in his undergarments, Elizabeth stole through the adjoining door.

"Lizzy." His face broke into a broad smile. He had done what the surgeon, the midwife, and the doctor had suggested. He had left her to heal and to decide on her own when she would return to his bed. As she approached in the candlelight, her expression revealed itself to him. She was not smiling. In fact, her face revealed nothing at all.

She took his hand and he stood to face her. She was dressed only in a shift and looked down as she took his hand in both of hers. He began to speak, but she gently touched his lips with two fingers to silence him. After a long moment, she looked up at him and led him to the bed.

How many times had they made love in this very bed? How many times had he touched and tenderly embraced her and whispered her name? How many times had she called his name aloud in the fury of passion? His name. How they struggled with it at first. Fitzwilliam was too cumbersome. William or Will did not seem to suit him. Fitz was unthinkable. When she was being playful, she would call him Squire as a private term of affection that only they and a few others understood. No, she called him what the world called him—Darcy.

"Touch me, Darcy," she said. Now, she had finally come to him and he would not disappoint her. Elizabeth relieved him of his remaining clothing and stroked his swollen member, and he quivered in anticipation. She turned from him and drew the shift over her head and tossed it to the floor. In the flickering candlelight, he marveled at how her body, despite two children and all its recent ravages, looked perfect. He desired her more than he could tell her.

He kissed her ardently and took her breasts in his hands, massaging them gently, running his fingers softly over her nipples. She ran her fingers up from his manhood, through the hair on his abdomen and over his chest. She kissed him on the nape of his neck as she guided him into her.

Darcy wanted so much to prolong this moment, but she would have none of it. It was just as well. All the emotion and desire for her that he had tried to contain over these past few weeks were channeled into this act of love.

She matched his every thrust, driving herself forward, impaling herself on him, her legs wrapped around him and her hands clutching his back. It was as if she could not get enough of him. He did not want to fail her on this night, and it took all his force of will to control himself until she was ready. When he felt her tighten around him, he dove into her one last time and felt her embrace him in her entirety. He kissed her neck and down to her collarbone and finally looked into her face.

He did not know what he expected: ecstasy, satiation? Even tears perhaps. What he saw, however, was a deep sadness, almost a flatness of expression. For a few precious moments they were one, and now, she retreated into herself again. It was usual for Elizabeth to ask him not to withdraw, but they would lie, connected to one another until that became physically impossible. Tonight, she rolled out from under him, retrieved her shift, and pulled it over her head to cover herself. No, this was not his Elizabeth. She turned and walked toward the door of her chamber.

"Lizzy," he called, a little too loudly. "Where are you going?"

"To my room." She was still walking, not looking back. Darcy leapt from the bed and caught up with her. He turned her to him. It was then she looked up at him, tears shining in her eyes. "I do not know what is wrong with me," she sobbed. "I…"

"Come. Come back to bed. You never have to explain yourself to me. Come back and sleep here with me. Do you… Do you want to do that?"

She looked up at him again, and he thought for a moment she would bolt like some small, frightened animal. Instead, she took both of his hands in hers.

"I am sorry for everything, my dearest." She looked down at the floor. "I have failed you, and I am sorry."

"Failed me? You have done nothing of the sort. You have nothing to be sorry for, dear, dear Lizzy." He kissed her forehead, letting his lips linger there. Then he put his arm around her shoulder, and she allowed him to turn her back to his bed. Their bed.

"We are together. We have two beautiful children. In fact, a family much like the one in which I grew up, Georgiana and myself." He lifted her chin and looked into her eyes. "I want nothing more. Nothing more. Only you, my dearest." She bit her lip and put her arm around his waist.

He lifted his nightshirt from the end of the bed and pulled it over his head. He then joined her in bed. She laid her head on his chest and he kissed her again.

"There is nothing that the two of us cannot overcome, Lizzy. You are not alone in your suffering. In everything you do, you take me with you. You know that, do you not?"

He could feel her nodding her head, but she would not look up at him. He sighed and turned from her to snuff the candles.

"I want to go home," she said in a voice so soft it was barely audible.

"We are leaving for Pemberley tomorrow," he said, confused.

"No," she said. "I want to go to Longbourn."

Chapter 2

Darcy was displeased, to say the least, that he would be returning home alone. It was decided that the Mayfair house would be closed for the season, and Darcy would return to Pemberley to take stock of progress on the farmland. His family would join him later. The planting season had passed, and full summer was upon them, so there would be much activity on the Pemberley estate.

Emma and Bennet would accompany their mother to Longbourn. Emma was about much wailing and gnashing of teeth. Among other grievances, she lamented that her life was now over, having been snatched from her inaugural year in society. Her father knew better. There would be other years, and other balls and assemblies and gossip and triviality. Unfortunately, there would also be other Edmund Montjoys. He suspected that all this anguish was partially due to her attachment to that rake.

As Darcy saw it, social amusements for her were stretching out as far as the eye could see. Whereas he dreaded such things, she embraced them as her life's blood. Nonetheless, she would accompany her mother to Longbourn. It would do her good to taste of family duty and obligations. If she was not a child anymore, as she claimed, then she could begin to take up the mantle of adulthood.

There was much to do for their departure, none of which concerned Darcy, so he stood helplessly watching the staff run to and fro. Finally, he retreated to his library. There was a heap of unopened post that had accumulated over the last fortnight that he should see to. It also allowed him to escape the hubbub and take his mind off his family's imminent departure.

As he casually sorted through one letter after another, an envelope caught his eye. The postage upon it was foreign, as was the look of the envelope. He knew its origin immediately. Rushing up to his wife's chamber, he opened the door to find her sitting among trunks that had been packed for Pemberley, dabbing her eyes with her handkerchief.

"What is it, dearest?" He strode toward her.

"Oh, I think I may be making a mistake. I should stay here or return with you to Pemberley. My place is with you." She spoke those words, but sounded unconvinced.

"I would not disagree for the most part," he said, kneeling on the rug next to her and taking her hand, "but your father has not seen you for a great while, and the trip will do you good. I will join you shortly. All is well. Do not worry." He did his best to reassure her, but from the look on her face, he was falling short of the mark. It was then he remembered the letter.

"I nearly forgot. This came for you." He handed it to her. "I am sorry that I let it sit upon my desk for so long, but…" He stopped talking when he could see the light in her eyes as she took the message from his hands.

"It is from Poppy," she said with more enthusiasm than he had heard from her in a long, long while. She held it in her hands, turning it over and over.

Poppy. It was she who had helped him in his deliverance of Elizabeth from all that carnage in Grenada the day Fedon ordered the English prisoners to be slaughtered. It was Poppy who'd risked her life for her friend, and then would not allow him to put her and her children under his protection. She had wanted to stay and take the chance that the rebellion would succeed, and she could be free. Save Elizabeth, Poppy was the bravest woman Darcy had ever met, although he had only met her a moment. A moment he would never forget, and for which he would be forever grateful.

The rebellion had not succeeded, and Poppy had disappeared. After Emma was born Elizabeth finally received word, Poppy was alive, safe, and free in New Orleans, a colony that changed hands between the French and the Spanish and was now a part of the United States. The United States with which the British were presently at war. He shook himself from his reverie.

"Are you going to read it?" he asked, smiling at her. She looked up into his face. For the first time in weeks, he saw a genuine smile on her face.

"Of course, of course." Carefully, she broke the seal and retrieved the missive.

"Darcy," she said as he turned to leave. The letter fell to her lap. She held her hand out to him. He stepped back toward her and she grasped his hand and drew him to her. Thinking she wanted to whisper something, he leaned in close. She then touched his cheek and kissed him, tentatively at first, and then with such lingering tenderness that it took his breath away.

When they finally parted, he looked at her, astonished. "I am trying, my love. I am." Her eyes filled with tears again.

"I know." He cupped her face with his hand, running his thumb along her cheek. He kissed her again on the forehead. "I will leave you to read your letter."

As he reached the door, he paused and turned to look at her again. The light had returned to her eyes for barely a moment. This helplessness he felt was intolerable. He felt as though he was reaching for her in the dark.

***

Darcy had a bittersweet homecoming. He brought with him not only his family troubles but also a sense of guilt that he had not stayed for the closing of Parliament. Still, they had again postponed arguments on the slave trade. The issue had surfaced in Parliament last year, spearheaded by William Wilberforce and supported by his Clapham Sect, and also by Darcy, but the rest of the members had not taken up the cause. Darcy was sure there would be a protracted fight. Perhaps the slave trade would not be banned for years, but he was willing to be persistent.

Ever since his adventure in Grenada, and meeting Poppy, he made it his mission to support the abolition of slavery. He and Elizabeth had even socialized with Wilberforce and his wife, Barbara, although he did not share their religious fervor. Still, Darcy believed the abolitionist's motives to be good, and Wilberforce could count on him as an ally. Darcy, for his part, was relieved to leave all the arguing and plotting that was the daily bread of Parliament behind him and return to his estate. The harvest would soon be upon them.

"Good mornin' to ye, Squire," Foster said as Darcy's horse cantered to a stop in the high meadow above the hayfields. The cows seemed to be contented enough to munch upon their grass and many did not even look up when the master of the estate approached.

"Good morning to you, Foster." Darcy dismounted. He offered his hand to his friend in a hearty handshake.

"It's good to see ye return, Squire."

"All goes well, I trust?" Darcy knew this to be true, for during his short ride this morning, he could see nothing amiss. For a former sailor and army scout, Foster excelled at running a farm. It was not a mistake to leave him in charge of overseeing Pemberley once Mr. Perkins retired to his cottage.

"Very well, sir. We had a good calving season in the spring, and there promises to be hay and corn a-plenty for the winter," Foster said, and then continued in a softer tone, "I am sorry to hear of your wife's troubles, Squire."

Well, there it was. The news had come ahead of him, as Darcy expected. Darcy merely nodded and looked away. Foster put a friendly hand on his shoulder. With that touch, Darcy turned to his friend.

Trying to stave off the descent into sentimentality, Darcy changed the subject. "And your family?"

"All's well there, sir. William has a family o' his own now, and Jemima, Peter, and Luke are all still goin' to school in the village. We are thinkin' of apprenticin' Peter to the blacksmith. Wouldn't 'urt now, would it, to 'ave a blacksmith in the family?" he asked, smiling.

"No, indeed it would not." The men stood in silence for a long while. The deference Foster showed Darcy always made him feel a bit awkward. After all, if it was not for Foster's tutelage aboard the *Marlin*, Darcy might not be standing here today.

How young he was and so filled with passion then. He threw over his gentlemanly ways and signed aboard a merchant ship as a deckhand. What he learned from Foster had many times kept him from falling to his death from atop the rigging. And Foster, for his part, left a good wage and position on the ship when they landed in Grenada to endure the perils of warfare and revolution and to stand by Darcy in his quest to find his beloved Elizabeth.

Every time Foster called him sir or doffed his cap to him, he was reminded that all that deference was due merely because of an accident of birth, and not the qualities of character such as honor and loyalty. In such matters they were equals. When Foster called him Squire though, his mind was at ease. That was his nickname aboard ship and an acknowledgment of all that had passed between them. Darcy welcomed it.

"You're awfully quiet, Squire," Foster said after a long while. "Somethin' wrong, then?"

"Nothing that I feel free to talk about," Darcy said, in more of an admission than he had intended.

"It's the wife, in' it?"

Darcy nodded. To whom could he speak of such things? His friend Charles was far away at Netherfield. And Elizabeth? She did not, or could not, say anything.

"'appened to us too. Lost one o' the little ones. Stillborn, 'e was. Nearly drove my Addy 'round the bend, it did."

Darcy looked up at his friend. How had he failed to learn of this? Again, his wealth and social class shielded him from events that happened right under his nose.

"And what did you do?"

Foster shrugged his shoulders. "What could I do? Dunno what a woman needs at a time like that. Tried to cheer 'er up. Tried to stay near. Eventually, she was 'erself again. Think 'er getting better 'ad naught to do wi' me." Darcy patted his friend on the shoulder and said nothing. They stood silently for a long while.

"I am thinking of putting a textile mill down near the stream. It might help put some of our poorer neighbors to work and would not do us any harm to process our own wool, now would it?"

"Don't know 'ow ye think o' such things, truly."

To think of things that would be a good political argument or a sound business idea were easy, but what of Elizabeth? Perhaps Foster was right, and there was really nothing he could do. He hoped this trip to Meryton and her family at Longbourn would accomplish what he could not.

***

The coach-and-four bounced along at a sprightly pace as Elizabeth tried to gather her strength for the oncoming onslaught. She should be comforted to return to her family home, visiting with her father, and seeing her sister Jane again. In fact, seeing most of her sisters again. Instead, all she felt was weariness. Looking up at her daughter Emma's bored face, she regretted her insistence that she return to Longbourn for a time. Her husband did this time as he did most times, acquiesced to her request. She was returning to her childhood home. He did not suspect that she knew he was at his wits' end trying to restore her to…what? A state of hope for the future? For some equilibrium? His ministrations, though well meaning, fatigued her even more. Returning to Longbourn might be a tonic for her. It would be a change of scene, at least.

Benji was asleep, leaning on her arm, his blond curls falling on her sleeve. She remembered how light her hair was as a child and saw herself in him a great deal. Darcy had the boy's hair cut short once he was "breeched" and stopped wearing his infant dresses. The long tresses and long dresses of his babyhood were gone, but his cheeks retained the remnants of his infancy. Elizabeth was glad he was with her.

Benji adored her father and it would do him good to spend time with his grandfather again. Ever since her mother had passed away suddenly from a fever last spring, her father sat alone in his house, buried as he always was in his library. Due largely to her mother's constant wailing about what she would do with five unmarried daughters with no fortune after her father died, she astonished them all by dying first. More surprising, for all her meddling and lack of grace, they all mourned her. She knew that her father did also…in his way. He may now be living a more peaceful life, and one in which the commotion had been removed. Perhaps he liked it that way. Perhaps she would ask him.

Elizabeth looked across the carriage at Emma, who caught her eye. Emma smiled weakly. Having taken her away from the London season before it closed was a crime for which, Elizabeth supposed, Emma would never forgive her mother. Elizabeth smiled back. It was so difficult to be a girl of eighteen, a girl of wealth, beauty, and breeding who had the world at her feet. So difficult. Her daughter knew so little of the struggles of life. Thinking of herself at that age, what had Elizabeth known? How much had she had to learn? She, like Emma, knew nothing of sacrifice, of endurance, of soul-crushing disappointment. Elizabeth wished that she had the energy to talk to her daughter, but of that she was incapable. It was an effort for her now to even rise each morning. She was as tired of her incapacity as she was exhausted by life.

Their coach came to an abrupt stop, and Elizabeth was greeted with a sight that warmed her heart. Jane and Charles, their children, her father, Mary and her bookish husband, a librarian at Canfield House, and Kitty and her clergyman husband and children came pouring out of their family home. Of Lydia, there was no sign. With the sight of such a lively crowd, even Emma seemed to rouse herself from her stupor. Benji, who finally revived from sleep, smiled up into his mother's face and then clambered out of the carriage into the waiting arms of his grandfather.

Jane was the first to embrace her. "Oh, Lizzy, welcome home." She nearly crushed her sister in her embrace. Elizabeth managed a smile and surrendered herself to the exuberance of her family. The younger Charles, Jane and Bingley's firstborn, Charlie as the family called him, was not among them. Elizabeth could see Emma searching the crowd for him. As the two eldest, they had become close over the years. Some even postulated that they might eventually marry. Elizabeth had her doubts, but one never knew. They all retreated into the house.

"Where is Charlie?" Emma asked eventually as they settled in the drawing room. The younger children were dismissed to play in the garden, much to their delight.

"Oh, so you have not heard?" Kitty asked matter-of-factly. "Charlie stayed in town. He was asked to stand up for a friend of his at his wedding. A fellow called Montjoy. Yes, that was it. Perhaps you know him, Edmund Montjoy?"

Emma did not answer but looked at her mother in wide-eyed shock. She brought her hand to her mouth and scurried quickly into the house. Elizabeth took a breath. She tried to warn Emma against a man like Montjoy, but her advice fell on deaf ears. All those hard lessons had to be learnt through one's own experience, and now what Elizabeth had dreaded, happened. She wanted to follow Emma and comfort her, but at that moment, she knew not what to say. Jane looked toward the retreating form of her niece and then turned to her sister as they all squeezed into the house.

"I am sorry, Lizzy. I had intended to write about Mr. Montjoy, but with all your troubles I did not think—"

"Why should you have written about this Montjoy fellow?" Kitty asked, peering at her two sisters with interest. "Is there something I should know?"

"There certainly is not," Jane stated firmly. Kitty was taken aback by the rebuke and turned away in a huff. Elizabeth looked over at Jane in surprise. Jane was usually so easygoing, so such a firmness of tone was completely foreign to her. Her look prompted Jane to speak again. "I suppose I speak to the children in such a manner." Her expression was quite apologetic.

Despite herself, Elizabeth laughed. "I understand completely."

When they entered the morning room, there were hardly enough places for all of them to sit. Her father insisted that she take his seat. At first, Elizabeth wanted to object, but then noticed her father looking out the window toward the garden where the children were playing. She knew that in a few moments he would escape there to play with his grandchildren.

The conversation turned to mundane topics, expertly led by the Simon Whitney, Mary's husband. It did Elizabeth's heart good to see how much he deferred to her sister, despite her occasional lapses during the conversation. It always amazed Elizabeth that one with as much book learning as her sister Mary always seemed so much at a loss for words, or worse yet, blurted out the most egregious non sequiturs. Her good husband did not seem to mind, or even notice. Emma was nowhere to be found.

By the time the tea was served, Lydia made her entrance from the upper floor. Elizabeth was shocked by her sister's appearance. She had not seen her in some time, having no choice but not to receive her or Wickham at Pemberley or in town due to their early disgrace, and so saw her only here, at Longbourn. Lydia's husband, George Wickham, Darcy's childhood playmate and subsequent near assassin, spent most of his time in the army. He had been invaluable to her and to Darcy during Fedon's Rebellion and became an ally of sorts to them both. Much to Lydia's chagrin, he was often absent, off fighting in the Caribbean, and then for much of his career, in France. How he survived, Elizabeth could not fathom. For all his faults, his womanizing, his self-serving nature, his complete irresponsibility when it came to his finances and his family, he did contain a tiny spark of honor, which would ignite occasionally and burn away his excesses, at least for a time.

Lydia had four children, all born in rapid succession, the last two having the most tenuous relationship to their father's presence in the country. How many children Wickham had roaming about the Caribbean or France was anybody's guess. Lydia's children were grown now, or nearly grown. Jacob, her youngest, and the child who bore the least resemblance to Wickham, was away at school. Elizabeth saw them even more infrequently than she did Lydia. To Elizabeth's mind, they suffered from a largely absent father and a mother who was not terribly fond of children.

From what Elizabeth had gleaned from her infrequent and uncomfortably scandalous conversations, they were primarily viewed by Lydia as the natural consequences of her own and Wickham's appetites. After Lydia mastered ways of preventing such consequences, she availed herself of these remedies whenever her husband deigned to come back to home and hearth and on other occasions when he was absent. Elizabeth was privy to such knowledge, not by her own inquiries, but by Lydia's shameless exchanges with anyone who would listen. To Elizabeth's mind it was one of life's cruelest ironies, that those who are indifferent to children or even neglectful or abusive to them can have as many as they desire, and those who long for them are frequently fated to not be so blessed.

"So, Mrs. Darcy," Lydia said loudly as she entered. "You have deigned to come back to your humble home." She was walking quite unsteadily, and Kitty's husband, the Reverend Andrew Mauldin, rose immediately to lend his arm. The irony of Kitty as a vicar's wife always brought a smile to Elizabeth's face. Perhaps it was Lydia's excesses and their consequences that led Kitty away from officers and in the direction of the church. "Thank you," Lydia continued as he guided her to the place he had recently vacated. All eyes went to Elizabeth. In her present state, she was not up to a sparring match with her sister, who should be grateful to Elizabeth's husband for saving her from ruin. Elizabeth knew not to expect much deference from Lydia on any account. The room was completely silent as Lydia wobbled and tried to remain upright. It was obvious to Elizabeth, and likely to all in the room, that her sister had been drinking heavily.

"So…you are no longer with child." An audible gasp went around the room. Elizabeth swallowed and said nothing. Lydia sat down heavily, poured herself a cup of tea, and brought it shakily toward her mouth. "Eh, well, just as well." Lydia spilled her tea into her saucer. Andrew, anticipating a disaster, quickly removed it from her grasp. As she spoke, she slurred her words. "You are lucky to have escaped with your life. Be grateful."

"Do not speak to my mother in such a manner," Emma said, stepping from the corner of the room. There had been such a hubbub of conversation that Elizabeth did not notice her until this moment.

Lydia turned to look over her shoulder at Emma, shrugged, and gave an unladylike snort. "I see you have not taught this one any manners, sister."

Emma made her way through the family to face her aunt, but before she could speak, Lydia's eyes rolled up in her head. She sagged against the back of the sofa and fell into a stupor. The servants were called to escort her to her room, which they managed with great difficulty. The party hastily adjourned to the garden for some fresh air.

Chapter 3

Darcy remained at Pemberley, ostensibly to look after the farm during its busiest season, but in truth, he stayed because he was attempting to stay out of Elizabeth's way. He hoped that Elizabeth would find solace in her family, though how anyone found solace in that noisy lot was a mystery to him. Jane and Charles had returned to Netherfield and would meet her there, of that he was sure. Of all her sisters, Elizabeth was closest to Jane. Perhaps she could do something to alleviate this black mood that had engulfed his wife.

After a long morning ride to observe the tenants' work in the fields, and meeting with the engineers at the site of his new textile mill, he returned to Pemberley for luncheon. The house was eerily quiet. It occurred to him that the silence was due not only to his children's absence, but also to the complete lack of music in the house. Pemberley missed his sister, Georgiana.

After a long search through the salons and great houses of London and a thorough scouring of all the balls and entertainments of Bath, Georgiana married an itinerant musician of Italian descent. To be fair, he was a concert violinist, but nonetheless.... Needless to say, Aunt Catherine was beside herself at the news of their engagement. He was not too pleased himself, at first thinking this musician was a fortune hunter and a gigolo. Matteo Ricci, though, proved himself to be a man of refinement who had amassed his own fortune as a violinist, conductor of operas, and composer.

Matteo fled Italy during the time of the French occupation and spent some of his initial years in England as first violinist and conductor at the Sadler Wells Theatre. It was at a performance there that Georgiana first met him. A friend who knew him personally escorted their entire dazzling group backstage to meet him. After a few pleasantries, it was divulged that Georgiana had a talent for the piano. A sonata for violin and piano was retrieved and Georgiana, through a hail of blushes and refusals, was finally persuaded to play a duet with the maestro. She told Darcy later that she knew from that moment she would marry Maestro Ricci.

Darcy had finished his soup when the sound of a great commotion assailed him from the entry hall. Since he was alone at Pemberley, he used the smaller dining parlour close to the front of the house, and it took him only a few steps to see what the uproar was all about. As he gained entry, he caught sight of his sister, Georgiana, bustling through the front entrance with Matteo by her side. When she saw her brother, a great smile, almost a grin, spread across her face.

"Fitzwilliam," she cried and ran to him. He was so surprised to see her, he did nothing, and she took advantage by throwing her arms around him, then kissing him on both cheeks. She had become completely Italian. "I thought you would still be in town. I hope you do not mind that Matteo and I have come to stay for a time."

"This is your house too, and always will be," he said, finally catching his breath. "Welcome, Matteo." It always felt awkward to Darcy to call his brother-in-law by his given name, but both he and Georgiana insisted. The violinist crossed the room in a few strides and Darcy held his hand out. Matteo ignored the gesture and embraced Darcy, kissing him on both cheeks as Georgiana had done. "Good to see you, my brother," Matteo effused. These outward expressions of affection were most disconcerting, but Darcy held his peace.

"So where is Elizabeth?" Georgiana asked, removing her gloves. Matteo said something in Italian to his wife, and she replied, "*Molto bene.*" Matteo disappeared with his violin in the direction of the music salon. Elizabeth turned her attention to her brother once more. "Elizabeth? Emma? Benji?" she asked, and then her expression turned suddenly somber when she looked into Darcy's face. She laid her hands upon his arm. "What has happened?"

***

Elizabeth could not sleep that night, and went wandering downstairs to the public rooms. Her sleep was fitful now and she could not find a remedy for it. Not wanting to wake the servants, she tiptoed into the kitchen to see if she could prepare a glass of warm milk. Upon entering, she felt no desire for it anymore and retreated to the hall.

From there she could see a light in her father's library. When she entered, she found him asleep in a chair, a book lying open on the floor. When she was a child, her father had lived in that library. Time had not altered that fact.

Seeing that he was asleep, she turned to leave. The door squeaked on its hinges, and her father's voice sounded behind her. "Is that you, Lizzy?"

Elizabeth turned and walked to her father's chair. It was old and threadbare now, but she could remember sitting on the floor by this chair as a child, her head leaning on her father's knee. On one particular day, twenty years ago now, she and her father were preparing themselves for his duel with George Wickham. Even now, with all that had passed, the mere idea of it sent shivers through her.

"Come, sit by your old father. I feel I can sleep better here in this chair than I can in my own bed. Is that not remarkable?"

Elizabeth sat at his knee, facing him. "I could not fall asleep."

"From the moment you entered the door, Lizzy, I could see that something was wrong. Talk to me. Is it the baby?"

Elizabeth sighed. "Yes, I suppose it is. That and so many other things. Emma is grown and already looking for a husband. Soon, Benji will be sent off to school."

"It is the nature of things, my dear. All of you grew up and left me, did you not?"

She looked up at him. "Oh, Father. In my mind, I know all these things. I know that life can sometimes be cruel, but that we must go on. It is my heart that does not understand. I feel I have disappointed my husband."

Her father sat up suddenly. "Has he said as much to you?"

"No. Certainly not." Elizabeth looked at her father's concerned expression. "In fact, he has told me the complete opposite. He is perfectly satisfied with our family and has no more desire for children."

"Well then." Her father relaxed back into the chair, his head resting on one of the wings, "I do not understand."

"I so wanted this child, Papa. I do not think Darcy understands how much I wanted this child," she said disconsolately. "Everyone tells me how I should feel, but no one can tell me how I can change my heart. For all my blessings, I can think of only my grief."

Her father said nothing but patted the back of her hand. "Time, my dear. Time heals all wounds. And besides, your children need you. Emma has had her heart broken, poor girl."

Elizabeth looked up suddenly at her father. "How did you know that?"

"There are no secrets for long in the Bennet Utopia," he said, laughing. "And your little son, my Bennet, he loves you so."

"I know, Papa. I know." She turned back and rested her head on his knee once again.

They sat in silence for a long moment. Finally, he spoke. "I miss your mother, you know." She looked up at him and he was smiling through shining eyes. "I know she was foolish and meddlesome and oh, her poor nerves," he said, softly chuckling. "But she worried so for you girls, and rightly so. Five daughters and no dowries. My goodness. I am afraid I was not much help in that regard."

Elizabeth turned and looked again at her father. "You sell yourself short, Papa. After all, was it not you who called upon Mr. Bingley when he first arrived at Netherfield and set all of our lives in motion?"

He looked down at her with a satisfied air. "You know, Lizzy. You are right." He then leaned heavily on the arms of his chair and pushed himself upright. "Come. It is late. Let us be off to bed."

Elizabeth held his arm and they made their way up the stairway.

***

What had started out as another solitary luncheon was now revived by the presence of his beloved sister and her exuberant husband. Darcy explained in general terms what had befallen Elizabeth in the last months and told her of the departure of their little family to Longbourn.

"It may a-help your wife to see her mama again," Matteo said.

"Her mother died last spring," Darcy stated flatly.

"Oh, I am a-sorry. I spoke out of turn. So sorry." Matteo was visibly embarrassed.

"Not at all. You could not have known. My wife is close with her father and her sister Jane. I am hoping they may cheer her." Even to himself, he sounded unconvincing.

"So, I hear that Emma is out in society," Georgiana piped in. "It must have been a splendid season for her."

Darcy knew she was changing the subject and was grateful. "I suppose it was."

"Really, brother, you are such a recluse. Did you not enjoy yourself at all?"

"I spent much of my time watching my daughter dally with some of the most notorious rakes in England."

Georgiana laughed. "Spoken like a true father." She then turned to her husband and gave him a significant look. "We sent for Daniel. He will be joining us here for a few days."

Darcy smiled. He liked their youngest son. Georgiana continued. "He is on summer holidays from school and we are taking him with us."

"Taking him with you? Where? Are you not remaining here for a time?"

"No. We have a, how you say, tour of concerts in Ireland, Georgiana and I," Matteo said.

"There are many great houses there. One I think belong to your cousin, *ho ragione*?"

Darcy gave his sister a puzzled look. She laughed. "We are to play at the house of the Earl of Fitzwilliam. They may be distant cousins."

"Undoubtedly they are, back in the mists of time. And Daniel will go with you?"

"He is our *critic musicale*, as you say, our music critic." Matteo laughed.

"Danny makes me quite nervous at times. He knows all of our pieces so well. He can hear every flaw."

"And he a-cannot play well himself. Ah well. Children, eh? They are all on their own path, not the one we set for them." Matteo sighed.

"Our hosts already have many things planned for Daniel especially. Travel is always good for the soul, do you not think so, brother?"

"It can be enlightening to be sure," Darcy said ruefully. "To be sure."

He was about to lose himself in reverie again when Matteo rose from the table. "Would you like a brief concert?" Georgiana's eyes lit up. How could he refuse? Darcy stood, made a slight bow, and gestured toward the music room. Matteo nearly ran ahead in his eagerness.

Georgiana took her brother's arm. "I am glad you are here," he said.

***

Emma spent the next few days avoiding her Aunt Lydia. She was angry, outraged even, at her behavior, but primarily by her outrageous treatment of her mother. As for her mother, she spent time sequestered with her Aunt Jane or alone in her room. If only they had not fled London so soon, she might have been married to Edmund right now instead of Juliette Hornsby. No doubt there would be news of the pair that would eventually filter down to Meryton.

They would go to Netherfield in a few days, and Emma welcomed it. Benji would have his cousin Simon to play with and would cease bothering her. She was in no mood for the antics of children. Looking one way and then another, she stepped outside the room she shared with her brother and made her way silently past her aunt's room. Lydia never woke early enough to eat breakfast with the family. Emma suspected that the reason for her late rising was drink.

A floorboard creaked and Emma froze. The door to Lydia's room opened and out stepped her aunt. Emma turned and gave her the most egregious look. Lydia's mouth curled into what looked like a smirk, but there was such a sadness in her eyes that Emma's anger abated somewhat.

"Good morning, niece."

"Good morning, aunt. You are looking well." She was not.

"Come down to the morning room with me," Lydia said.

"I really..." Emma began. She did not want to exchange pleasantries with her aunt and if her aunt was in a haranguing mood, she did not think she could hold her tongue.

"Come. I have need to speak with you." Emma descended the stairs. Once they were alone, Lydia turned upon her.

"I am sorry about your mother," she said flatly. Emma was taken aback. This condescension was not what she expected. "I was not myself the other day." And turning away, she looked out the window.

Emma was tempted to retort but refrained. Lydia continued. "I am not sorry, however, about your troubles with Edmund Montjoy." Lydia turned back and looked at Emma with such directness that she was speechless for a moment.

"I... I... How dare you?" Emma was flustered.

Lydia laughed ruefully. "I dare, little miss, because I have stood in the shoes that you stand in now. Sit down."

Emma was so taken aback that she did as she was told. "Men like Edmund Montjoy—"

Emma interrupted, "Do not speak of him. You do not know him."

With that Lydia began laughing, cackling really. "Oh, my dear niece. I know of him and his ilk. I am married to a man like Edmund Montjoy. You do not know it now, but you have escaped a dire fate. A dire fate indeed."

Emma did not know if she was angry or hurt or mortified. All she knew was that tears began to gather, and she wiped them away quickly when her aunt turned toward the window again.

"I do not know my Uncle George, so I cannot verify the veracity of your words," Emma said, trying to contain herself. She was determined not to cry in front of this woman.

"Uncle? Uncle George. Ha. He was not even a father or a husband, much less an uncle. I am sure your mother has told you how your noble father, on his deathbed, forced George Wickham to sign a contract promising to marry me in exchange for his freedom and not an insignificant income."

Emma had risen to confront her aunt but collapsed back in her seat as if she was pushed. What was she talking about? How could her father do anything from his deathbed? He was alive. This was also the first time she heard of a bargain between her father and George Wickham. Lydia looked at Emma's stricken face. "Oh my. You did not know of this, did you?" Her aunt's expression softened. "I suppose your mother and father kept many things from you while you were a child. Now you are grown, my girl, out in society, and you should know how your father traded my life for your mother's respectability."

Emma closed her eyes for a moment, gathering her thoughts. She knew of her Aunt Lydia's penchant for exaggeration, and invention even, so she took little notice of the later part of her speech. She would ask her mother to tell her the real story later. The matter of a deathbed, however, she wanted to know now.

"Why on earth would you say my father was on his deathbed? He is alive and well and at Pemberley."

Lydia looked at her, wrinkling her brow. Emma suspected that she was thinking of some preposterous lie. Finally, she spoke. "George Wickham shot him in a duel."

"That is a lie," Emma spat.

Lydia laughed. "Go and ask your mother if do not believe me. Shot him and nearly killed him. Go, ask your mother, and be grateful you escaped the likes of Edmund Montjoy."

Oh, yes, Edmund. That was about whom they were talking. Emma's head was spinning. "I will. I will ask my mother." Emma found her feet again and left the room, slamming the door behind her.

She had no intention of asking her mother anything due to the state she was in. She would find out the truth, though, from her father. They must leave soon, and not for Netherfield as planned. They must leave for Pemberley, for home.

***

Darcy welcomed his nephew, Daniel, who arrived a day later. He looked hale and hearty but was disappointed that Benji was not at home. No matter. The three of them were leaving in a few days for an adventure in Ireland. The visit with his sister was a tonic after having spent the last weeks wracked with worry about Elizabeth. When he found himself looking in the glass in the morning, he noticed the touch of grey at his temples. Time and life moved on inexorably, he supposed. Although Elizabeth was not yet forty, he had passed the mark by four years.

Watching Georgiana and her family and witnessing their great happiness, he was determined to restore that happiness to his own family. Spending time at Pemberley and resuming his rounds of the tenants reminded him again of his own privilege. Did any of them even think of happiness as within their reach? Did most of them not live day-to-day and think only of their survival and that of their children? Still, many of them seemed satisfied with their lives, and even happy. Foster, who married soon after he arrived at Pemberley nearly twenty years ago, married a woman more than ten years his junior. When Darcy would visit their cottage, besides the great deference he was shown, he noticed smiles on the children's faces and good-natured banter at the table. No, wealth was no guarantee of happiness.

When the trunks were stowed in the carriages and the demonstrative good-byes were said, Darcy was left alone again in his great house. He had received a short letter from Elizabeth in the interim and one from Benji, who told him that his cousins were happy, and his mother and sister were sad. No, this state of affairs was intolerable. He must do something, but what? As evening weather grew rainy and dark, he sat alone in the drawing room. The servants lit a fire in the grate as the room had grown dank, and as he swirled his brandy and listened to the distant thunder, he gave way to melancholy.

He had been so immersed in his concern for Elizabeth, his responsibilities in Parliament, his return to his duties here at Pemberley, and then the unexpected visit from his sister, it was not until this moment that he gave way to the grief he felt for the little one he had lost. He dared not show his sorrow to Elizabeth. She had enough of her own and felt in some way that she disappointed him. No, he could not show her anything. But here, alone save for the servants, he could let a lump form in his throat and tears course silently down his cheeks. There was at least one advantage to being alone.

The next morning the storm had cleared, and Darcy woke to the sun streaming into his bedchamber. He dressed early and went out into the garden before breakfast. For the first time in weeks his head felt clear and his spirit light. He took a brisk walk around the pond while all the parts of the puzzle that had been his life in recent weeks seemed to fall into place and coalesce into one strange and impossible idea. His path was clear before him now. As he entered the great house, he knew exactly what he must do.

***

The plan had been to stay with Jane and Charles for a time before returning to Pemberley, but Emma, of all people, expressed a desire to return to Pemberley, and Elizabeth posed no opposition. In her mind, one place was as good as another. They bid farewell to her sister Mary after only three days, since her husband had duties to perform. Kitty was in and out of the household since she and Andrew stayed at a nearby vicarage. Lydia returned to her house in Brighton more out of ennui than anything else. Although her family with all of its noisy tiffs and reconciliations did divert her attention for time, the grief always returned, seeming to dwell somewhere near her heart, ready to overwhelm it if she turned her thoughts inward.

Thus, trunks were packed, and good-byes were said. A messenger was sent ahead the day before to let Darcy know of their imminent arrival. Her father, who seemed older and frailer than before their visit, embraced Elizabeth wordlessly before she entered the carriage. Benji was wiping his eyes as he sat down next to his mother and would not speak or look at her or his sister. With a jolt, the carriage was off and the three of them were off for Pemberley.

***

"What do you mean they left already?" Darcy asked Mr. Bennet as he entered the drawing room.

"They departed this morning, Mr. Darcy. Emma wanted to go home," Mr. Bennet said with a confused look on his face.

"And Elizabeth agreed? How odd."

"Elizabeth has not been herself, as you know. Neither was Emma once she heard of Mr. Montjoy's marriage."

A sense of relief passed over Darcy. So that rogue Montjoy had married. He could guess at the circumstances. But now, there was a matter of intercepting his family.

"Do you know on which road they are travelling?" The servants were summoned, and Elizabeth's maid intimated that the plan she heard discussed, not that she was eavesdropping, mind you, was to visit Netherfield for tea and then begin their journey. This was good news for Darcy, and he left his carriage at Longbourn, borrowed a horse from Mr. Bennet, and rode off at a gallop.

***

Benji was in the front garden digging near the rose bushes with his cousin when his father approached. He was filthy as usual. The boys did not look up from their work until he was nearly upon them.

"What will your mother say now that you have spoiled your clothes?" Darcy called out, and Bennet looked up at him.

"Papa, Papa, Papa," he shouted and ran to Darcy as he dismounted his horse. He threw his grubby arms around Darcy's legs.

"Here now, let go. Mama will scold me too if I arrive covered in mud." He laughed, and Bennet looked up in his father's face and let go of his legs.

"I am most happy to see you, Papa. We were going home. Go ask Mama." He put his grimy hand in Darcy's.

Hugo, Jane's youngest, stood stock-still. Darcy turned to him. "Are you coming with us, Hugo?"

"Yes, uncle." His voice was meek and barely audible.

"Come along. Take my other hand. We will all get scolded for our folly together." Hugo grinned. "What were you boys doing there by the rosebushes?" They strolled toward the house.

"We were digging a hole to China," Hugo said proudly.

"And we were almost there," Bennet rejoined.

Darcy shook his head. He could remember such antics when he was a boy. "I will tell the gardener to go fill it up at once, lest we are invaded by Chinese warriors while we are having tea." Both boys stopped and looked back at the hole and then up at Darcy with wide eyes.

Hugo stated uncertainly, "You are joking, uncle."

"Am I?" Darcy asked and smiled to himself as the boys stole furtive glances behind them as they entered the house. The two boys ran into the morning room to their respective mothers ahead of Darcy.

"Oh, Hugo, what a sight you are," exclaimed Jane. "What have you been doing?"

At that same moment, Darcy could hear his wife, "Benji, you are filthy. What did mother tell you?"

Darcy entered the morning room. They all looked up. Charles was the first to nearly jump from his chair and greet him, "Darcy, old man, what a surprise. Do come in. Come in." He shook Darcy's hand. Elizabeth was upon them.

"Hello, Lizzy."

She said nothing but embraced him there. When she released him, she looked up at him quizzically. "Whatever are you doing here?"

"I am afraid you have wasted a trip, my friend," Charles continued. "They were on their way home to Pemberley this morning."

"No," said Darcy. "We are not going home to Pemberley." He looked about at the confused and incredulous faces, and it caused him to smile slyly.

"Back to London, then?" Elizabeth asked. Darcy shook his head.

"No, my dear. I have a surprise for you all."

Chapter 4

They were in the carriage by that afternoon, headed in the direction of Portsmouth. Emma began asking questions as soon as they were out of sight of Netherfield.

"What do you mean I am having my Grand Tour? A Grand Tour begins in Paris."

"How much of a welcome do you think we would receive in Paris right now?" Darcy asked in return. "We have been at war with the French for nearly twenty years."

"The Balkans then?"

"No, not the Balkans."

"I do not think it appropriate that my little brother accompany me on my Grand Tour, or my mother and father either, for that matter. A companion of some sort is in order. An older, refined gentlewoman."

"I am sorry, my dear, but you are travelling with your family. Be grateful that we are travelling at all."

"But you have not told us where we are going," Bennet said.

"All will be revealed tomorrow," Darcy responded.

Elizabeth looked quizzically at her husband. This trip seemed ill-conceived and not at all typical of Darcy's temperament. How had he arranged everything? Why, now, decide to take Emma on a trip? The crisis involving Mr. Montjoy had passed and there was no reason to remove Emma from England.

"I am afraid I do not understand," Elizabeth said. "How can you leave Pemberley?"

"Foster has things well in hand. I have seen to the accounts and everything is in order."

"But Parliament?"

"I have given Parkson my proxy and instructed him as to how to vote in my absence. We should be back in London by the new year."

50

***

They reached the Blue Anchor Inn near the port, and Darcy had most of their belongings sent to the docks to be stowed aboard ship. He still had not intimated where they were bound, and Elizabeth could already feel a weariness settle around her. Why did he not take only Emma on this adventure or, as she had said, send her with a companion? But to where? Europe was in shambles.

Darcy had secured a room for them all, and when Emma was settled in a large chair with a book and Benji was asleep on a cot, Elizabeth and Darcy sat on the small balcony to take tea and talk.

"Whatever are you doing, my love?" she asked, setting her cup down and taking his hand. "I do not feel I have the strength to make an ocean voyage, much less a tour of some foreign land. Perhaps Benji and I should return to Pemberley and you and Emma go on."

"I am afraid that is impossible." He enfolded her hand in his. "I wanted to wait until tomorrow, but I see I will have to tell you now. We are going to New Orleans."

Elizabeth let out a soft cry and covered her mouth with her hand. She looked over her shoulder into the darkening room and saw Emma still contentedly reading and Benji curled in a ball asleep. She whispered to him, "How is that possible? We are at war with the United States."

"Yes. Technically, we are."

"Indeed we are." Her whisper was more forceful this time.

"The war is concentrated in the north near New York and even Canada. It will not touch us thousands of miles away in New Orleans."

Elizabeth was skeptical and her expression must have shown it, for Darcy continued, "I also have it on good authority that there are plans to send diplomats to Ghent to sign a treaty ending all hostilities. What could possibly happen?"

Elizabeth knew full well what could possibly happen. She had lived through warfare. It sprang out of nowhere and ripped away her dignity and thrown her into bloodshed and abuse. Darcy knew it too, firsthand. He had snatched her up from the jaws of death. She looked over at him, and his gaze never wavered from her face. When she did not speak, he continued, "Besides, Poppy and Monsieur Peschier are expecting us."

She finally found her voice. "How can that be?"

"I sent a letter by dispatch boat immediately after you received your letter from Poppy. I told them that we might possibly come for a visit soon. Of course, we may arrive before the letter does."

She looked at him a long while wondering how in the name of all that is holy, after all they had been through together, he could not understand how she felt? How could he not see it? An ocean voyage was the last thing on earth that she wanted to embark upon. "Oh, you are an impossible man," she said, and stalked off back into the room.

***

This was not the reaction that Darcy had expected. When playing it over in his head, he envisioned his Lizzy throwing her arms about his neck and kissing him, taking a breath only to thank him for his kindness and understanding as a husband. But no. She was angry. Angry? How could she be angry after all that he had done? He found a merchant ship of Belgian registry willing to take them as passengers. He secured the best cabin for the four of them so that they might be comfortable during the voyage. He left all his affairs in order, which took a great deal of doing, so that he might be free to spend time with his wife and children and help her heal her mind and spirit. Had he not been attentive and patient with her? Had he not taken up the mantle of both mother and father when she was indisposed? And now, he was taking her halfway around the world to see her dear friend, and what did he get in return? Anger. Anger and resentment. If he were to live a thousand years, he would never understand women. Never.

***

When the sun rose, the tempest seemed to have lifted somewhat. Without any protestation from Elizabeth, the Darcys boarded the good ship *Veronique* bound for the mouth of the Mississippi River. Her anger with her husband had abated and she realized that he was only attempting to restore her spirit. Why did men always think that they could mend what cannot be mended? She supposed it was in their nature. In spite of herself, the smell of the sea air was already lifting her spirits.

Darcy had booked the most spacious cabin, save the captain's, which he could not arrange. He also organized for provisions with some of the other passengers, so their voyage, at least at the beginning, would be comfortable. Her bad temper was dissipating with every step. It really was ungrateful of her to throw this *Grand Tour* back in her husband's face. There was a larger bed, bolted in the left corner of the room near the door, that she assumed she and Darcy would share. A smaller bed was on an elevated platform with drawers beneath on the other side. There was a table in the center with four chairs, and enough room to walk about. There was even a small library filled with books near the aft section of the cabin. The room was flooded with light from the row of windows along the rear wall. The sailors were bringing in their trunks and stowing them along the walls.

"Are we to be trapped in this…this prison for weeks?" Emma asked shrilly. That was a relief. Now Elizabeth could be angry at her daughter for a while.

"I think it is quite nice," Elizabeth said, looking at Darcy rather than her daughter.

Emma crossed the deck and began to peruse the books in the library. "All these books are in French."

"The ship is Belgian, Emma. One must expect—" The ship's captain knocked on the already open door.

"I 'ope you are 'appy wit your accommodations?" he asked Darcy in what sounded like a thick French accent. "Thees ship was used during de war to transport many 'igh ranking officials. They liked their comfort, *n'est-ce pas*?"

"It is quite nice, thank you," Elizabeth said.

Suddenly, Benji piped up. "Where am I going to sleep?" They all looked about the room.

"Ah," the captain intoned. "If the young man would not mind." He shouted something in French down the passageway, and in a few moments a deckhand arrived with a hammock in his hand. As he hung up one side of the hammock on a post near Emma's bed, Benji let out a cheer, "Hoorah, hoorah, hoorah, hoorah," he cried, jumping up and down.

"Benji, do control yourself," Elizabeth said sternly, even though she had to smile at the boy's excitement. As soon as the hammock was up, Benji clambered into it.

"This is the best day of my life," he proclaimed, folding his fingers and putting them behind his head. "I hope this voyage never ends."

"Well," Elizabeth said as soon as they were alone, "we should begin our unpacking."

***

The shoreline had disappeared from sight days ago, and Emma kept to her cabin a great deal. She did not want to admit to her parents that she did not feel well at sea, but her mother probably guessed as much. This *Grand Tour* of her father's was nothing more than a visit to her mother's friend in the New World. It was all right, she supposed. She knew her father was correct in his assumption that France, and even Italy, had no place for them now. Stupid war. Stupid Napoleon.

As she arrived on deck the morning of the fourth day, having only had some tea and a biscuit for breakfast, she walked to the rail, hoping that the fresh air would alleviate her constant nausea. It was there she heard her brother call to her, "Emma, Emma, come here."

She looked about, but did not see him. Some of the other passengers were at the rail, but she could not see her brother among them. Then, from the bow of the ship where the sailors were sitting, mending sails and doing all manner of work, came her little brother.

"Look, Emma," he fairly gushed. "Look what I made." He was holding up a rope with some sort of convoluted knot in it.

"What is it?"

He puffed himself up. "It's a monkey's fist."

"It looks revolting."

"On the contrary, it is quite astounding," her father's voice sounded from behind her. She turned suddenly to look at him. He took the knot from Benji, who was beaming from ear to ear.

"Did you make this, son?"

"Yes, I did. I have been practicing. Mr. Harwick there, he taught me." Benji pointed over to the group of sailors at their work. One of the men nodded in deference.

"Look, Lizzy. Look what your son has done," he said as Elizabeth joined them. He smiled at her. "During my entire voyage, I never learned how to tie a knot like that, and Bennet has done it in less than a week."

"Perhaps your nautical skills were passed on to him."

Emma looked at them suspiciously. "What voyage, father?" She looked from one parent to the other. "And when does a gentleman on a voyage learn to tie knots with common sailors?" She was beginning to think that her Aunt Lydia was telling her the truth after all. Her father cleared his throat.

"It was a long time ago," he said cryptically, then looked over at her mother. "We will tell you the whole story at another time."

Benji chimed in. "I want to go up there." Squinting his eyes in the sunlight, he pointed up to the rigging. "I want to go to the crow's nest and look about and search for whales."

"This is not a whaling ship, silly boy," Emma said.

"You are forbidden from climbing that rigging." Darcy's tone brooked no argument. Benji looked down at his shoes. "It is dangerous and no place for a little boy."

"I am not so little. I am almost seven." He looked up again toward the sails and the crow's nest beyond.

Emma looked up at the swaying masts, and her stomach churned. "I am unwell, Mother." She made a hasty retreat toward the gangway.

***

This voyage had been the first Elizabeth made since her homecoming from Grenada when she was only a girl of twenty. The days at sea brought back memories of the first voyage she made with Edward Home and his sister Barbara. Although this ship was of foreign design, it was similar enough that at every turn, she was reminded of her days of excitement and adventure, and also of the grief she tried expunging from her heart when she thought of her Darcy, cold and alone in his grave.

She did not know he lived still. She did not know many things. It was on board ship that she first began to learn of the horrors of slavery due to the Quaker couple who voyaged with them. It was when she began to consider a new turn in life, one that might keep her in Grenada indefinitely, perhaps as the wife of Edward Home. So many thoughts and memories: so much she was to learn after that first voyage.

It was well after ten bells in the evening when she stood at the railing, watching the black and silvery water slip noiselessly beneath them. She listened to the creaking of the rigging and the soft banter of the seamen on night watch. She had to admit that stirrings of excitement began to bubble up in her for the first time since that fateful day when she experienced her latest loss. It would be so good to see Poppy again. She tried to imagine her now, the mistress of her household. It made Elizabeth smile. She was so lost in thought that she did not hear Darcy approach from behind her.

"I wonder if I may speak to you, Miss Bennet," he said in the darkness.

"Perhaps, sir. If you can keep a civil tongue in your head," she answered, teasing him.

"Are you still angry with me, Lizzy?" He did not seem amused, so solemn was his tone. She could see only the outline of his features in the moonlight, but knowing his so well, she knew he had been beleaguered with his own thoughts.

She looked up at his shadowy countenance. "I was never truly angry with you, my dear husband." She sighed in spite of herself. "It is just that…" The words would not come. "Dear heart, you cannot erase all that has happened."

"That was not my intent."

"I am putting it poorly." She turned from his gaze and looked out again to the sea. "I will not be restored to the person I was, no matter what you do, or even what I do. That person is gone. She died with her baby."

Darcy said nothing, but she felt his arms encircle her. Leaning back, she let her head rest in the crook of his neck. They stood there for a long while, and then he spoke. "We have been through much together, Lizzy. More than most. We both have changed from where we started. I would like to think that those changes were, in the most part, for the better. Do you not think so?"

She turned in his arms and looked into his face. "It seems that I will spend my entire life misjudging you," she said, trying to control the emotion in her voice.

"Ah, well." He gently tucked away a strand of hair that had fluttered in her face with the breeze. She wanted him at that moment.

He bent his head to her, and kissed her, gently at first and then again and again, each one becoming more ardent than the last. She could feel her body grow weak in his embrace. This was not the kiss of a man who was her helpmeet and her spouse, but the kiss of a young and ardent lover. A kiss of passion. Alas, with two children in their bedchamber, it was to be only a kiss. But, perhaps, longing is the better part of desire. When she finally looked into his eyes, she saw the Darcy who had sacrificed everything for her. She finally felt something awaken in her that had long been covered in a blanket of sadness and despair.

"May I escort you to your cabin, miss?"

"If you can do so without creating a scandal." She adopted her arch manner once again.

"I can tell you, my dear Miss Bennet, that I am quite prepared to create a scandal, but my prediction is that we will find our youngest sitting in his hammock waiting for us to bring him a glass of water."

Elizabeth could feel it now, that flicker of happiness burning steadily if not yet bursting into flame. It was enough. They stood before the door, and she kissed him again. When they opened it, there was Benji standing in the darkness, looking out of the stern watching the waves.

***

Phillipe Peschier dismounted his horse and bounded up the stairs to the veranda of the brightly colored plantation house. He looked along the eight French doors that lined the outside and opened the two at the center. He was overly warm in his coat, and tossed it aside as he entered.

He looked about empty sitting room. "*Maman*," he called. "Papa. Where is everyone?" His mother came out of the bedroom on the east side of the house, her mending basket in her hand. "*Maman*, you have servants to do such work," he chided, shaking his head.

"Speak English. Wit' me you speak English, wit' your papa you speak French. Remember?"

"I hate the English, and you are changing the subject. You should not be doing servants' chores."

"I was not born to do nothin' on dis eart'. And do not say you hate de English. You are half English. And what you expec' me to do all day?"

"I do not know, but not this," he said, lifting up some worn stockings of his father's. She laughed at him.

"I am conten'. Leave me alone," Poppy said, smiling. "So what da news you bring from town?"

He sat next to his mother and held out a letter in his hand. "This has come for you. Is there lemonade?" He dabbed the sweat from his brow and his upper lip with his handkerchief.

"In the dinin' room." The dining room was directly behind the main parlour, so as he filled his glass, he could see his mother looking earnestly at the letter. When she did not open it immediately, he reentered the room and sat down next to her.

"Did you see? English," she said, staring at it but not opening it.

"It must be from your friend Mrs. Darcy," he said casually, drinking deeply from his glass. "Open it."

"It not in her hand," his mother whimpered. "Somethin' happen'. Somethin' has happen' to 'Lizabet'."

Philippe looked at his mother. "You do not know that. Read it."

"You read it to me." She held the letter out to him. He looked at her impatiently. "Please, son."

He took the letter from his mother and broke the seal. It was definitely a more masculine hand. He looked over at his mother, fretfully chewing her lip, and began.

My dear Mrs. Peschier,

I am Fitzwilliam Darcy, Elizabeth's husband. I am writing to you now as my last hope.

"Oh dear." Poppy covered her mouth with her hand.

"Please, *maman*. Let me finish." His mother nodded.

My wife, your friend, has recently lost our last child and nearly lost her own life, and is in the depths of despair. Nothing I do seems to help. The only light I have seen in her eyes of late is that which you have brought her by your last letter.

I am sorry to burden you with our troubles, but I am at my wits' end and do not know what to do. I was hoping that perhaps a journey to see you and your family might distract her from her difficulties and bring her some peace of mind.

As of now, I am not sure that we will be coming, but if that is to be, we should be there by the end of September. I hope this does not create a burden for you or Monsieur Peschier. We will make accommodations in the town of New Orleans for ourselves, so you need not worry that we will inconvenience you.

If we come, I will bring my eldest daughter, Emma, who is eighteen as you probably know, and our little boy, Bennet, who is six. I do not know if this will reach you in time. We may arrive before this letter. We may never arrive. As I said, I am at my wits' end at what to do.

I do thank you for all you have done for Elizabeth both now and all those years ago when you saved her life and thereupon my own.

I am most respectfully yours,
Mr. Fitzwilliam Darcy, Esq.

"Ha, ha," Poppy exclaimed, jumping up from her seat. "She not dead. She comin' for a visit." Poppy suddenly hugged her son, who still held the letter in his hand.

"It does not sound like it will be a happy visit," he said skeptically.

"Oh, we make her quite well again. Yes, we will." Poppy rubbed her hands together. "I go now and see what we have in de larder. Oh, happy, happy day." She clapped her hands and was off.

His mother left her basket of mending on the settee and sped off through the house to look at their supplies. The English. In his house. Despite his English blood, he renounced them and all they stood for. In his mind he was French, and a former slave. He would tolerate his mother's visitors, but only for her sake.

Chapter 5

By the time they reached the Bahamas, Emma confided to her father that perhaps this unusual *Grand Tour* was not as intolerable as she had first supposed. He made it clear that he was glad to see her joining them on deck during the day and sitting with some of the other passengers for card games in the evening. Judging from her mood and mobility, he judged that the seasickness must have left her.

On one fine morning, they were rounding Great Abaco with a heading to the Straits of Florida. Emma and Elizabeth were standing at the rail after breakfast when the island came into view.

"Oh, look, Benji, we can see land," Emma called. There was no answer from the boy. Darcy looked about, but Bennet was nowhere to be found. He was about to ask Emma to go look for him when he heard a faint cry.

"That is Benji," Elizabeth said immediately. They all looked about and then Elizabeth's eyes grew wide and she looked overboard. Darcy's blood ran cold. Then, they heard the cry again. It was coming from above them.

Darcy looked heavenward and, stepping so that his eyes were not blinded by the sunlight, he looked up into the rigging. There in the crow's nest was his son, waving to them.

"My God," Darcy said and brought his gaze down to Elizabeth. All the blood had drained from her face. She swallowed hard and looked up to her son.

"Come down from there this instant, young man," she shouted, at which Darcy shook his head furiously. At this point, the ship entered the channel between the islands and swayed slightly from side to side. Darcy looked up and could see his son attempt to step down onto the rigging only to propel himself upward again and grasp the railings attached to the small wooden platform that served as a crow's nest.

A sailor approached Darcy. "The boy should come down," one of the Belgian sailors said in his best English. Darcy looked at him in amazement.

"Yes, we know that," he replied, trying to keep the sarcasm out of his voice.

"I send my men," the sailor said. By this time, they could hear Bennet crying. His face emerged over the edge and he seemed to be hanging on for dear life.

"I can't get down," he wailed. "Help, Papa."

One of the men arrived with a length of rope wrapped over his across his body diagonally. "I get him and bring him down."

Darcy held out his hand. "Indeed, you will not. Give me that rope." The sailor looked at him curiously as Darcy sat down unceremoniously on the deck and removed his boots. "I will get my boy," he stated, standing in his bare feet.

"Whatever are you doing, Father?" Emma cried. "You will both be killed." Darcy removed his jacket and a smile momentarily crossed his lips as he handed it to Elizabeth. They exchanged a look that could pass only between the two of them.

Elizabeth laid her hand on Emma's arm. "Your father knows what he is doing."

Darcy tilted his head, cupped his hands around his mouth, and shouted, "Hold on tight, Bennet. I am coming."

He could hear some muffled cries, but no distinct words. He hoped his son would not attempt to descend the rigging without him. By this time, a small crowd of sailors and passengers had gathered around. The captain approached.

"*Monsieur*, we need to get ze sail in as the wind becomes strong. Ze channel, she is treacherous."

Darcy nodded. "Let me get up, and I will remain there until you get the sail in."

The captain scrutinized Darcy skeptically. "You are a sailor, *monsieur*?"

"I have sailed before," Darcy answered, his hands already on the ropes.

"*Tre bien*," the captain said, and began shouting orders to the men on deck.

Darcy stole a quick look at Elizabeth, gave a wink to his daughter, and began his ascent. It was gratifying that his body remembered how to clamber up the ropes as if he had done it yesterday. Still, his feet were not as toughened as they were twenty years ago when he first made such a voyage. No matter, in no time his head appeared through the opening in the crow's nest and he was momentarily blinded when Bennet's arms were thrown round his eyes.

"Bennet, let go," he shouted in the wind. The mainmast was swaying rather forcefully now, but as he clambered into the small space, he knew that they were safe enough for the time being. The structure, fortunately, had spindles that ran up from the circular floor to a railing but also had cross-pieces of metal that held them in place. It looked quite open and terrifying, but it was strong enough and closed enough for Darcy to sit down and lean against its sides. Bennet scrambled into his lap.

"Papa, Papa," the boy cried, hanging onto Darcy's neck.

"You have been a willful and naughty boy, Bennet," Darcy said as sternly as he could considering how relieved he was that his child was still with them. "What did I tell you about climbing up the rigging?"

"Not to do it," he replied, blubbering. "I am sorry, Papa. Now we are both going to die."

Darcy knew this situation was no laughing matter, but he could barely contain his amusement at so much drama. The poor child was frightened, so he turned a sober face to his son. "We are not going to die, Bennet. I am going to get you down, but you have to do everything I ask of you." Bennet nodded. "First, we need to stay here and wait."

The swaying of the ship decreased as the crew did their duty and reduced the sail. After some time, Darcy looked down and saw that their work was nearly complete, so he began to unwind the rope he carried up with him.

"Now, listen carefully, son. I am going to move up to this hole in the floor and put my feet through. You need to stand up and then sit behind me and hold on to my back."

Bennet was wide-eyed with terror and began vigorously shaking his head. "I cannot."

"You very well can," his father barked at him, "and you will. I have no intention of spending the rest of my life in this basket."

Bennet quickly wiped his eyes and removed himself from his father's lap. He stood and grasped the railing of the crow's nest.

Darcy looped the rope around his own waist, crossed it in back, and when his son sat down behind him, crossed it again though Bennet's legs, back over his own chest and then around Bennet's shoulders. Thus, he wove his son onto his back and secured all with a knot in front.

"I wish I could tie knots as well as you," Darcy said, as he stood upon the rigging and hoisted Bennet up off the floor.

"Is it going to slip? Are we going to fall?" Bennet yelped.

"We will be fine if you do exactly as I tell you." Darcy endeavored to keep his tone even so as not to panic the boy.

It would be a struggle to get both of them through the opening that led to the rigging, but holding his breath and wriggling down, they were finally through. Bennet clung to his father's neck to the point where Darcy told him to loosen his grip lest he lose consciousness from lack of air.

The ship was moving more smoothly now. Darcy descended gingerly from the crow's nest, down the rigging to the deck. When they reached the bottom, a great cheer and applause resounded, much to Darcy's chagrin. The entire ship's company, passengers and crew, seemed assembled for the spectacle. Quickly, he untied his son, and the boy threw himself into the arms of his mother. Darcy handed the rope back to one of the crew.

Now that they were safe, Emma muttered, "How undignified," and floated across the deck and down toward the hatchway. Elizabeth was alternately embracing and scolding her son. She took Bennet by the hand and led him along the deck toward their cabin. "And if you ever do anything like that again..." she chided, her voice faltering.

"I will not, Mother. I promise. I have learnt my lesson," Bennet cried, clinging with his free hand to her skirts. She held him by the hand until they were down the steps of the hatchway and in sight of their cabin. Darcy followed close behind, his stockings and boots in his hand. They were the only passengers below decks.

"Go to the cabin now, Bennet Fitzwilliam Darcy, and do not come out until I tell you to do so," she said sternly. Bennet looked from one of his parents' faces to another.

"Yes, Mama," he replied and ran off. As soon as the door slammed, Elizabeth turned to her husband. Darcy expected her to say something, but she only threw her arms around his neck and kissed him over and over again.

"Now I am not angry with you anymore," she said between kisses.

"But you told me that…" He knew it. She had been still angry with him. No matter. He kissed her longingly, tenderly on the mouth, on the eyes, and down her neck. They would have remained that way for a time, if they did not hear a faint, but imperious voice whisper, "How undignified." Then a door slammed.

Darcy held Elizabeth to him and laughed with relief.

***

They were now several weeks into their journey and Emma could contain herself no longer. She tried several times to speak to her mother about what her aunt Lydia said. Now, with her father running up the rigging of a ship like a common tar, she was filled to bursting with curiosity. Benji ran off directly after his lessons to mend sails or something else completely beneath him, and their father was on deck, so she approached her mother, who was securing Benji's supplies against the movement of the ship. She thought she would never get used to all this constant movement.

"Mama," she began, while her mother busied herself with capping the inkbottle. "Did Father ruin Aunt Lydia's life?"

Elizabeth looked up at her daughter with a stunned expression. "Whoever told you that?" she asked, and then quickly added. "No doubt it was your Aunt Lydia." She laughed ruefully.

"She said that Father forced her to marry Uncle George Wickham in order to save your reputation." With that her mother burst into laughter.

"Oh, Emma, that is the most ridiculous interpretation of events that I have ever heard. How can you believe such a thing of your father?"

Before she could continue, Emma interrupted, "And she said that Uncle George shot Father in a duel."

"That is almost entirely accurate." All mirth had evaporated from her mother's manner. "Come here, Emma, you are old enough to know the truth of our past, and I can tell you now, if you like."

Emma felt she was of two minds. She wanted to know but was afraid to know. She sat down next to her mother on her bed.

"Your Aunt Lydia was away on a trip, away from us, unprotected. There she met George Wickham again, who was acquainted with our family though your Uncle Charles and your father. Without anyone there to properly supervise her, she ran off with Wickham. They were not married."

Emma brought her hand to her mouth in shock. "Your grandfather and my Uncle Gardiner went in search of them. So did your father. It was your father's intention to offer a settlement on Mr. Wickham to marry your Aunt Lydia, which would save her and all of us from ruin. Unfortunately, my father found them first. One thing led to another and George Wickham challenged your grandfather to a duel."

Elizabeth paused in her story for a moment. Then Emma looked up at her. "Grandfather? A duel? How did that lead to Father being wounded?"

"He acted as my father's second. Wickham decided at the last moment not to fight and threw his pistol in the air. It hit the ground and discharged, badly wounding your father. He insisted on having George Wickham released from gaol to sign papers promising to marry your compromised Aunt Lydia in exchange for a monetary settlement, otherwise all of us Bennet sisters would have been unmarriageable due to Lydia's folly. Your father had the papers brought to his bedside where all were convinced he would die. I know this to be a fact. I was there."

Emma leaned back and gazed at her mother in surprise. "You were attending my father in his sick room?"

"Indeed, I was, and did thereafter. All through his illness." Her mother looked up into the air, her past clearly playing through her mind. "We were not married either, although I told everyone that we were engaged."

Emma stood up and gazed down at her mother. "That cannot be true," she said skeptically.

"In fact, not long after, we all thought your father was dead. I was so distraught, I left the country with friends and travelled to the island of Grenada. There I became engaged to a man called Edward Home, the son of the lieutenant governor." Emma shook her head as if that movement might dislodge her denial.

"And Father? Why does he know so much about sailing?"

"When he could not find a ship that would take passengers, he threw off his gentlemanly airs and signed aboard a ship called the *Marlin* as a common seaman."

This news was almost too much to hear. Emma continued to shake her head and drifted toward the row of windows in the stern of the ship. There she gazed out onto the water, where she sought some sort of resolution to the turmoil in her head. She turned and looked at her mother.

"I find this story hard to believe," she said finally, trying to regain her composure. Her mother looked frighteningly calm. How could she have lived with these two people her entire life and never hear a breath of this incredible saga? How much did the Bennets know? How much did her Aunt Lydia?

"Who knows of this family history?" she asked.

Her mother sat serenely. "Most know of the duel and of my journey. No one but you, your father, Poppy and I, and, I suspect, her family know of your father's journey. Oh, and of course, George Wickham."

Emma paused again, trying to digest the incongruity of this tale. "And what of Edward Home?"

"He was killed in Fedon's Rebellion."

"Oh," Emma said.

Why did George Wickham know of her father's journey as a common seaman? Did her mother love another called Edward Home? What was Fedon's Rebellion? She had more questions, many more, but did not think her brain could cope with any more of her mother's disclosures. She sat down in Benji's chair, the one he used for his lessons. She felt she needed to put distance between herself and her mother, at least for a time.

Finally, she said, "Thank you for telling me." Elizabeth rose, and rather than take her daughter's hand or touch her shoulder, bent down and embraced her.

"There is more to the tale," she said softly in Emma's ear. "When you are ready, I will tell you all."

Emma was convinced that she would never be ready. This voyage was proving to be more of an education than Emma had ever dreamed.

***

On a sunny morning a day after they passed through the Straits of Florida, the captain asked for a meeting of all the men, passengers and sailors alike, on the aft deck. He wanted the women and children to remain below. Darcy was apprehensive.

"Men," the captain began in French, "we are entering the Gulf of Mexico, which is filled with pirates." The men began to murmur amongst themselves. "I have made this voyage many times. I have encountered Jean Lafitte himself and he has taken my ship from me, and killed many of my men. Those of us who were left were set into small boats and allowed to row ashore."

Darcy spoke up. "Perhaps it would be better to show them no resistance to minimize the bloodshed, or perhaps to find another route."

"I would not advise it. I am sure you men do not want to hand over your women or your children. And, sir, there is no other route. We must go close to Grande Terre where they hold their slave auctions, and directly past Barataria, their headquarters."

There was more conversation, which grew louder and more agitated. "You must protect us," someone called out.

"My men and I will do what we can, but in my experience, it is not always enough. For any of you who want a weapon and will commit to fighting with us, I will gladly give you a cutlass, or even a pistol, if you know how to use one."

This was a turn of events that shook Darcy to his core. The captain explained further. The pirates of Barataria were notorious, raiding English ships, any ships for that matter, that ventured into the gulf. Lafitte was the scourge of the Spanish, English, and the French, raiding merchantmen and their slave ships and then hoarding the booty. Slaves were sold wholesale in illegal auctions on Grande Terre and Barataria. Many ships were relieved of their cargo and a lucrative but illegal market had sprung up in New Orleans supplied by legions of privateers who crisscrossed the Gulf of Mexico. The Creole French treated Lafitte as something of a folk hero, having no great love for their American government, which they found restrictive. This adulation lasted, of course, until he plundered one of their ships or undercut their businesses.

Darcy descended the steps to his cabin and opened the door to see his wife teaching Bennet his lessons, and Emma sitting in her bunk, engrossed in a book.

"Emma, Bennet, go up on deck for a moment. I need to speak with your mother," he said sternly, so sternly in fact, that both of them looked at him wide-eyed and left together without a word.

"Dearest, what is it?" Elizabeth asked.

"A moment." He opened the door of the cabin and glanced in both directions. There was no one there.

"Why all the secrecy? What has happened?"

He stood with her by the row of windows at the stern that flooded their chamber with light. Then he opened his coat slightly and showed her the pistol secreted in his waistband.

"What does this mean?"

"Pirates," he said. "We are in grave danger of encountering pirates." He studied her face. He knew all she had suffered at the hands of lawless revolutionaries all those years ago, and he half expected fear or horror in her aspect. Instead, all he saw was resolve. "I am so sorry, Elizabeth. I did not consider the danger we would face here when I conceived of this idea. I did not stop to think."

She did not speak for a moment but looked up at his face as if she was studying it. "It does not matter now, does it? We are here, and that is that. Go to the captain and ask him for another cutlass."

"Whatever for?"

"For me, of course. If any brigands come for my children, they will have to go through me first."

"No, they will have to go through me first."

"I will rely on you to keep them at bay. But we both know how rapidly circumstances can change." She turned from him and looked about the room. "We cannot stay here. It is the first place they will look."

"The captain suggested the cable tier," Darcy said, quite taken aback by his wife's commanding tone.

"If most of the women and children will be there, we will find another place. First, we will hide from them. Then we will fight."

"I have married a lioness," Darcy said affectionately. "Hopefully, it will not come to that."

"Yes, husband, we can hope, but it is best to be prepared." She tapped her fingers on her lips in thought. "Ask for two cutlasses. Emma should have one too. I will not have her endure what I endured, at least not without a fight."

"I expect the captain will not issue weapons until the danger is upon us." He watched the expression on her face. She did not look frightened, only thoughtful. "Have you ever killed a man?" Darcy asked, already knowing the answer.

"No, of course not," Elizabeth answered.

"It is a terrible thing," Darcy said, half to himself and half to her. She looked up him and touched his cheek.

"I will do anything to protect my children," she said fiercely.

"And I will do anything to protect all of you."

She sighed, and then looked straight into his eyes. "Mr. Darcy, we will show them what we are made of."

***

Elizabeth spent the next few hours searching for a suitable hiding place for herself and her children. Even though she asked Darcy, to the point of begging him, he would not acquiesce to hiding with them. She knew he would not, for that was not the man he was. Although she was putting on a brave face, she was terrified. Twenty years before she had faced the brutality of such men, and it had left her with scars. A feeling of helplessness, of having no control over what was happening to one's own body, was distressing, to say the least. Now, it chilled her to her soul to think that something that horrific might be in store for her children. She would do everything in her power to prevent it.

After finding a small storage locker that she thought might do, she returned to her cabin and took Emma aside to explain what might happen and what to expect. Elizabeth was not of a mind to shelter her daughter too much. It was nearly time to tell her of the events in Grenada. The facts of life had already been explained to her. Elizabeth felt that she did not want her daughter to be as naïve as her mother was at her age.

"Mother," Emma said as Elizabeth returned from her scouting task. "What is happening? Where is Father?" She was no longer calling them "Papa" and "Mama."

Elizabeth met her daughter's gaze. "Your father is on deck with the other men. I have to speak to you both."

Benji was drawing at the table and looked up at his mother. "Are we nearly there, Mama?"

"No, we have some distance to go, and it is of that I wish to speak. We may be encountering some danger along the way."

"What danger?" Emma asked, her eyes widening.

"Come here, Benji, close to me," Elizabeth said and took her children's hands in hers. "The captain said that we *may* encounter pirates in these waters."

Benji clapped his hands together with glee. "Hoorah. Pirates."

Emma scowled. Elizabeth continued. "We are not playing at pirates, Benji dear. These are dangerous men who might mean us harm. I want you both to come with me and I will show you a place where we will hide." She stood up and Emma stood with her.

Benji ran to the door. "I am going on deck to help Papa. I will show those pirates."

Elizabeth caught him by the collar before he reached the hall. "You will do no such thing. You will come to the hiding place with us, and you will be utterly quiet."

Benji stuck out his lower lip and pouted. Elizabeth tried another tack. "Do you not want to come and protect your sister and your mama? If you go on deck, we will be all alone and unprotected."

Benji looked up at her with narrow eyes and paused for a moment. "Do not worry, Mother. I will protect you."

Elizabeth wanted to smile at her blustering boy as she led him and his sister through the bowels of the ship to a place where she hoped against hope they would be safe.

***

The next few days went by without incident, but tension had gripped them all. According to the captain, they were nearing the mouth of the great Mississippi River and would soon gain access to the deep-water route that would take them safely into New Orleans. One of Lafitte's strongholds, the island of Grand Terre, was near that route, and even after they gained access to the river, they would still have to pass his headquarters at Barataria. The captain's assurances that most of the piracy took place in open water did not assuage Elizabeth's anxiety. She would not feel safe until their feet touched the ground in New Orleans.

They were all on deck one evening to take the air after dinner when a cry went out from the crow's nest. "Ship ahoy."

With the other passengers and some of the crew, they gathered at the ship's rail and gazed out over the water. In the distance, barely discernable to the human eye, was a speck on the horizon. The entire ship's company watched with bated breath and the speck grew larger. It indeed was a ship, and it was headed in their direction.

"Pick me up please, Papa, I cannot see," said Benji as the crowd pressed together. "Can you see the Jolly Roger?"

Although all had been explained to him several times, Benji still was more excited than fearful at the thought of pirates. Darcy lifted him up so that he could see above the crowd. He held him there for a moment and then let him down. He looked up into his parents' faces. "I wish I had a telescope," he stated disconsolately.

The captain began barking orders, "Women and children below. Break out ze weapons." The small ship, Elizabeth learned, was armed with four small cannons, two forward and two aft. Not much of a deterrent for pirates, she imagined. Still, they were not without some protection. The men gathered near the mainmast and were issued various large knives and cutlasses. Elizabeth stepped forward at Darcy's side.

"I will require two of those," she said, pointing to the large wooden crate containing the weapons on the deck. A silence fell over the men.

"Do not worry, madame," the captain said. "We will protect ze ladies and ze children."

"Just the same," she continued, looking right into the captain's eyes, "I will require two weapons. One for myself and one for my daughter." Some of the men sniggered.

"Do as she asks," Darcy ordered gruffly. When no one moved, he took two large, machete-like knives from the chest and handed them to Elizabeth. She looked up into her husband's eyes and disappeared below decks. Meanwhile, the ship that was a mere dot on the horizon moments ago began to bear down on them.

Emma and Benji were not on deck. When she ran down the steps of the gangway, she saw her two children stood frozen at the door of their cabin. She handed Emma a cutlass.

"Use this if you have to," she said. "Come along." She held out her arm for them to proceed.

Both Emma and Benji looked more frightened than she had ever seen them, but she resolved not to betray any emotion until the crisis was over. They followed her mutely to the locker they had occupied before. Benji was the first to enter.

"But how can I protect you if I am all the way back here?" he asked as he folded himself into a small space at the end of the tiny chamber.

Elizabeth had no answer, but Emma provided a good one. "You are our last line of defense," she said and patted her little brother on the head. That statement seemed to satisfy the child and he sat down quietly. Emma, cutlass in hand, went in next with Elizabeth at the front. With effort, she pulled the door shut and they were engulfed in darkness. No one spoke. The space was hot and unbearably stuffy. From time to time, Elizabeth opened the door and peered into the mid-deck. No one was about.

There was no telling how long they stayed in such a cramped position, but suddenly, there were sounds of feet tromping the upper deck and voices.

"Mama," Benji squeaked.

"Hush now," Elizabeth whispered as forcefully as she dared. She wanted to add, "Our lives may depend upon it," but she did not want to frighten him further.

The voices grew louder, and she could tell from the sounds that men were descending the stairway to the lower deck. One set of footsteps was louder than the rest and seemed to head directly toward them. Elizabeth's heart was pounding, and she could feel Emma's hand grip her shoulder.

The door to their hiding place flew open. Elizabeth raised the cutlass above her head and lunged forward.

"Elizabeth, it is I," Darcy shouted as he raised his hands to protect himself while jumping back to avoid her attack.

Elizabeth stood frozen for a moment and then heard the cutlass clatter to the ground. Darcy clasped her to him with one arm and embraced Emma with the other. Benji ran and threw his arms around his father's legs, nearly toppling all of them over.

"It is all right now. The danger has passed. There will be no pirates. That ship brought us news. The Americans have burned Barataria."

Chapter 6

Now that the crisis was over, the crew and the passengers assembled on deck. By now, night had fallen, and yet they could see the first hint of land. Beyond, however, a glow was cast in the night sky that betrayed a raging inferno. Barataria was ablaze.

The captain of the agile schooner that outran them had finally stopped them. He was an American, and told them that a raiding party, with the object of securing the coast against a possible invasion by the British, had mounted a sneak attack on Jean Lafitte and his pirates. Catching them by surprise, they burned and sank their ships and caused them to flee in every direction into the Louisiana swamp. To the great surprise of their attackers, the pirates left much of their ill-gotten booty behind. The Americans proceeded to confiscate what they could and then set Barataria ablaze. It would be some time before the Lafittes were able to threaten the shipping channels of New Orleans.

With this news, Darcy breathed a sigh of relief. He found it strange, however, that the Americans were concerned with a British invasion. Surely, the war between them was drawing to a close. Certainly, the cause of it, British captains stopping American ships to recapture deserters, was no longer a concern. The war with Napoleon was over. The British Navy had no more reason to impress men into service.

Darcy had to admit, the Americans had every right to object to their citizens being *recovered* from British ships. Who could tell which sailor was which? In any case, he put this tiny problem out of his mind. The danger had passed, and they all were safe. In a day or two, they would be at the Peschier Plantation and all would be well.

***

Their ship wound its way through the lush vegetation of the southernmost Louisiana islands. The water turned from azure to a muddy brown as the great Mississippi River emptied itself into the swampy islands and the bayous. The landscape was a great change from the scenes one encountered docking in Porstmouth. The land here was lush and green and seemed nearly even with the water. The river itself was nearly as big as the ocean from whence they came.

They arrived at the dock at the Port of New Orleans in late morning. The sun washed the stone and wooden buildings in a soft, pink light. Bennet was already on deck, peering over the railing.

"Look, Mama, we are here," he said joyously.

Elizabeth smiled into Bennet's beatific face. "Yes, through God's mercy, we are here, safe and sound."

It was a surprise to Elizabeth that the river was so deep their ship could anchor so close to shore enabling them to disembark by gangplank rather than on smaller boats. Even the Thames did not have so deep a draught. As she looked along the shoreline as they were approaching, she did not see any roads along the shore, or anything really, except greenery and fetid swamp. It was a wonder anyone would choose to live in such a place. Still, it was Poppy's home, and a place where she could be free.

In no time they stood upon the dock, their trunks and belongings beside them, and she saw Darcy looking about for a conveyance of some sort to take them to the nearest hotel. It was then she noticed a small Negro boy running from one passenger to another, only to be rebuked. Finally, he lighted upon them.

"*Êtes-vous* Monsieur Darcy? he asked rapidly. "Are you Mr. Darcy?" he asked again in heavily accented English, closing one eye as if preparing for a blow.

"I am," Darcy replied in French. "Who are you?"

The boy smiled widely. "I am glad to meet you, sir. I am Antoine De Peschier," he said with an exaggerated bow belying his ragged appearance.

"Peschier?" Elizabeth asked. "It is the Peschier family we are here to visit."

"I come from the plantation," he said in French. "We have waited for you." With that he ran off, and a few moments later, two men and a woman, all dark-skinned, came forward.

"Come. We go by boat."

Elizabeth took her husband's arm and saw Emma roll her eyes as her brother said, "Oh dear. Another boat."

This boat, however, was flat and open, loaded with their luggage, and quite far from where they disembarked. The air was humid and warm, not at all like England, in fact, similar to Grenada. Many memories of that time flooded Elizabeth's mind. These people who were helping them. They were the slaves of the Peschier Plantation.

The boat was finally loaded, and they were off. Since the plantation was upriver, the boat was equipped with oars that were being used only to steer. The power to bring them upriver was provided by what Elizabeth guessed was a mule on shore that was tethered to the conveyance. Their progress was slow, but steady. Soon they were out of sight of the city, and on their way through the land of plantations.

Benji insisted on sitting in the back with the little slave boy, Antoine. Even though there was a language barrier, the two boys began to play a game in which Antoine took a pebble and hid it behind his back, switching it from side to side. Benji, after much pantomime, understood that he was supposed to guess where the pebble was and so they amused each other with simple games. She knew her son was desperate for the company of other children. There were only a few children aboard their ship, and they were either too young or too old to be of any interest. She had hoped that she would bring a new sibling into the world for him, but it was not to be.

Her husband must have been studying her in her reverie, for he spoke to her now. "What are thinking of, Lizzy? You look so pensive."

"I was thinking of how similar this place is to Grenada." She did not want to talk about her troubles again. Of course, the past had its own haunting memories.

"I was thinking the same thing myself. The climate, the vegetation, the French," he said, emphasizing the last.

"They do seem to be everywhere."

"As do we English. And both of our people bring with us the slavery of others," he murmured.

"You will try not to quarrel with Monsieur Peschier," she said as more of a question than a command.

"I have learned enough from this life not to make any hasty judgments, but still…" he trailed off.

"Please, Mr. Darcy, you will try not to engage in parliamentary quarrels." She smiled at him.

"As you wish, madame." His eyes were twinkling.

They had to be rowed across the river to arrive at their destination, and so were pulled almost a quarter mile past it and then, with the expertise of the oarsmen, they landed at the dock of what Elizabeth presumed was the Peschier Plantation.

The boat gave a great knock as it was maneuvered into place, and that sound brought a great rush of humanity from the household. In all the hubbub, Elizabeth heard the lilting sound of Poppy's voice shouting out, "They are here. They are here."

As Elizabeth stepped out of the boat onto the landing, she saw her friend Poppy. She had not much changed in the intervening years, her face unlined, yet showing a testament to the years she lived. Her dress, however, was much changed. She wore a dress of current fashion, with a high waist and cap sleeves of a fine, floral fabric. And on her head, she wore an orange scarf that covered her hair. It was adorned with feathers. Poppy looked every part the lady of the household.

For a moment, the two women stood and looked at each other from a distance. Then, all at once ran to one another. Poppy nearly crushed Elizabeth in her embrace.

"Oh, my friend, oh my dear friend," she kept saying over and over. "You are here. You are finally here." Elizabeth could feel the tears well in her eyes. When Poppy loosened her hold and beheld her friend, her face softened into the smile Elizabeth remembered so long ago. Poppy gently brushed the tears from Elizabeth's cheek. Then she reached out her hand to Darcy, who took it. "Welcome to you, my dear Mr. Darcy. Thank you for bringing my friend to me." Before Darcy could reply, Poppy put her arm about Elizabeth's waist. "Come. Come into the house. We will have lemonade and meet the family."

Poppy and Elizabeth led the parade to a splendid wooden building, painted every colour of the rainbow. The main house was yellow, but the trim had many colours and gave the house a gay, tropical feeling. The house stood well above the ground, supported by tall brick pillars set every few feet. With the river so close by and so expansive, Elizabeth guessed that it flooded its banks from time to time, hence the need to elevate the house beyond ground level.

The façade was interrupted by French doors, which were placed every few feet along the front of the house. Two staircases parallel to the house led to a landing that protruded from the veranda, which was wide enough to set a bed upon, and ran the length of the house. When they reached the central door, Poppy opened it and they all gathered in the sitting room or main parlour. Immediately, a tall, slim, aristocratic white man who appeared to be about sixty years of age stood and bowed with a slight incline of the head as they each entered.

"This is my husband, Francois Peschier," Poppy said as she released Elizabeth. Poppy crossed the room and took hold of her husband's arm.

"*Monsieur*," Darcy said, extending his hand.

"Welcome to our home, Mr. Darcy," Peschier said with a heavy French accent and, letting go of Darcy's hand, took him by the shoulders and kissed him on both cheeks. Elizabeth looked at her husband's face and could hardly contain her mirth. This was not a greeting to which her Mr. Darcy had adjusted, even after all these years of suffering his sister's husband's salutations.

Benji moved over to his mother and held her hand, observing the introductions. Peschier took her hand and kissed it and likewise Emma's uttering, "*Enchanté*." Elizabeth thought she could detect a blush of pink rise from Emma's neck to colour her cheeks.

All this time, Benji was holding his mother's hand, hiding behind her skirts.

"An' who is this young man?" Poppy asked.

Elizabeth bent and gave Benji a little push forward. "Tell Madame Peschier what your name is," she whispered.

Benji let go of his mother's hand and, taking a breath, stepped forward. "I am Bennet Fitzwilliam Darcy, your humble servant," he said solemnly, extending his hand. Poppy took it and bid him welcome. Monsieur Peschier stepped forward and Benji's eyes became as wide as saucers. "He is not going to kiss me, is he?" The boy looked horrified. The entire company dissolved in laughter and was suddenly interrupted by the entrance of a tall, well-built, well-dressed young man. The sight of him made the skin prickle down Elizabeth's arms.

He had Edward Home's face, but with a slightly wider nose and fuller lips. The young man was almost a perfect combination of

Poppy and Edward. His eyes were his most striking feature. They were a hazel color with the slightest hint of green and gave his face quite an arresting aspect. As they exchanged formalities, Elizabeth watched her daughter closely.

"So pleased to make your acquaintance," he said carefully in well-crafted English with only the slight hint of a French accent. "I am Phillipe Peschier. Welcome to our home."

He kissed Emma's hand. She stared at it for a moment, and this time, the blush Elizabeth observed before was more robust.

"I am pleased to meet you also," Emma said rather timidly. "You have a beautiful home."

"I will show you about, if you like," he said gallantly. Emma smiled and blushed again.

"Plenty time for dat later," Poppy said. Elizabeth was gratified that her friend's Caribbean accent had not disappeared. She could listen to it all day. There was a bustling of activity on the veranda, and two young women close to Emma's age came rushing through the French doors, their parasols collapsing as they entered.

"Oh, *maman*, we are so sorry," cried the young girl with the chestnut-coloured skin dressed in a pink frock. She ran to her mother and kissed her on both cheeks.

"Yes, we are sorry, *maman*," the other echoed, her cheeks pink and flushed with exertion, her blond hair escaping from her bonnet, which matched her blue frock.

They turned immediately to Elizabeth. Poppy nearly jumped from her seat; putting an arm around the girls' waists, she brought them forward.

"Dis is my daughter Elizabeth Ann," she said, smiling all the way to her eyes as she presented the girl dressed in a lovely pink frock to her friend. "And dis my daughter Adele. We call dem de twins," Poppy said giggling.

Elizabeth took each girl by the hand. "So wonderful to meet you both." In the French style, they both embraced her and kissed her on both cheeks. To Elizabeth, they seemed bubbling over with energy.

"You will meet my Manon and Cecile when we go to town," Poppy explained. "Dey grown and married now. Come. We show you where you will sleep and then we have something to eat."

"Oh good," Benji said. "I am hungry."

Poppy laughed and ran her hand over his head. "Little boys always hungry."

Then Benji looked up into his mother's face. "After that, can I go out and play with Antoine?"

Poppy looked over at Benji. "You talkin' of de little boy who come with you upriver?"

she asked.

"Yes, madame," he said politely. Elizabeth was gratified that her lessons on deportment were taking hold in her youngest.

"Dat boy have work. He don' play 'til evenin' time," Poppy said. "Now come. We get you settle, and den we eat. Francois," she called, interrupting her husband's conversation with Darcy. "Can you and Philippe show Emma and Master Bennet der rooms, please? Den we come back and you tase our New Orleans dish, jambalaya."

***

Emma was not used to food with so much spice and heat, and her first taste of jambalaya was challenging. It was fortunate that she had such a keen appetite as they had not eaten all day. She watched her father and mother, and they did not seem to notice the spices at all. Perhaps their mysterious trip to the Caribbean was the origin of their expanded palates. Not to be outdone by her parents, she made no complaint of the heat of the food but gave everyone the impression that she had been eating such delicacies her entire life. They say that travel broadens the mind, but apparently it also broadens the palate.

Her little brother made an attempt at the dish but made a face and a painful swallow. Madame and Monsieur Peschier found his machinations most amusing and then brought some boiled meat, cheese, and something called *greens* that looked a bit like cabbage, but a much darker green. This dish Benji ate with dispatch.

Emma was determined to give a good impression to Poppy and her family, most especially to her eldest son, Philippe. Of course, she could never be really interested in him, considering his origins, yet she found him compelling. He spoke eloquently of the raid that they had witnessed from afar on Barataria and seemed to know a great deal about the politics of the area. Of course, it was nothing compared to her father, who was a Member of Parliament, which was a national, not a local, institution. With the defeat of Napoleon,

Britain was the most powerful country on earth. New Orleans, by contrast, was a tiny backwater city. Still, Phillipe was most attractive, and she felt herself colour whenever she looked at him.

With dinner over, Phillipe renewed his offer to show off the plantation. Benji insisted on joining them, and Emma did not know why that so annoyed her. Did she want to be alone with Philippe? She must remind herself that she was a young lady of breeding and must not let herself be swayed by foreign good looks. She had been fooled once by Edmund Montjoy, who was unworthy of her. She would not be fooled again.

***

Poppy left Elizabeth and Darcy in their chamber at the end of the house. In fact, the Darcys occupied a wing of the house that extended out from the rest of the house. The wing began in a parlour next to the one in which they were received, and went on to a hallway that led to three rooms: first Emma's, then Benji's, and lastly Elizabeth and Darcy's. Theirs was an airy room at the end of the building with three windows on each side, she guessed designed such to catch the breeze. Gauzy white curtains fluttered there. The headboard of the bed leaned against the far wall, and compared to their cramped quarters aboard ship, there seemed to be oceans of room. Poppy had encouraged them to rest after their long journey, but judging from the look in her husband's eye from the moment the servants left their things, a rest would have to wait.

With Benji gone on a tour of the plantation, and the cooks sequestered in the kitchen, there was no one about either inside or out and they were quite alone in their room. Elizabeth suspected that this was Poppy's and Francois's room, as it had the look of a master chamber. She was grateful for her friend's consideration. It had been weeks since she and Darcy had touched each other save a few furtive kisses at the taffrail.

The fog of misery that had clouded her spirit was lifted day by day as their journey progressed. She could feel now the full blossoming of her desire, a desire for Darcy's touch that the prolonged abstinence of the voyage sharpened into an aching need.

At the beginning of their marriage, there was the shadow of her ordeal at the hands of the revolutionaries on Grenada that overshadowed the pleasure she took in her husband's lovemaking. Darcy was understanding and gentle with her then, but also possessed of a young man's ardor. Now, as their bond deepened over the years, he could caress her in a long and lingering act of love.

Darcy was at the washbowl washing his face and hands, his jacket already draped over the chair in the corner of the room. She joined him and took up the towel and began to daub his face. He said nothing as she then dried his hands, taking her time with each finger.

He reached up, taking her face in both his hands, and gently kissed her. Her desire for him was so aroused she felt she had not patience for the buttons on his shirt or the front of his pantaloons. He kissed her below her ear, and then his mouth traveled along her neck and along her shoulder. His hands had pulled her sleeves down and she left off with his garments and pulled both her arms out of her sleeves and then ran her fingers along the scar on his side. She looked into his eyes. Darcy untied the ribbon round her waist and her dress puddled to the floor. In a moment they were in each other's arms in bed, no clothing between them.

Their bodies glistened with a thin film of sweat, and Elizabeth could feel a most pleasant tingle with each puff of breeze. Her husband looked straight into her eyes, and then began his slow and pleasantly unnerving descent to her breasts, where he ministered to them with his hands and his mouth. It took every bit of self-control she had not to cry out with pleasure. She ran her hands along his back and felt the tautness of his muscles. She touched his face and brought him back to face her.

"I missed you," she whispered, and began to kiss his cheeks, his eyes, then the curve of his jaw. When she reached his lips, he opened his mouth to her with such passion and desire that she felt herself breathless with happiness and desire.

He pulled away and looked at her. "I missed you too, Lizzy. For a time, I thought I would never get you back."

She was so touched by his words and his tone that she cradled his head against her neck and wove her arms around him in an embrace that she hoped would be more eloquent than her words. He kissed her neck and rolled onto his back so that they were side by side. She could see, from the sheet that covered them, his member in full standing.

"I am so sorry," she began, but he touched her mouth with two of his fingers, and then she saw a rueful smile play upon his lips.

"What happens to one of us happens to us both. I mourned too, Lizzy."

It was the first time she had considered that he also mourned the loss of their child, the loss of each one that was never to be. As it was in most of their marriage, she knew he felt it his duty to be the protector, the guardian of their lives, and would not betray his doubts or his feelings if he believed they would cause her any pain.

She could feel the tears well in her eyes, and she wanted now to be the protector, the only one who could assuage his pain. She kissed him passionately, deeply. She wanted to be close to him, to be one with him, to have him inside her.

He responded to her every touch. She peppered him with kisses down his chest and all the way to his rigid manhood. Gently, he turned her on her back and, taking his time, touched and caressed her in her most private of places. When the pleasure of it nearly became pain, she guided him into her liquid center. He entered her and then stopped, looking first into her face and then kissing each eye, each cheek, and then her waiting mouth. She could feel him moving slowly inside of her and wrapping her legs around his; she moved with him, engulfed him, embraced him.

His slow ministrations took on a more urgent rhythm, and then, when she felt she would burst from yearning, she rode with him over the precipice. Elizabeth could feel herself tighten around him.

She wanted never to let go.

"Do not withdraw," she asked of him. He nestled into her neck, relieving the weight of his body from her, but not leaving her. They lay like that for a long time, and then he began to move again, slowly. She could feel him harden again within her. She moved with him, taking his head in her hands, and smiled at him. "Why, Mr. Darcy," she said playfully. "You *have* missed me." Then with what she hoped conveyed her boundless love for him, she whispered, "Thank you for this journey."

"It is not over yet," he replied, smiling, and they enjoyed each other once more.

Chapter 7

Phillipe stood on the veranda of the house waiting for Emma Darcy. His mother insisted, in no uncertain terms, that he be the perfect gentleman and, dare he say it, friendly, to these English visitors. The English: the people who enslaved him, his mother, and his sisters. He was the product of slavery. Edward Home took his mother whenever he liked but did not recognize him or his sisters as his own. The dreadful man had his own children as his slaves. Phillipe shuddered at the thought.

At last Emma emerged from the house, her head covered in a bonnet. Phillipe gallantly produced a parasol and offered it to her.

"Thank you, kind sir," she said. From the expression on her face, he could not tell if she was mocking him or not. He remembered his mother's words: "Be kind to the Darcys. Their mother is my dearest friend." He would be gallant for his mother's sake. Her little brother arrived in her wake.

"Good afternoon, Master Bennet," he said with a slight bow.

Benji grinned. "Good afternoon, Monsieur Peschier," he replied, bowing low. "You may call me Benji. Everyone does."

"Benji then."

Phillipe offered Emma his arm, and they set off. Benji skipped along behind them, or in front of them, or wherever it was that small boys wandered. They descended from the veranda, and Phillipe brought them into the cool of the cellar. It was quite deep and expansive and built so much below ground level that they could stand upright in it easily.

"The river will sometimes flood," he began, "so all the plantation houses are built high."

"Why do you not build farther away from the river?" Emma asked. "Then you would not have to worry about flooding."

Insolent girl. What does she know of anything? Phillipe breathed a sigh and controlled his reaction. Really, it was an innocent question. He must stop letting his hatred for the English colour his treatment of his guests. He was, after all, a gentleman.

"We need the breeze from the river. It cools the house. As I take you farther back to where the fields begin, you will see what I mean," he stated with forced calm.

By this time, they had emerged to a brick courtyard that filled the space between the two wings of the house where he pointed out the windows of her room, and Benji's, and those of her parents.

Phillipe directed her to the two long buildings built a short distance behind the house. The first was the kitchen. The place was alive with activity with black women in kerchiefs tied over their heads, and a large blonde woman with a florid face stirring a pot. There was much chopping of meat and vegetables, and all manner of cooking. Small Negro children bustled about carrying water and firewood. They all acknowledged him as he strode through, calling him *Monsieur Phillipe,* and he smiled and spoke to them in French. The place was stiflingly hot, even with the windows open.

When they were outdoors again, Phillipe spoke to Emma. "The food prepared in that kitchen is for everyone, master and slave alike," he said rather proudly. "They eat what we eat. I believe that is not so in your country."

Emma looked at him askance. "We have no slaves in my country," she said haughtily.

He looked at her, trying to hide his aggravation at her impudence. The English always felt themselves so superior. "But you have tenant farmers whose fortunes rise and fall with the land, the weather, and the market for their goods while you remain untouched." From the look on Emma's face, he could tell that she did not readily have an answer for him. That pleased him greatly. "And what of the destitute of your cities?"

Emma paused for a moment, looking vexed. "We do not buy and sell human beings."

Phillipe stopped and looked at her. "But your country dominated the slave trade and only abolished it quite recently."

"And my father was one of those who spoke out most vehemently against the practice and was instrumental in stopping the slave trade."

He was about to ask her if what she said was true but stopped himself in time. "I did not know that." He would withhold judgment momentarily. Perhaps there was more to these Darcys than he thought. "But, although your country abolished the slave trade, it did not abolish slavery itself."

She looked at him through narrowed eyes. "And you own slaves."

After that remark, she looked at him with a self-satisfied air. It irritated him. There was so much that she did not understand. What right had she to be so arrogant and condescending to him? This was his land, to be accurate, the land of his family, and she was a guest. He was proud, and rightly so, of all their accomplishments. She had no idea the arguments he had with his father about using slave labour at the plantation, and how it hurt his heart to see that he was holding people in bondage as he had been held.

They had arrived at the overseer's cottage. She was silent. Perhaps he had been rude to speak to her in such a manner. Still, he detested interlopers such as herself, questioning his way of life. What right did she have? He had to admit she had a point, but would never admit that to her.

"Benji, come look," she said to her brother, turning away from Phillipe. Benji ran to join them. "Did you see this cottage?"

"It looks like Mr. Foster's house, but with many more colours," he said and was off again.

"Who is Mr. Foster?" Phillipe asked, hoping she would favour him with a reply. It would not go well with his mother if this Miss Darcy arrived back in the house in a huff.

She deigned to speak to him. "Foster is someone who helps run my father's estate. In fact, he does run it when we are in town for the Season." He thought her tone sounded as if she was talking down to him from a great height.

"He is your overseer, then."

She paused a moment, and then spoke. "In a manner of speaking," she admitted. She stood looking at the cottage with its wide veranda and surrounding garden. She ran her hand along the white wooden fence that contained a multitude of flowers in front. She had long since dropped his arm that he had offered when they began.

He led her back onto the brick path that led to the garden behind the kitchen. This plot was nearly a small farm. "We grow all our own vegetables here."

Phillipe was proud of the grounds, which were neat and well-kept, with many of the slaves engaged in every kind of activity. On the other side of the plantation, opposite the cottages, were chicken coops and a cattle barn. Benji trailed along behind them or ran in front of them, but rarely walked alongside and contributed little to their conversation. Phillipe noticed that Miss Darcy was keeping a watchful eye on her brother and frequently turned from Phillipe to observe the little boy's movements.

At last they were quite far from the house, in view of his family's great fields. "Sugar cane," Phillipe said as Emma gazed past the many small houses arranged at the back of the property. "It is the lifeblood of our plantation. From here you can only see a small portion of our land. Unlike our neighbors, whose plantations are long and thin, our land extends back, but widens considerably. We have the largest sugar plantation in the delta." Emma looked back at the cane. He surmised that she had never seen anything like it before, but if he asked, she would never admit it.

Benji began to run toward the plants. Phillipe shouted after him, "Be careful. The leaves are sharp." Benji froze immediately and looked back at the two of them.

"I will be careful," he shouted back and continued running toward the cane.

"He will not," Emma said to Phillipe.

"Do not be concerned. Unless your brother tries to harvest the cane, he will undoubtedly be all right. Pulling up the old cane is the most difficult," he said, turning her toward the small houses. "The cane you see here is beginning to regrow. Our older plants, farther back in the plantation, must be pulled up and new ones planted. It is backbreaking work. I will take you there so that you may see."

"This is the work your slaves do, I expect." She had the supercilious air about her again.

"Without slaves, there would be no sugar. No white man or free man of color would work in the cane fields for any price. Without sugar, there would be no pastry in France, and no cake in England." He waited for her reaction.

"I saw a white woman in the kitchen, and some servants in your house are also white," she said, changing the subject.

"They are German. Immigrants such as we are, but with little or no fortune. There are many such people in New Orleans." He waited for her response but received none. "And these are the slave quarters," Philippe said, as they walked along the path that led to some impossibly small houses, shacks really. They were sound, painted white, but so small that a man could walk from one end of the building to the other in twelve paces, perhaps less.

"An entire family lives in such a tiny place?" Emma asked incredulously.

"Two."

"Two what?" Emma asked, looking into his face in disbelief.

"Two families. Two families live in each building. There is a smaller room at the back for washing, perhaps for cooking. The families have no need of a kitchen, really," he continued. "As I said, the kitchen for the big house cooks for everyone."

Emma said nothing but stared at him, her mouth momentarily agape. He knew that a girl of her wealth and upbringing would undoubtedly have a bedchamber larger than two of these buildings. Before she could speak again, he said, "Come. There is one more thing I would like to show you."

"Benji, come along," Emma called, and waited until her brother was alongside once again. Only then they proceeded to a building behind the caretaker's cottage. It looked unimpressive, like a barn or some other outbuilding, but Phillipe smiled at it with pride.

"This is my workshop." He opened the doors of the large outbuilding and led them into the coolness inside. "It was once a barn," he explained, "but after I returned from Paris, I needed a place to conduct my experiments."

"You were in Paris?" Emma asked, surprised.

"Yes, of course." He opened the shutters as the dust floated in the sunlight. "It was a time when the French and the British had a temporary peace. It did not last long. I was sixteen at the time. My father sent me there to studying engineering."

"I have never been to Paris," Emma said wistfully.

"It is beautiful and the people there are open-minded," he said absently, then added, "not like the English."

Emma turned and glared at him. "I do believe, sir, that you are deliberately trying to provoke me."

Phillipe laughed. "I am only saying what I have observed. The French looked past the color of my skin. The English never did. But let us not quarrel. I wish to show you something."

By this time, Benji was nearly dancing about what appeared to be large metal barrels on their sides, held up by three-foot legs, and were connected by metal crosspieces.

"What is it, *monsieur*?" Benji asked.

"It is a sugar crystallizing machine," Phillipe stated and then commenced to explain his experiments using steam to extract sugar from the cane. He looked over at Emma from time to time and could tell by her bored expression that she was uninterested, uncomprehending, or more likely, still angry with him for his characterization of the English.

"And why do you need such an apparatus?" she asked.

"The method we use now requires men to transfer large, boiling kettles of sugar. The liquid, if spilled, causes dreadful burns. I would like to prevent that."

"Make it go," Benji demanded excitedly.

"Not today, I am afraid. I am still working out some problems. Someday, though, it will change everything."

"Perhaps you should also invent a machine to harvest the sugarcane so that you do not need the slaves," Emma retorted.

Emma Darcy will have her own back, he thought. Without moving he pointed to a darkened corner. "I am working on such a machine. It is over there," he stated flatly.

"Does it work?" She strolled toward it.

"Not yet. Everything takes time."

***

Elizabeth and Darcy had emerged from their chamber to find their children had disappeared into the plantation. Elizabeth watched Emma return to the house from her place of repose near her bedroom window and met her daughter in their wing's hallway. From her expression, Elizabeth knew that a storm had gathered. She put her arm around her daughter's waist and directed her to her room. As soon as Elizabeth closed the door to Emma's chamber, the lightning bolt was released.

"That Phillipe Peschier is the rudest man I have ever met," Emma hissed as she removed her bonnet and then sat upon her bed. "He actually insulted the English," she said in an exasperated tone. "Right to my face."

Elizabeth smiled. "What did he say?"

Emma thought for a moment. "He said that the French were much more open-minded than we are."

Elizabeth was about to speak, but Emma continued, "And he had the gall to defend slavery to me. I cannot understand it. He was a slave himself. Has he forgotten the ignominy of it?"

Elizabeth felt that her daughter was on dangerous ground. She herself had questioned that foul institution with the Home family in Grenada and was rebuked for her efforts. The situation here at the plantation was not what Elizabeth expected, but she had learned to bide her time. In her younger days, she had to admit that she often spoke before she thought.

"Be careful you do not misjudge him," Elizabeth cautioned. She could tell by Emma's pout that was not what she wanted to hear.

"Are you taking his side?" she asked shrilly.

"My dear," Elizabeth said soothingly, "there are no sides. Please try to be patient, and remember that you are a young lady with impeccable manners. People are not always what they seem on first examination."

Emma huffed and crossed her arms. "Am I expected to stand there and accept his insults?"

"Emma, dearest, he did not insult you personally. As for England, I believe she can stand up for herself."

"You are making fun of me." Emma's eyes narrowed.

"No, I am merely saying that you need to watch and learn before making judgments. In my youth, I too was hasty to judge your father and take the part of another who was unworthy. It is a predilection of youth." Gently, Elizabeth pried one of Emma's hands loose and held it. She looked down into her lap. "You do not know Phillipe's history."

Emma bent her head to look into her mother's face. "Perhaps you should tell me, so that I might better understand."

Elizabeth looked up. "Yes, I do believe it is time." She told her daughter of her engagement to Edward Home in Grenada, and her subsequent discovery that Edward had taken his slave, Poppy, as his mistress against her will, and that she bore him four children, the last of whom was born after his death in the rebellion. The eldest was Phillipe. He was eight years old when Elizabeth had met him, and the boy was well aware that his father was the lieutenant governor's son and he let his mother, himself, and his sisters continue to live in slavery. Phillipe was in the camp with his mother and sisters and watched the English attack.

Elizabeth stopped short of her own abuse at the hands of the rebels. She could see in her daughter's eyes that she was shaken by the revelations she imparted, and as such, did not wish to reveal any more.

Elizabeth waited a moment and then asked Emma a simple question. "Why do you think slavery is wrong?"

Her daughter did not hesitate. "Papa says it's wrong, so it must be." Elizabeth sighed but did not address the subject further.

"And do you think the English are superior to other people?"

"Oh, well, Mother." Her tone was condescending. "We are most assuredly superior to the French." Elizabeth shook her head, kissed her daughter on the cheek, and left to find her youngest.

Chapter 8

The days passed peacefully. One early morning, after Elizabeth rose from a peaceful sleep, she went to awaken her children and found her son's bed empty. Dressing quickly, she looked for him in the public rooms of the house. He was nowhere to be found. As she stepped out on the veranda, she spied him. He and Antoine had yokes about their necks connected to a bucket on each side. They were coming from the river. She thought to call out to him but decided instead to watch. As they neared the veranda, he had not yet seen her. They passed the house and she ran to one of the dining room windows that gave a full view of the kitchen buildings. There she watched as they emptied their buckets into a large barrel at the front. They then took their yokes and began running again toward the river.

"Mama, you should call Benji in at once. What he is doing is most unsuitable." Emma had approached quietly from behind and startled Elizabeth.

"You sound like your Uncle Charles's sisters."

Emma came around to look directly at her mother. "That is unfair."

"Yes, I suppose it is, I am sorry, dear." She took her daughter's hand and then looked again out the window. "Look how happy they are. How can you deny your brother a playmate?"

"But he is not playing, is he? He is doing the work of a slave. At home, he would not even be allowed to play with the village children and here…"

Elizabeth was afraid that her face betrayed her.

"Mother," Emma's voice was rising in pitch. "You do not allow him to play with those urchins from the village?"

Elizabeth smiled and shrugged. "Sometimes I take him on my visits, and he disappears into the cottages or the gardens. Really, Emma, what is the harm in it?" With emphasis, she said, "There are only the two of you and there will be only the two of you. I am sure you do not want to spend your days entertaining your brother."

Emma shook her head. "It is not proper. There are some things that are acceptable in society and some that are not."

"By unacceptable I take it you mean, for example, a young woman from Longbourn, from the middle classes as it were, marrying a man of your father's social class. Is that what you mean?"

Emma did not say anything, but her lips were pulled tight. Eventually, she commented haughtily, "Sometimes, Mama, you are quite vexing."

Elizabeth smiled and patted her daughter's hand. "I think I have heard something similar from your father." She did not argue with Emma, as she hoped her daughter would consider her words when she was alone and could contemplate them.

Elizabeth turned again to the window to see the boys again empty their buckets into the barrel. Antoine disappeared for a moment and then returned with white powder in his hand. He threw it into the barrel, and the two boys commenced stirring. Elizabeth and Emma watched them for a while. Poppy arrived and joined them at the window.

"What are they doing?" Elizabeth asked, still watching the boys.

"They stir alum in the water. It take the mud from the Mississippi, den de water safe to drink."

By this time, the servants were bringing in pastry and coffee for breakfast. Apparently, Emma had requested that her breakfast be brought to her room as she watched one of the servants leave with a laden tray. The rest of the family had not yet risen, and Poppy and Elizabeth sat down at the table to talk.

"This pastry is quite delicious." Elizabeth bit into a delectable treat.

"De Arcadians call them beignets. Eat dem hot w' lots o' sugar. Dat's de bes'. She smiled as the sugar coated her lips. They sat for a moment, enjoying the pastry. Poppy got up from the table and looked out the window, her expression suddenly serious. "I teach de slaves to read."

Elizabeth smiled almost to a grin. "You do? That is wonderful."

Poppy turned and looked back at her friend. She paused a moment and Elizabeth waited for her to speak again. "You wonderin' how I can keep slaves when I know what slavery like, is it not so?"

Elizabeth was not going to bring up the subject at all. With the Home family and with her Quaker friends, she felt she could talk about it, but here in her friend's home, she felt it was not her place. She said nothing, but Poppy must have read her expression. Even though they had been apart for many years, because of the intensity of their shared experience, they understood each other well.

"It's Francois. He a planter. Always was a planter, even when de English take everyt'ing from him in Grenada. It all he know. He hide some gold from Grenada an' when we come here, we have money to start again. He took four chil'ren not his own to himself, and a slave woman as his wife. What can I say to him? He say to me, 'You cannot grow sugar wit'out slaves.' What could I say?"

Elizabeth said nothing but reached out and held Poppy's hand. Poppy continued, "After Edward Home, I t'ought to myself, 'No udder white man ever gon' touch me.'"

Elizabeth understood. After what happened to her in Grenada, it took a long time and an understanding husband to overcome her aversion to men, and she had not suffered to the degree that Poppy had suffered.

"But," Poppy said, looking up, her tone suddenly brightening, "here we are. He a good man, Elizabet'. He been good to my chil'ren and to me. We happy here. Nothing perfect in dis worl'."

By this time, Benji's bouncing footsteps were heard on the back stairway. He joined them in Emma's room. He ran to his mother and kissed her on the cheek and then ran and did the same to Poppy. He took his seat next to his mother and she filled his plate. He took a bite immediately, chewed twice, and then began to speak.

"Toby and I were playing carry the bucket."

"Do not speak with your mouth full, Benji," Elizabeth chided.

"No, Mama," he responded with his mouth full. He chewed a few more times, and then spoke again. "I want to stay here forever."

"Then they will call us, The Darcys of New Orleans," Darcy said with a laugh from behind them. Poppy and Elizabeth turned at the sound of his voice.

"That is a good idea." Benji stuffed his mouth again.

"Who is Toby?" Darcy asked as he sat down to breakfast.

"Toby is Antoine. He said I could call him by his secret name."
Benji suddenly covered his mouth with both hands. "Oh no. I was
not supposed to tell."

Elizabeth looked at Poppy quizzically. Poppy smiled. "Mos' de
slaves have a name dey master give 'em and then dey choose another
that only dey friends and family use. Toby mus' be Antoine's udder
name. We all still call Toby "Antoine". Don' you worry."

Benji seemed much relieved at the news and set to consuming
his third beignet with much enthusiasm.

***

Emma did not see Phillipe for the next few days. He did not join
them for dinner. She had taken to strolling down the banks of the
river with her mother's namesake and her sister Adele. The two
girls, who looked so different from each other, seemed to be of one
mind. A cross word never passed between them. Emma was
fascinated with their stories of boarding school at the Ursuline
Academy in the city. Adele was admitted without question, and at
her father's insistence, and a sizable donation to the order, her sister
Elizabeth Ann entered as well.

To Emma, it seemed the height of adventure to go away to
school as a boy would do in England. Her own education was had
under the guidance of tutors and her governess, and was not confined
to music (which she learned from her Aunt Georgiana) and decorum.
She'd learned the arts, languages, reading, writing, some
mathematics, and outdoor education according to the ideas of
Rousseau. Her parents considered themselves progressive in their
attitudes toward girls' education, but she did not go away to school.
Even though Adele and Elizabeth Ann were only down the river
from their family home, Emma thought it a great privilege to
actually attend school. Still, they had never crossed the ocean as she
had. And it also seemed to her that they spent an inordinate amount
of time on religion, and the Catholic religion of all things.

They were seated in the shade under a live oak hanging with
what the twins told her was Spanish moss. Emma looked at the girls
and felt a pang of jealousy.

"It must be nice to have a sister, but you two…" She trailed off,
wishing she could take back the last few words.

Adele looked at Elizabeth Ann and smiled. "We have always been together. I cannot remember a time when we have ever been separated. Even though we did not have the same mother and father when we began, we have the same ones now."

"But you do not share the same blood, do you?"

This time Elizabeth Ann spoke. "Whatever blood we have, from a French father or an English one, from a Grenadan mother or a French one, God has seen fit to make us sisters. That is enough for us."

Emma thought she had something to say in response but stopped herself before awkward words escaped again. If these two considered themselves sisters, who was she to say otherwise? They seemed blind to their differences and saw only their family connection. Again, oddly, she felt a pang of envy.

Elizabeth Ann patted Elizabeth's hand. "For the time you are here, you can be our sister also. You may tell us all your secrets and we will tell you ours."

Emma was startled and pleased by their announcement, but was skeptical as well. "I thank you for that, but you may find my secrets too scandalous."

Adele's eyes were dancing. "Those are the best kind."

Emma smiled in spite of herself. "Do you two have any secrets?"

They looked at each other and nodded and then both of them began scanning their little resting place for eavesdroppers. "We will tell you, but you must promise not to tell *maman* or Papa."

Emma traced an "X" with her finger over her heart. "I promise. Now tell me."

Elizabeth Ann leaned over and whispered in Emma's ear. Indeed, it was a most surprising secret, and one Emma could never have guessed.

By early evening, the trio arrived back at the plantation house and the two sisters retired to their rooms before dinner. Emma was not tired, and she did not want to join her mother and Poppy as they did their needlework. Her father had disappeared with Monsieur Peschier to somewhere on the plantation. What men found so interesting about farms was a mystery to her.

She passed the wing of the house that was theirs and walked along the pathway toward Phillipe's workshop. As she approached, she noticed a young man at a distance running toward the building.

He had come from the direction of the cane fields. He was bare-chested and was wearing only breeches tied at the waist. He wore no stockings and was barefoot. He slowed his pace to a walk, and not wanting to be seen, Emma secreted herself behind a cypress tree to observe him.

He stopped at a barrel near the workshop and began splashing the water over his heated body. When he turned toward her, she realized that the young man whom she assumed was a slave was none other than Phillipe Peschier. His body glistened with water droplets, which ran in rivulets down the taut contours of his body. A tingling sensation travelled from her nether regions and up her spine.

She decided then not to reveal herself and then she noticed that his arms, chest, and back were covered in small cuts. He cupped the water with his hand and attempted to splash it down his back, but the method proved unfruitful. She stepped out from her hiding place.

"May I assist you?" she asked.

He spun around as if propelled and stared at her. "Are you spying on me?" He stood glaring at her with his arms akimbo. He did not seem embarrassed by his state of undress and spoke to her without showing any signs of discomfort. She wondered herself how she had been so bold to reveal herself.

"No, of course not," she said, perturbed. "I was strolling about and saw you approach. At first, I did not know who you were."

He stood for a moment, considering her. "Well, then, *mademoiselle*, if you really want to assist me, come into my workshop."

Emma bit her lower lip. She did not wish to seem fearful or naïve at his suggestion, and did not want to find herself in a compromising situation. While she was thinking, he slid the barn door open and waited for her.

"All right," she said and followed him into the shop. She did not know what to expect, but as her mind sifted through the possibilities, she found herself comparing him to Edmund Montjoy, of all people. She would never have followed Edmund into a deserted barn. Still, she did not know what she would say if her father caught her there.

Phillipe walked to one of the many shelves lining the walls of the workshop and drew out a bottle and a small rag. He handed both to her and sat down on a small barrel. The bottle contained a colorless liquid. When she pulled the cork, she smelled strong spirits.

"If you think that I am going to have a drink with you, sir, you are very mistaken," she said most decidedly. He turned and looked over his shoulder at her and rolled his eyes.

"I have no desire to drink with you, Miss Darcy, only that you should dab some of this spirit on the wounds on my back. It will staunch the bleeding and I will have less to explain to my parents."

Wordlessly, she dabbed the rag and then, cautiously, began to apply the spirits to his back. He flinched only once but then sat quietly while she ministered to him.

"How ever did this happen?"

"I was out working in the cane fields," he said matter-of-factly.

She stopped momentarily and turned to face him. "Whatever for?"

"Because a man cannot expect others to do for him what he will not do for himself."

She was silenced by this disclosure and returned to her task. As she touched his back, that feeling of physical pleasure continued to pulse through her. She began talking again, hoping that it would subside.

"Were you pulling up the sugar cane?"

"And planting the new."

"What does your father think of you engaging in such a practice?"

"He does not know, and if he does, he does not speak of it to me."

"What do your slaves think of you? How can you maintain your position as master if you stoop to working...to doing work below your station?"

"The station in which I find myself I is not the one to which I was born. I cannot claim the privilege under which I live as easily as you," he stated.

She gritted her teeth and looked at the bottle in her hand. She wanted to strike him over the head with it. "I do not understand you," she said, leaving off her task, which she had nearly finished.

"And I do not understand you, Miss Darcy, but I thank you for assisting me. I can carry on from here." He retrieved the bottle from her.

She turned to leave, and he called out to her. "You will keep my secret, won't you, Miss Darcy?"

"I believe you may now call me Emma, since we are now so intimately acquainted."

"And you may call me Phillipe." She smiled at him. "So, you will keep my secret?"

"I suppose so, if you will keep mine," she said, smiling. He looked momentarily confused.

"Yours?"

"Of course. What would my father say if he knew I was alone in a barn with a man in such a state?" She gestured toward him with her hand.

"He would undoubtedly challenge me to a duel." She knew he was teasing her for his tone was light and he was grinning at her.

"He has fought in a duel and lived to tell the tale, so you will mind your tongue." She was enjoying herself, joining in with his banter.

"Your father is a surprising man, and one to be reckoned with. Indeed, I will keep your secret for my own safety's sake."

She smiled in spite of herself. As she entered the sunlight outside the workshop, she heard him call after her. "*Au revoir, mon cher.*"

She felt that pulse of energy again. It really was most unsuitable, and most pleasurable.

***

Mr. Darcy felt content, more content than he had been for a long time. His little son was growing slightly wild, chasing about with the children of the servants and of the slaves. Bennet and Toby had grown to be friends, and he hoped that this taste of a life other than the protected, rarified status he enjoyed at home would stay with his son as he became a man. In his own life, this discovery of the worth of people he had once found beneath him had a jarring effect on Darcy, so much so that he felt lost for a time until his dear wife suggested he run for Parliament. He entered that body with such idealism and so many ambitions, but now realized that change in policy happened by much compromise and by many small increments rather than in a blinding flash of inspiration and energy.

His daughter Emma also had changed for the better. She befriended Poppy's two younger daughters, who were not much older than she, and the twins' devotion to each other and their good natures seemed to him to have a steadying effect on his daughter. He also noticed an abrupt change in her attitude toward Phillipe, whom she'd so despised when they first arrived.

The biggest change, however, was in Darcy's beloved Elizabeth. The despair that had descended over her after she miscarried was so profound that he thought it would never lift. Now, the joy in her returned and so then did the joy in him. He knew that every one of those losses she endured were still with her, but for now they were tucked away. Her friend Poppy had brought her spirit all the way back the same as she had delivered her physically from harm all those years ago.

They had finished their evening meal and were adjourning to the veranda when they encountered Phillipe in his shirtsleeves on top of a ladder with one of the house servants, nailing a contraption to the ceiling. It was a complex device with blades that were tilted on a slight angle and arranged in a circle from the center of the apparatus like the spokes of a wheel. There was a rope that descended from two sides of the device. Darcy took his spot on a rocking chair facing the house, and Phillipe's father sat next to him. Both men swirled a glass of French cognac and sat looking up at the invention.

Poppy and Elizabeth claimed a hanging bench that swung gently back and forth when they propelled it with their feet, and Benji nestled himself between them. Emma leaned on the railing of the veranda, looking up at Phillipe as he finished his work. His sisters sat in two chairs near their mother.

"There," Phillipe said with a satisfied air.

"There what?" his father asked, amused.

"It is a fanning machine. It will keep the air moving and keep us cool. Watch." He took one end of the rope in one hand and one in the other. Pulling on one side, the fan blades began to rotate. As they slowed, he pulled on the other. The blades continued to rotate in the same direction.

Darcy put his glass down on the veranda railing and stood up to examine this amazing new device. "Now is that not a marvel to behold?" He gazed at it admiringly.

"But what good is it if you have to stand beneath it and keep pulling on the ropes?" Francois asked.

"I will do it," said Benji, jumping up from his seat.

"I can get Toby or one of the other…"

"No," Benji shouted. "Please, let me do it."

Phillipe handed the rope ends to Benji and he began to pull on them one after another. The fan blades whirled round and round as the boy stood beneath watching them.

"Not so fast," Phillipe told the boy. "It is to make a gentle wind, not a hurricane." This provoked laughter from them all. Benji's face took on a studious look.

"Do you feel cooler, Mama?" he asked, still looking up.

Elizabeth smiled. "Oh indeed. Much cooler."

"We have de mos' modern plantation on de river," Poppy said, looking admiringly at her firstborn. "It would been nice to have such a t'ing in Grenada, don' you t'ink, 'Lizabet'?"

"Yes, indeed."

"It was a long time ago, Grenada. But we are not from Grenada, are we, *mon cher*?" Poppy asked looking up at her husband with a mischievous smile.

"No," he said, and before he could utter the words himself, his entire family chorused, "We are from Saint-Domingue." They all burst into gales of laughter.

"What does that mean?" Emma asked, and all eyes were upon her.

Poppy looked at Elizabeth and then to Darcy. "We can tell you de story if you want to hear."

"I want to hear," Benji said, not breaking his rope-pulling rhythm. Elizabeth nodded.

"It was some time after you lef'," Poppy began, looking at Elizabeth. "De English army was finally destroyin' Fedon and his revolution. Every day, we lose more men. De English get closer."

"Why did you not run away?" Benji asked.

Poppy looked up at Francois. He continued with the story, "We could not run because we had two small babies, the twins." He looked over at Elizabeth Ann and Adele. "My second wife, Louisa, had little Adele, and while the baby lived, Louisa did not."

"And I had just give birt' to Elizabet' Ann," Poppy added.

Bennet looked from Francois to Poppy and then to the two young girls. "Is that how twins are born?" Poppy eyes crinkled up for a moment and then she began laughing her tinkling laugh and Francois gave an ungentlemanly guffaw, and soon they all, save Bennet, were laughing.

"I do not understand what you find so funny," he said with a pout. This made everyone laugh once again.

"I will miss this boy when he goes home," Francois said and leaned forward to ruffle Bennet's hair.

"Do go on," Darcy said. "I never knew exactly what happened. Elizabeth was beside herself with worry about you, Poppy."

"I know. I was worryin' too. After dat day you come get her, I don' know if she alive or dead."

Bennet was looking back and forth from his mother to his father and then again to Poppy with a confused look on his face.

Francois continued, "So there we sat, staring into the fire in Fedon's mountain camp with these two little babies between us. Poppy was sitting with these two little loaves of bread, one in each arm, singing and cooing to them, her three children behind her looking at me with wide eyes. I could not think. My heart was in..." he stopped for a moment, and looked to his son, "*comment dites-vous en anglaise....lambeaux?*"

"Tatters," Darcy said.

"*Merci.*" He inclined his head to Darcy. "My heart was in tatters."

No one spoke for a time. Darcy looked up at his wife. Such stories were never told around the fire at home.

Francois Peschier continued. "It was perhaps a week, perhaps two, we received word that if we move quickly, we can catch a boat to Saint-Domingue."

"I was still nursin' de lil' ones, but I was able to travel. Der was no choice. We all had to go."

"I had some money, in gold, that I kept safe and we bought our passage. We went together. My baby needed a mother, Poppy and her children needed me. I thought, *We need to stay together at least until we are away from Grenada.*"

Poppy looked up. "You never told me dat. I t'ought you always t'ink we goin' wid you wherever you go."

Francois smiled. "I could not think at all, *mon cher*. I had lost my wife, all my possessions, all chance of regaining my family's plantation on Grenada, and now I had a baby. My mind would not work. All I could think of was survival."

Darcy looked over at his daughter. She was transfixed by this tale. They all were. Only Poppy kept at her needlework, looking up from time to time to steal a glance at her husband.

"When we arrived at Saint-Domingue, we were exhausted. I can see it in my mind as if it was yesterday. Poppy put Adele in my arms and was carrying Elizabeth Ann. We walked down the gangplank to the shore, and I looked down at this little bundle and I thought, *What am I going to do now?* It was then I turned to look back at Poppy and the children and thought: *This is my family now, if they will have me. I need them and they need me.*"

"Dat was de truth," Poppy said.

"That does not sound particularly romantic," Emma commented.

Poppy laughed. "We all need to survive, so he ask me if I will marry him, and I say, 'in church?' and he say, 'in church.' Then I say, 'will you rec'nize my chil'ren,' and he say, 'of course, they my chil'ren now and dey free.' Dat enough romance for me."

"At the time in Saint-Domingue there were rumblings of revolution even then. I found a priest who was a freed African slave and he married us in church," Francois continued.

"I have de paper," Poppy said impassively, "and we change the chil'rens' names from English to French. Philip was now Phillipe, Molly was Manon, Cecilia was Cecile, but I would not change Elizabet' Ann. No, no. If dey ask me, I would tell dem why she have dat name. Our Adele now, she already was French.

"So why do you have to say you are from Saint-Domingue?" Bennet asked. Darcy did not think the boy was listening, but he had been hanging on every word.

"That is a smart boy," Francois said. "He remembers how this whole tale began." He turned his attention to Bennet. "We need to tell people here that we are from Saint-Domingue because when we left Grenada, many slaves escaped. Some were caught and enslaved at other places. With me as the head of the household, we could tell them we were from Saint-Domingue where there are many free people of color. They would believe that my wife and my children were free."

"So, you told a lie," Bennet said.

"A small lie that did much good."

"We need to keep our marriage a secret here too," Poppy said. "A white man may not marry a colored woman, even if she free."

Phillipe abruptly left his seat and went into the house.

Emma followed him with her gaze. "How can you live in such a place?" Emma asked, still looking at where Phillipe had been.

"Ah well, one must live someplace. Here we could begin again, and New Orleans society is much like its river. It ebbs and flows. We can go along for a time and then we find we can go on no longer. We have reached a spot where the river has turned in on itself, so we must paddle back along the same route from whence we came. Eventually, though, we find our way to the sea."

Emma shook her head and again looked in the direction in which Phillipe disappeared. Darcy watched his daughter carefully and began to have concerns that she was again embarking on an impossible journey that would cause her pain.

Chapter 9

"We going to a ball," Poppy announced one morning at breakfast. "We leave for the city in a few hours. My daughter Manon invite us to her house in New Orleans and we will show you de city."

Emma's spirit lifted. Finally, they were to dance and meet people. She felt here as she felt at Pemberley. It was all well and good to be among family and friends, but she wanted to be in town. Being away would also afford her an escape from Phillipe, who was now constantly in her thoughts. She found herself rising early and standing by the window in the hallway outside her room to catch a glimpse of him as he donned his slave attire and ran out to the cane fields. If he remained at home, working or supervising the plantation, she sought him out to talk to him as though drawn by an invisible force. She knew in her heart that any attachment between them was utterly impossible. Even if he were free from family responsibilities and came back with them to England, they would inevitably be ostracized from polite society even though she was the daughter of Fitzwilliam Darcy.

How they would fare here, she did not know. She also was unsure of herself. Could she leave everything she held dear—her friends, her family, her country—and become the mistress of this backwater farm? Would she be the mistress here if she and Phillipe were forbidden by law to marry? She also did not know how Phillipe felt about her. He seemed to despise her one moment and flirt with her the next.

Nonetheless, she longed to be near him even though they could not seem to agree on anything. He was a proud man, but carried many prejudices that had to have been wounds he suffered as a result of his origins. Her life had been sheltered, and she had difficulty comprehending the depths of his pain. She could understand his hatred of the English and wondered if that wall, which he had built around his heart, excluded her as well. In a way, she hoped it had, for anything beyond friendship was impossible.

Her mother was bustling from Emma's room to her brother's, making decisions on what clothing to bring for their latest excursion. She was grateful to help, so as to quiet her thoughts.

At last the time arrived for their departure. The luggage was loaded into the flat boats and they all gingerly embarked. All the ladies were carrying parasols to protect them from the sun, and the gentlemen carried their gloves and hats in their hands. Monsieur Peschier told them that from the moment they docked at the quay, they needed to look as elegant as befitted their standing in society.

Emma was seated next to Phillipe, who chatted amiably to her of their upcoming visit. He seemed eager to show off this little town, and Emma put aside her first impressions and decided to open her mind to its possibilities. After all, there was no point in being cross. They were here and they were to attend a ball, and she was pleased and excited at the prospect.

Two fine carriages awaited them when they arrived, and they arranged themselves comfortably. It was a fine day and the carriages were open to the air.

"Are we to be put on display, Phillipe?" she asked in as coquettish a voice as she could manage.

"But of course," he replied. "We are the news of the town. We will first go to my sister Manon's house to situate ourselves and have some refreshment, and then Papa and I will show you the sights. My sister lives in what we call the *Vieux Carre,* or the French Quarter."

They arrived shortly at the home of Manon and her husband, Jean Jacques Cheval, and their children. It was located on Chartres Street, a good distance from the river. Emma caught a glimpse of the town square as they were passing, and Benji jumped from his seat pointing to the spires of St. Louis Cathedral. Emma did not know what to expect, but the sight that greeted her was a surprise. The Cheval house rivaled any town house in Mayfair in its tasteful splendor.

The entire building was made of brick, with six large arched windows as large as doors along the street level. There was a large front door that stood in the center, decorated with carvings along the doorframe. The most delightful aspect of the house was the upper two stories. They imitated the ground floor exactly, but along each level ran a balcony with a beautifully decorated, black wrought-iron railing.

When they disembarked, a Negro butler greeted them at the doorway. *"Entrez, s'il vous plait."* He bowed low. What greeted her then was most impressive. The floor in the entryway was inlaid wood with a curved staircase on the right within a few feet of where they entered. All the walls were plastered and white, and tastefully decorated with works of art, and occasionally a mirror in the French style. Almost immediately after they arrived, a young woman, elegantly dressed, her hair done up in a tignon, entered to greet them. She was beautiful, with dark oval eyes and dark skin much more akin to Poppy's than to Phillipe's.

"Oh, welcome, welcome. I am Manon Cheval." She took their hands in both of hers and kissing them on both cheeks. Emma had to smile watching her father. His usual reserve was being tested every day in this strange place. She imagined that he had not been kissed by so many strangers in his life. Admittedly, she liked these French ways. She knew she should not, since they had recently been through the most brutal wars with France, but this seemed a world apart and free for her to enjoy.

"You must come and refresh yourselves, and we will eat," Manon entreated. "I have the most marvelous cook from Bordeaux, and she makes the most exquisite dishes. Come, I will show you to your rooms."

Before luncheon, Monsieur Cheval arrived and greeted them. He was slightly shorter than his wife and a bit more rotund, with a jovial disposition and a welcoming smile. Emma liked him at once. Their two small children, Gustave and Henri, joined them. Gustave was younger than Benji, but near enough in age that the boys requested to be seated next to one another. Henri was only two and, after being introduced, was taken away by his mammy to sleep.

The luncheon table was relaxed and boisterous, much more so than their table at the Peschiers'. How different the manners were of these French-Grenadan-American people. Emma had felt a certain disapproval at first, and tried to retain the formality that she had been taught, but soon the laughter and the good-natured camaraderie drew her in. She glanced at her parents more than once, to gauge their reactions. Her father was cordial, but appeared a trifle uncomfortable. Her mother seemed completely at ease. The noise and laughter were typical of the Bennet household more than the Darcys'.

After luncheon and a short rest, the Darcys, hosted by Monsieur and Madame Cheval, embarked on a tour of the city. Poppy remained at the house with Monsieur Peschier, who begged to be excused, and Benji, who had found a playmate in Gustave, disappeared into the walled garden behind the house that stretched between the main house and the servants' quarters. With everything in readiness, they again set off in open carriages.

In a short time, they were in a large square in the middle of town near the river. At the center of it was St. Louis Cathedral, built by the French. Flanking it was the city hall, the *Cabildo*, built by the Spanish, and the priests' *presbytere*, which was newly completed. They began with a tour of the cathedral. As the rest of the party continued along the aisle to look at the nave and the altar, Phillipe drew Emma into a small room in the back of the darkened church that contained a statue of the Virgin and a bank of votive candles in blue-colored glass.

He was close when he whispered in her ear. "Would you like to light a candle?" he asked.

"Whatever for?" she whispered back.

"To make a request. To say a prayer."

"The Church of England does not believe in idolatry. Do you find comfort in this statue of the Virgin?" she asked. Emma never thought too deeply about religion. She grew up with all the ceremonies of the Church of England, but never considered herself a true believer. Religion was there to teach a moral code, nothing more.

He did not answer, but took a long, thin stalk of wood that sat with its brothers in a small container of sand near the candles. He removed it, lit it with the flame from one of the votives, and then handed it to her. She took it from him, and then he did the most remarkable thing. He took her hand and guided it to one of the candles where they lit the votive together. Then, his hand still enclosing hers, he snuffed it out in the sand from whence it came. He was standing quite close, and when she looked at him, his eyes were closed, and his face contained an almost beatific expression. She was still staring at him when he opened his eyes.

"Have you made your entreaty?" she whispered.

"Indeed, I have." He looked at her with such intensity that it nearly took her breath away. He was still holding her hand.

She did not realize it until she heard her father's voice. "Ah, there you are, Emma." Phillipe dropped her hand as if it was on fire.

Phillipe cleared his throat. "We will see the *Cabildo* next. It was built during the time of the Spanish," he said a little too loudly. Emma saw him glance up at her father, whose expression she recognized. It was the same expression he wore whenever she spoke of Edmund Montjoy.

Emma and Phillipe led the party into the sunlight. Once they were in the plaza, Emma could find her footing again. There was something about the harsh glare of sunlight that brought her to her senses. She smiled at Phillipe, and again took his arm.

Phillipe and Monsieur Cheval were explaining the history of the various buildings as Emma's mind began to wander. She had to admit that this *little backwater city* was more impressive than she first supposed, and that her *Grand Tour* was more interesting than she expected.

Only a few months ago, she'd railed against being deprived of things she could not have, but today she felt more accepting of the way life had revealed itself. Her mother appeared to be happier than she had seen her for a long time, and her father as well. The change in her brought about a change in him. It seemed odd to her that men, who were so insistent that women had no place in public life, were so dependent on them in private.

"Whatever are you thinking?" Phillipe asked as they walked along in silence. "Your face took on a most pensive *mien*."

"I am thinking about men," she said, her eyes dancing. She could see that she shocked him. Perhaps he hoped that she was thinking about him.

He said nothing for a moment and then muttered, "Next time I will mind my own business." She laughed and he joined her. He could be quite charming when he made an effort. She could not help but consider that all the times he had been disagreeable were designed to keep her at a safe distance.

***

With their excursion finished, Darcy and Elizabeth were finally alone in their room at the Chevals'. She turned to her husband. "Do you think our daughter is attracted to Phillipe?"

"I was about to ask you the same question. If we have both observed it, then the question answers itself."

"I was happier when she thought him arrogant and vexing."

Darcy looked at his wife with narrowed eyes. "Perhaps he finds her argumentative and spoiled."

"Mr. Darcy, how can you say such a thing about your own daughter?" Elizabeth asked in mock outrage. She smiled, and then became serious. "We did spoil her, did we not?"

Darcy took his wife's hand and kissed it. "Perhaps a little. She is young and is easily infatuated. We will not stay here so long as to give them time to form an attachment."

"As I recall, it does not take a young man much time or encouragement to form a strong attachment even if the young lady is not at all encouraging."

"My dear Mrs. Darcy, whatever do you mean?" He pulled her to him. He kissed her once, and then his expression changed. "You are concerned for her, as am I. I do not want to see her heart broken again." Darcy sat down heavily on the bed. "He is a bright young man and I do not believe he intends to lead her on. His father thinks the world of him. Under any other circumstances, I would welcome him, but—"

She interrupted him. "You do not have to explain yourself to me, my darling. All of us are mindful of what the world is like and the impediments that stand between them. Poppy has expressed the same concerns to me as you are now." Elizabeth sat beside her husband.

"She has noticed their growing attraction too, then?"

Elizabeth joined her husband and leaned her head on Darcy's shoulder. "Perhaps we are worrying for nothing. Phillipe is well aware of the insurmountable obstacles between them, even if our Emma is not. Who knows what is in their hearts? I will talk with her if that will ease your mind."

"It will not ease my mind until I know what she has to say."

***

"Cecile was married in church," Poppy said as the carriage rolled along the cobbled street toward the center of the *Vieux Carre*. "Her husband is a blacksmith in town. He a free man of color too and have his own business."

Today they were not dressed in all their finery. Elizabeth felt it would draw too much attention to them as Poppy explained that her second daughter did not live in the same social circle of her first.

"You never ask about Manon, Mr. Darcy." Poppy was looking at her husband intently. "You wonder about her and her lil' Frenchman. No, dey not marry in church or any udder way. Dey cannot. We have agreement between our two families. I arrange everyt'ing when he express his desire to take her into his house. Every day I pray he never decide to marry a white wife."

"Would that be possible?" Elizabeth asked. She knew in her heart that indeed it would be possible. Edward Home had attempted to marry Elizabeth in Grenada while having Poppy and their four children. Still, the circumstances were not the same. Poppy did not consent. Poppy was not free.

"Oh, mos' certainly. Some white men who have free coloured women also have a white wife. Some do not. Dey call our Monsiuer Cheval a bachelor even though he have my Manon and two chil'ren. I am hoping he be a bachelor all his life."

Elizabeth looked over at her husband and tried to read his expression. When he took her as his wife, he had ruffled some feathers in his circle, to be sure, but their lives were secure. These arrangements here were a different kettle of fish entirely. He did not look completely satisfied, but she knew him well. His sense of good manners stood in the way of satisfying his curiosity. She and Poppy, however, did not have the social niceties standing between them.

"What of their children?" Elizabeth asked.

"Oh, the chil'ren will inherit and Manon will also. De law will stand by dem. Dis a differn' place den Grenada. Free people o' colour have many rights. Not as much as white folk, but many rights."

Poppy then pointed out one of the other sights, and then continued. "And if de chil'ren pass, den everyt'ing be all right for dem," she continued matter-of-factly.

"Pass?" Darcy asked, finally finding his tongue.

"Pass for white. Maybe dese chil'ren not pass, but if dey marry light-skin' women, maybe der chil'ren pass. If dat happen, dey have all der rights and can do whatever dey like."

The entire party was silent for a moment. Darcy sat back against the seat of the carriage and looked off into the distance. Elizabeth knew she should leave him to his thoughts.

"What about the other way around?" Emma asked, startling Elizabeth. They had been so deep in conversation that she momentarily forgot her daughter was there.

"What'chu mean? A free coloured man and a white wife?" Poppy asked, her voice rising slightly.

All eyes focused on Emma. She looked from one of them to the other. "I am asking hypothetically," she said casually, though Elizabeth did not believe it for a minute.

"What is 'hypo…'?" Poppy began but left off without finishing.

"Hypothetically means she is not asking for herself, only to…" Elizabeth began, but stopped in confusion.

Darcy rejoined. "Only to know in case something like that would ever happen to someone else." Elizabeth looked over at her husband. She tried to communicate her dismay without words.

Poppy eyed them all with a doubtful expression. "Well hypo or not, it could not be. I have never heard of it. A free black man can only marry a free black woman, or if he want, he can buy a slave and free her and den marry her. Der are many laws. Oh, here we are, and der is Cecile and Valentine. Hello, hello, *bonjour*," she called, waving to the two young people who emerged from a modest shop of horseshoes and anvils.

As they disembarked to greet Cecile and her husband, Elizabeth watched as Darcy handed Emma from the carriage. Her daughter's eyes were cast downward and would not meet her father's gaze.

***

The next evening Emma saw Cecile's husband, Valentine, again. She saw him, but he did not see her. It was quite late, past midnight, when she heard the crunch of gravel in the drive and the sound of horses. Looking out her window, which faced the front street, she saw several men, all men of colour, dismount and walk their steeds to the back of the house where there was a large outbuilding. She knew she should return to bed but was filled with curiosity. That curiosity peaked when she heard a door close downstairs and saw Phillipe outside, greeting the other men.

Dressing quickly, she made her way down the stairs and stood by the kitchen door. Fortunately, the top of the door contained windows, and she could secrete herself in the darkened house, and yet observe all that transpired. Still unable to hear what they were saying, she waited until the last man entered the back building and then stole across the lawn, following them.

Light flooded from the windows, so she had no difficulty picking her way along the side, looking for an open window. She crouched beneath it, able to hear the conversation. They were all speaking French.

"I say we send a petition to Washington asking for full suffrage." Phillipe was speaking.

"You are mad, sir," said another. "How many years ago did we ask for the right to vote on taxes? It was ignored."

"You cannot make one attempt and then give up," Valentine said. At least she thought it was he.

"Indeed, brother, you cannot. We are men of property, wealth, education, even many of our women own property."

"Surely you cannot advocate for women's suffrage?" The men laughed.

"Not today, *monsieur,*" Phillipe said. "But our petition is another matter. I can see that it is delivered before the white landowners even know it has been drafted."

"You seem to have a great deal of faith in this American government, my naïve friend," said yet another man.

"Faith or no faith, they are now our government. It says in their Constitution that we have many rights."

"*They* have many rights. The white men. We must fight for ours."

"Perhaps," said Phillipe, "but does it not make sense that we should fight on paper before we shed our blood?"

There was some grumbling among the men, but eventually they seemed to reach an agreement.

Emma ducked her head and made her way back to the house. *Phillipe Peschier is an idealist.*

He became more interesting with each passing day.

Chapter 10

Emma insisted on accompanying Manon, Phillipe, and their family to the cathedral for Sunday Mass. Monsieur Cheval, acting the perfect host, arranged for a carriage to take Elizabeth, Darcy, and Benji to the Episcopal cathedral on St. Charles Avenue. The journey was some distance from the *Vieux Carre*, but Emma knew her father could hardly refuse such a generous offer. The look her father gave her as he entered the coach was intended as a warning. She had seen that look before. She had ignored it before. Smiling, Emma watched as the coach departed, and she rejoiced at having the watchful eyes of her parents momentarily focused on her brother instead of herself.

At the cathedral, before Mass, Phillipe took her again to the alcove to light a candle, which Emma accomplished without assistance. They took their places and Phillipe gallantly placed Emma on the aisle so that she could observe the service. She had never been to a Catholic mass before, as none of her class would dare go. Although she did not understand a word, the ritual did have a soothing effect on her spirit, and the wafting of the incense she found most pleasing. Although she knew her history, she still did not understand why there was so much conflict between two religions that seemed so similar to her.

"It is much like the Church of England," she said as they emerged from the cool darkness into the brilliant sunlight after Mass concluded.

"There are many important differences, Miss Darcy, of which you are well aware," he said, calling her by her more formal name in front of his sister and brother-in-law.

"You are so severe, Phillipe. You should be grateful that your guest is so open-minded as to attend at all," Monsieur Cheval commented.

"I suppose you understood every word of Latin," she said, determined to match his quarrelsome mood.

"I learned Latin at school. I also speak French and English, of course. Also, I speak Spanish," he said haughtily. "We belonged to the Spanish for a long time, you know."

"Of course, I know," she said, even though she had no idea. She did not understand him. On one hand he could be exceptionally accommodating, even charming, but then this distasteful pride would emerge, and he became quite intolerable.

He offered his hand to help her into the waiting carriage. When they were seated alone together, he spoke. "After luncheon and rest, I will take you to see something quite remarkable."

"What is it?"

"A surprise."

By three in the afternoon, they were again in a carriage moving across the *Vieux Carre*. Her parents had not yet returned, so she made the decision to accompany him on this adventure. They had only a young Negro boy as driver and chaperone, so really, she was quite alone with Phillipe. Such an outing in London would create a scandal that would not die away for months, but here she felt freer. There were almost no familiar signposts from which she took direction in her English life, so she felt she had to put her trust in someone to guide her in this new world. Even though she argued with him nearly all the time, and thought him supercilious at times, she trusted his word as a gentleman.

Thus, they were on their way to who knew where without her father's knowledge or her parents' permission. She found herself smiling at the idea of it. The carriage took them through the many Spanish-style houses of the *Vieux Carre* until they emerged outside of it altogether in a large, open field surrounded by bushes and copses of trees.

There were many dark-skinned people milling about, selling foodstuffs from baskets. Some set up makeshift stores and lean-to booths from which there was a lively trade in goods ranging from fresh fish to coffee. People of every colour and style were walking to and fro, shopping and buying things from the various vendors. Phillipe instructed his driver to take them around the outskirts of this activity. They stopped at a stand of trees and vegetation a distance from the festivities.

"Why are we stopping here?" she asked.

"Here we will not be seen."

"I do not understand," she said as he gave her his hand and she descended to the ground.

"In many ways New Orleans is an open city. Much exchange between your people and mine is tolerated, but the two of us together, alone, would attract attention…much unwanted attention. You understand."

He led her into the thicket where a live oak stood, trunk bent nearly to the ground. She did not exactly understand what he meant by "your people" and "my people." Did he mean the British and the French? Did he mean the people of colour and the white? Poppy made it quite clear to her that, although there were matches made between the European and the African, they were exclusively one-sided. Not wanting to display her naiveté for him to see, she kept silent. Where were they going?

He led her to the base of the old and gnarled tree. The grass surrounding it was trampled upon and most of the area was hardened mud. There was no one there but the two of them.

"Whatever are we doing here?"

"We will climb this tree and then can observe the goings-on from a safe distance."

"Climb the tree?" She was horrified. "You cannot be serious."

"If you would rather not, we can leave now." His calm demeanor and steady gaze annoyed her. This type of remark was what irritated her the most about him. He would argue with her without arguing with her. The onus was on her. Not wanting to appear fainthearted, she attempted to look at him without expression.

"If you can find a way to help me ascend, I will do as you ask." He smiled and extended his hand. She put hers in his. It was calloused and dry to the touch.

The trunk of the oak nearly touched the earth, so with a little effort and some balance they merely walked up until they reached the limbs. He took her higher and higher, she following his lead. Then, to her dismay, he began to creep along the length of a limb to the outer branches.

"This is difficult to do in a long dress," she complained, and they crawled along the length of the limb.

"Do what you must about your dress, I will avert my eyes." He was playing with her and turned his head toward the square. She pulled at the skirt until it was above her knee and that facilitated her passage. By the time she reached him, he was sitting in the crook of a limb, and beckoned her to sit next to him. From their perch, they could observe the goings-on easily.

"This is my place. I discovered it as a child and have availed myself of it often."

"Surely you can walk about freely on your own or with your family." Again, she was making assumptions, but had no other way of learning the ways of New Orleans.

"Indeed, I can, but many times do not wish to. I enjoy watching people candidly, from a distance." She looked over at him, but he did not return her gaze. He seemed pensive, and she did not want to disturb his thoughts.

When he finally roused himself and paid attention to her, she spoke. "What is this place? A sort of market?"

"We call this place Congo Square. It is where the slaves come on their day of rest to do business with one another, and later to dance and sing. You will see. Now, though, you must try these."

Phillipe took some peculiar-looking beans from a small sack that he carried in his pocket. They were a tan color and mottled. He held one of the beans, which seemed to be in a dimpled pod similar to peas, but the pod was brittle. He crushed it easily between his fingers. Inside were two smaller beans that were brown in color and covered with a paper-like skin.

"Here," he said, dropping these odd beans in the palm of her hand. "Try them."

She held them in her hand but did not move. He took another, crushed the outer shell and then popped the funny beans into his mouth and began chewing. She did the same, chewing them as he did. This odd food was really quite pleasing to the palate. He watched her face with an expectant expression.

"So, do you like it?"

"Yes, it is quite nice. What is it?"

"The African name is *nguba*, but we call them peanuts."

"Oh, so they are nuts like a walnut or a…"

"No. They grow in the ground."

What a strange place this was. Nuts grow in the ground. Slaves walk about freely one day a week.

He pointed to a large circular area that was empty of stalls and sellers. "The slaves will begin their music and dancing soon. You must see that. It is quite remarkable."

She wanted to ask if he ever played such music, or even danced here. She could picture it in her mind, but in her imagination the dances looked like English dances and she knew that could not possibly be correct. She looked at him and smiled. "Are some of your slaves here?"

"I expect so. Selling things they grow or make enables them to earn money to buy their freedom." He offered her another peanut pod, which she broke apart herself.

"Really? You allow them to work for their freedom?"

"Many slave owners do. It benefits us all. In order to buy their freedom, the slaves are hired out to do many public works about the city. Joseph, Antoine's father, has hired himself out many times to work on the levees. My father takes some of his wages, and he keeps the rest."

"Should he not keep all of his money? He earned it." She caught herself again arguing with him.

Phillipe was silent for a moment. "That is a, how do you say, bone of contention between my father and me. His argument is that the slave belongs to him and if he wanted to, he could keep all the money. He is being magnanimous by letting Joseph and the other slaves keep any of it."

"And you disagree."

"I have been a slave, my dear Emma. I must disagree."

He called her by her Christian name and said "my dear." Why was such a small thing so thrilling it made her heart race so wildly?

They had a spectacular view of the large, empty area where slaves were gathering, making a circle ringed by drummers who took their places. Among the spectators were well-dressed people of every color. She noticed that although there were white men with wives of obviously African descent, the opposite was not true. She and Phillipe were an anomaly even in this place. She wondered why this was so, but she would ask him another time. He may even conclude, however erroneously, that she was inquiring because of her feelings for him. That would be incorrect. Even if it was correct, he should not have this knowledge.

The rim of the circle was now several people deep. There were complicated rhythms coming from the many drummers who occupied the first row of spectators. There were also sounds coming from bells, shakers, and all manner of homemade instruments. What caught her attention was one odd-looking guitar-like instrument that had a long neck and a round body.

"What is that?" she asked excitedly. "And what are the names of these drums and where do they come from in Africa?"

Phillipe laughed. "Emma, you do ask many questions. All will become clear soon."

A tall Negro man, bare-chested, stood in the middle of the circle singing. He would sing out a phrase in a language Emma did not understand, and the crowd would answer him back, adding harmony or extra melody above or after in the most marvelous fashion. Emma had seen many concerts in which a choir would stand singing and a pianoforte, or an organ, would accompany. Everyone would rehearse many times to get the music to come out perfectly, and here were these people who began playing and singing impromptu, and the music flowed out of them in a naturally perfect, unmatched symphony of beauty and dynamism. She had never heard anything like it before.

Then the dancing began. Women, their heads covered, began to move in a circle, their hips swaying provocatively. Each knew the movements as well as Emma knew the dances at home, but these were not the dances she knew. Their feet moved in complex stepping and stamping patterns, and they began to move their arms about. Some took to the center of the circle and even got down upon their knees, flailing their arms and singing with abandon.

An odd sensation crept over Emma as she watched them. She felt as though someone was caressing her intimately and most pleasurably. A tingling sensation rippled over her skin. She felt as though she wanted to fling herself from her perch and rush in to join in their dance. Phillipe must have noticed how enraptured she was, for she felt him staring at her. She returned his gaze and noticed for the first time a smoldering wildness in his eyes. He laid his hand upon hers and she quivered. At this moment she knew she would surrender to him then if he would only ask. They sat for a long time, watching and listening. Emma did not notice the passage of time.

He was the first to break the spell when he took his hand away. "We need to be going. Night is fast upon us."

With his words, the music seemed to fall away. She did not want it to end, or to remove herself from such a place. Nonetheless, she followed him with her gaze as he swung his legs back to the limb and began to move along it toward the trunk of the tree. Securing himself, he extended his hand to her. "Oddly, it is much more difficult to climb down than up."

In the gathering darkness, Emma looked down from where she sat. For the first time, she felt anxious. The flickering light from bonfires that had been built to illuminate the dancers leapt over the contours of his face and she took his extended hand.

"Do not look down, Miss Darcy. Look only at me."

He made an easy request for her to look only at that handsome face. She put her hand in his and he guided it to each crook and handhold in the tree. They were nearing the trunk and she began to relax her vigilance and then it happened. She lost her foothold and her balance and could not retain her grasp. She gave out a small cry and felt herself come away from the branches. Within a moment, however, a strong arm caught her and blocked her ungainly descent. Desperate to prevent herself from falling, she threw her arms about him and clung to him for a moment. Looking down, she saw the ground a good distance from where they precariously perched. Her heart was pounding.

"Oh goodness," she gasped, still looking down at the hard ground nearly ten feet beneath them. When she looked up, her face was inches from Phillipe's. One arm was above his head, holding on to the branches, and one was wrapped securely around her waist. Her arms were about his neck. They were both breathing hard. She wanted him to kiss her at that moment, but again her foot slipped, and she felt his grip tighten as she felt her foothold fall away. With a great deal of effort, he swung her in front of him on the limb, and her feet were again on a solid surface. He indicated with his eyes and she let go of him and grabbed onto the branches. She began to descend ahead of him down the large trunk of the tree. Neither of them said a word.

When they reached the bottom of the tree, his carriage and driver awaited them. Emma breathed a sigh of relief, but also felt a great disappointment. If only she had not slipped again. What would now be between them? She had no time to reflect on such things for she heard branches crack and footfalls coming from every direction.

"So, what 'ave we 'ere?" said a voice from the darkness. Emma felt a hand reach for her. Turning, she saw Phillipe take hold of her arm and pull her behind him. In the flickering firelight she could make out three figures who made a semicircle around them. The live oak was at their backs.

Phillipe spoke to them in French. "Make way. We are leaving," he said boldly. Emma did not feel bold at all. She was terrified.

"Not without your purse, and, perhaps, even your woman," one of them sneered. The pounding drums from Congo Square matched the thrumming of blood in her ears.

Chapter 11

The Darcys returned from services to find Emma and Phillipe gone. Elizabeth grew more and more anxious as the hours stretched on. As night fell, and they still were not at home, her husband and Monsieur Cheval made preparations to conduct a search.

Poppy tried to reassure her that all was well. Phillipe was a sensible man, not at all impetuous, and wherever they were, Emma was safe with him.

Darcy looked like thunder. His daughter was out, unaccompanied, with a young man in a strange city, and the sun had set. Elizabeth knew he was more worried than angry, and she feared for the confrontation that would undoubtedly take place once the two young people returned home.

The rules of conduct here were much more in flux than they were back in England. She remembered that buoyant feeling of freedom she had in Grenada, walking about on her own with Poppy as her only chaperone, meeting people without a formal introduction, clandestine parties with the disenfranchised French. Edward had introduced her to such a society, and she was transfigured by it. Now Emma was having her own adventures. She hoped they were benign. How lucky her mother was that she had no idea what her younger self had experienced. Would her mother have worried so? She would never know.

"May I come with you?" Benji asked his father.

"Certainly not. Whatever do you think you could do?" Benji looked crestfallen, and she watched her husband crouch down until his head was even with his son's. "Better you stay here and keep your mother safe. She is quite worried, you know." He looked up at Elizabeth and smiled slightly. Benji ran to her.

"Where will you begin?" Elizabeth asked Monsieur Cheval. He looked from one of them to the other.

"We will begin 'ere, close to 'ome," he said hesitantly. "They are no doubt nearly 'ere already."

Elizabeth was not comforted by his expression or his plan. She believed that he had no idea where they were, and their search could be fruitless. Monsieur Cheval excused himself and went outdoors to see to the horses. Darcy took Elizabeth out on the veranda in the gathering darkness. They could see the slaves igniting torches to light their way through the shadowy New Orleans streets. He put his arm about her shoulders and whispered to her.

"I do so hope we are not on the same search as we were for Lydia," he said.

Her heart leapt to her throat. She had been so intent on comparing her daughter to herself that she had not considered the possibility that Emma was following in her Aunt Lydia's footsteps.

"Oh, surely you do not think..." She looked up into her husband's face, the panic rising in her.

He looked at her intently. "I would not have mentioned my fears to you if I thought you had not thought of them yourself."

Elizabeth shook her head in disbelief. "No, no. It cannot be," she said more to reassure herself than to him. "I do not think they have formed any such attachment, and Phillipe is nothing like Mr. Wickham."

Benji was leaning into his mother's skirts. She felt his head rest against her. Looking down, she ran her fingers through his hair.

"Is Emma coming back?" he asked softly.

"Of course, she is," Darcy said firmly, but Elizabeth, looking into his eyes, could see the worry in them. "And she will be scolded roundly when she does."

Benji looked up into his mother's face. "Good," he said, smiling. "She never gets scolded like I do." He let go of his mother's skirt and skipped back into the house.

Darcy smiled weakly and kissed Elizabeth on the forehead. "We will find her. I have searched for errant girls before."

She knew he was trying to comfort her and loved him for it. But where was Emma?

***

"Do not make me injure you," Phillipe said calmly. Emma's heart was in her throat. She could see the knives the other men were carrying glint in the distant firelight. Suddenly, one of the men rushed at Phillipe. Emma screamed, but the instant he was within striking range, he was down upon the ground clutching his stomach. Phillipe never touched him with his fists but kicked him hard in the center of his body. Emma watched as Phillipe removed a knife from his boot, and crouched, brandishing it as the other two rushed him at once. Phillipe's high kick connected with one man's jaw and he spun to kick the other one in the neck. Both fell to the ground. By this time, the first man retrieved his knife and took a step toward Phillipe. He took only one step forward, noticing his two comrades on the ground, looked back and forth between them and then, turning heel, he fled.

"Come along," Philippe said as he handed a shaking Emma into the carriage. His driver, who was a young boy, was hiding behind the carriage with a large branch in his hands. He dropped it when he saw it was his master and resumed his seat. The carriage moved off into the darkness.

As soon as the crisis was over, Emma dissolved into tears. Phillipe, who was sitting next to her, removed a handkerchief from his breast pocket and dabbed her face gently. Emma's first thought was that in England, a gentleman would hand a lady a handkerchief, but this action was much more intimate. With the touch of his hand, she ceased crying, but still felt as though a cold wind was blowing through her. She also felt quite dizzy.

Through the flickering moonlight, he could see him keenly observing her. "Are you quite all right?"

"I... I... believe so," she answered shakily.

He put his hand over hers. "I am sorry if you were frightened. There really was no danger."

She pulled back from him instantly. "No danger?" She could hear the shrill tone of her voice and looked at him incredulously. "We were nearly murdered."

"They were merely ruffians. I knew from the start I could defeat them handily." How smug he was. "As you can see, they did not lay a hand on me or you. They did not even muss my clothing." Emma shook her head. Now she was no longer frightened. She was irritated.

"What sort of fighting was that? You did not even make a fist."

"It was something I learned in France." He straightened his shoulders and brushed his cravat. "When you have the look of someone with money, and your skin is brown, sometimes you need to fight," he continued casually. "We French do not box, like you English. It damages the hands. We use only the feet."

Emma was grateful that they escaped with their lives. She was so grateful that she would let this insult to the English pass this time. This time.

"When we arrive at home, we will tell your mother and father what has transpired. They will be curious why we have been so long."

"No, we will not," Emma said firmly. "This adventure will be our secret. I will tell them of Congo Square, but nothing else."

Phillipe laughed softly. "You enjoy your secrets, do you not, Miss Darcy?"

"Indeed, I do, Monsieur Peschier," she said, smiling at him in the darkness. When the fear subsided, Emma felt an elation she had never felt before.

Being here with Phillipe, the throbbing rhythms of Congo Square, even the attack on them was thrilling beyond anything else she had ever experienced. And Phillipe. He was so different from the men of her class back in the salons of London or Bath. When she thought of them now, even Edmund Montjoy, they faded into a bland nothingness. This was a man, and moreover, a man whom she could trust with her life.

Alas, he was also a man she could never possess.

***

Darcy and Cheval returned to the parlour to make last-minute arrangements. The horses and torches were ready outside, and they were taking their leave. When the crunch of gravel revealed the return of the carriage, Elizabeth rushed to the door. There was a flushed and smiling Emma, followed by a contrite Phillipe.

"Where in heaven's name have you been?" Darcy roared from behind her. The thunder had broken into a storm.

"I am afraid that it is my fault," Phillipe said apologetically.

"Indeed, it is your fault, *monsieur*," Darcy bellowed. He strode across the room to confront the errant couple. Elizabeth took his arm and laid her hand on it, catching his eye. He let out a deep breath and changed his tone. "We were concerned." He was emphatic, but no longer shouting.

"I apologize if I have given you any concern," Phillipe said evenly. "We were seeing some of the more out-of-the-way sights in the city and the time escaped us."

"Oh, Mama, we saw the most incredible dancing and people playing drums, and—"

Poppy asked angrily, "You did not take her to de Square?"

"It is one of our great wonders."

Poppy shook her head. "Sometimes I despair of you, my son."

"It was wonderful," Emma interjected. "Phillipe was the perfect gentleman. I did so enjoy myself." She looked over at Phillipe and they exchanged a glance.

Elizabeth knew that sort of glance well. There was more to the story, but she would not press her daughter. She and Darcy had brought her up to be a young lady of good manners and morals, and they would trust her, at least for the moment. Relief flooded Elizabeth, and good manners dictated she would not make a scene in Poppy's daughter's home. Phillipe did not strike Elizabeth as an impetuous young man. She was prepared to let the matter rest. She looked up at her husband. Darcy was looking from one to the other. She knew he was making a sort of social calculation. Should he question the young man or let the matter drop?

"We will discuss your antics further in the morning." He glared at his daughter.

Emma was nonplussed. "I am famished." Phillipe made a gesture with his hand toward the dining room.

"I will have something prepared for us," he said gallantly. He then turned to Darcy. "I do apologize again, sir. Your daughter was completely safe in my company. I assure you." He extended his hand. Darcy hesitated and then took it.

"I will rely upon your word as a gentleman."

"I thank you, sir." Phillipe met Darcy's gaze, and then he and Emma retreated to the dining room, leaving their confused and rather suspicious parents behind them.

***

At Elizabeth's insistence, Darcy tried to compose himself. But the night did not bring its usual solace and Darcy found himself pulling on his dressing gown and wandering the house, anger and worry each taking their turn tumbling round his brain. As he ascended the stairs to try again to lay his head to rest, he came upon Poppy quietly closing the door to her room. She started at seeing him there, standing like an apparition on the staircase holding a flickering candle.

"Oh, Mr. Darcy, you did give me a fright."

"I do apologize, madame, I could not sleep." They were both whispering so as not to wake the household.

Poppy nodded. "Nor could I. You worry about our chil'ren who are no longer chil'ren, *n'est-ce pas*?" Darcy sat down heavily on the top of the staircase and Poppy joined him there. "I don' know what Phillipe was thinkin' takin' her dere an' stayin' out after dark. He know bedder."

"She also knows what is proper and expected of her. I do not understand her behavior either."

"She young and in a new place. She trus' my son and I trus' him too, Mr. Darcy. You have no reason to worry dat he take advantage o' her. He never do dat."

"I meant no insult to your son or to your family."

Poppy patted him on the arm. "I know. I know." She took a deep breath and let it out slowly. "A papa worry 'bout his girls more dan he worry 'bout his boys." He looked into her face and she had a rueful smile fixed upon it. The candle burning upon the step below them threw both of their faces into sharp relief, and each expression became a caricature of itself. There would be no hiding of emotions tonight.

"Do you think that they are forming an attachment to each other?" Darcy asked, looking straight into her eyes, trying to divine the truth they contained.

"I truly do not know. If dey love each odder, dey travel an impossible road. I cannot talk to my son. He tell me that he is jus' showin' your daughter the sights of our gran' city and has no design on her. He knows more dan mos' dey have no future here. Dey have no future no place."

Darcy let out a sigh. "Do not mistake me, madame," he began and then hesitated. He would try to explain his concern without casting aspersions on her son or his origins. Poppy began to laugh softly.

"It jus' us two, Mr. Darcy. Jus' call me Poppy. We been tru' too much."

"Very well, Poppy. Please call me Darcy. Even my Lizzy does so." He paused for a moment and looked at her. "As for my daughter, I do believe she is developing feelings for your son. She is younger than he and full of romantic thoughts."

Poppy nodded. "I hope my Phillipe don' break her heart. I don' know his mind, but he say he don' wan' hurt her."

"Perhaps we should cut our visit short and return to England before Christmas." Darcy noticed he was wringing his hands. He forced himself to stop.

Poppy sighed. "Maybe dat be for de bes'. Her tone was resigned. "I hate to see you go, an' dat de trut'. I be so happy to have my Miss Lizabet back."

"I know. I know. This journey has done wonders for her spirit." He took Poppy's hand and squeezed it. "Thank you for that."

Darcy's natural reserve was on the verge of slipping into a maudlin display, so he picked up the candle and rose quickly, clearing his throat. "I believe I will sleep now." He offered the candle in its holder to Poppy.

"No, I go back too. We solve de problems of de worl' tonight."

He smiled at her but did not see her return it as she opened the door to her room and entered silently.

***

Dawn was breaking when Elizabeth heard a soft knocking upon their door. Her husband still slept. A few hours before, she woke briefly as he left their bed and later heard his voice and Poppy's nearby. She could not hear their exact words but smiled to herself that they had become confidantes. Her daughter's behavior concerned her too, but she felt that some passage of time and a good night's sleep might blunt the edge of their anger and distress. She rose from their bed, put on her dressing gown, and opened the door slightly.

There stood Benji.

"Why are you awake so early?" She blinked several times and rubbed the sleep from her eyes. A moment later he was in their room. He seemed agitated.

She sat upon the stool near the dressing table and whispered to him. "Your father is still sleeping. What is it you want, Benji?"

"I have to tell you something, Mama." He was doing his best to whisper. "A voodoo princess is coming today."

She smiled. "What is a voodoo princess?" Sometimes he was so sweet and delightful, it was everything she could do not to squeeze the breath out of him in her embrace. She refrained from that now.

He looked from one side of the room to the other as if the walls themselves were listening. "I do not know exactly, but I think I am worried about it."

She hugged him close, and then pulled away slightly, her hands upon his shoulders. "How do you know this princess is coming?"

"Gustave told me. His mammy said it too. The voodoo princess knows how to heal people. She can read minds. I wanted to tell you yesterday, but Emma spoiled it by not coming home. Did Papa scold her?"

"Papa did not scold her," she said and saw his face fall. "But he will speak to her this morning."

"Good. She thinks she can do anything she wants. Papa will tell her." He folded his arms in a determined fashion.

Darcy began to stir, and Elizabeth did not want to wake him. She knew he had had a restless night.

"Benji, I think the Chevals would not invite anyone here that would do us harm, do you?"

He screwed up his face in thought. "No, I do not believe they would, but I still want to see her and see if she can tell me what I am thinking."

Darcy's voice came sleepily from the bed. "I can tell you what I am thinking. I am thinking you need to go back to bed, young man."

Benji's eyes grew wide and he put his fingers to his lips. "I think we need to be quieter."

"I think you need to crawl back into your bed." Elizabeth hugged him close, then turned him around and gave him a pat on his bottom. He stopped at the door and turned to her as he opened it.

"I do not know why you are sleeping when the sun is up," he said. She made a face at him and he scampered off, closing the door behind him.

***

Phillipe wished that he could forgo the upcoming social occasion with his two younger sisters. They had attended a few of these balls, and the girls danced reluctantly with each suitor in turn but did not seem to have much enthusiasm for the whole proceeding. He remembered his sister Manon's introduction to society. It took only an initial meeting at the cathedral and then two or three events of that sort before she settled upon Monsieur Cheval. At the time, he could not see what she saw in him, but as the years went by, he proved to be a good match for his sister and a devoted father. He could see by the way he treated Manon that he adored her, and Philippe was happy for his sister. The youngest two had proved to be intractable thus far.

Adele could do as she wished. She had no African blood and therefore had her pick of New Orleans society. He did not even know why she would attend with her sister Elizabeth Ann, for this ball was not designed for a white woman. He suggested that perhaps Elizabeth Ann preferred a free man of color for a husband, but she showed little interest in any of the men whom Cecile and her husband arranged for her to meet. The two young women really did seem inseparable, and Phillipe worried that they might never marry. Of course, they need not really. The family could support them throughout their lives if need be.

The breakfast table was emptier than usual. Mr. Darcy had not risen when Phillipe sat down for his meal, and he saw nothing of Emma.

"Phillipe, whatever were you thinking taking our guest to Congo Square? You were unaccompanied and came home so very late. It was quite an embarrassment to our entire family," Manon scolded him as he silently poured his coffee and heaped peach jam on his beignet.

He tried to ignore her admonitions. "These are awfully good when they are still warm."

"Really, Phillipe, your sister is right. What does your mother say?" Monsieur Cheval was not allowing the matter to drop.

"I explained everything to her, and she is satisfied. You should be too. Am I not to be trusted with a family friend? You behave as if I am capable of compromising her honor or my own for that matter."

"But how does it look?" Manon asked.

"How does it look to whom?" he rejoined. His sister was too concerned with what people thought. "We were well hidden and were observed by no one. Emma will leave in a few weeks and all will be well. No one of her society has seen us together."

"Even if they did," Emma said as she entered the dining room, "I would be proud and happy to introduce Monsieur Peschier as a close family friend."

Monsieur Cheval stood up at Emma's entrance and grew quite red in the face. Phillipe was heartily amused. He began to like this proud and forthright young woman. He could not help but smile.

"Nevertheless," Manon continued, "I will apologize again to Mr. and Mrs. Darcy." She turned to Emma. "You must be careful here, my dear, there can be grave consequences for flouting society's rules."

Phillipe could see Emma bridle at this remark, but she did not reply as he expected. "I will be careful, madame, and heed your advice." Then she took her seat next to Phillipe. He could feel the warmth of her body even though she was not touching him.

She looked directly into his eyes in that confident, piercing way of hers that sent shivers down his spine and excited his manhood. He must control himself. This attraction to her was growing stronger by the day, and he knew it was doomed before it began.

***

"Emma," Darcy said as he entered the dining room, "I would like to have a word." The sound of his voice silenced the entire company as they turned their gaze upon him. Emma rose slowly from her seat and met her father. Gently, he took her arm and led her out into the deserted garden. A walk among the flowers and shrubs helped him gather his thoughts. He led Emma to a stone bench he'd espied earlier and bade her sit down. He was struggling to control his anger. Elizabeth had entreated him to keep his temper in check, and he knew from all the other encounters with his headstrong daughter that raising his voice would lose him the argument. And there would be an argument, to be sure.

As she finished smoothing her skirts and finally looked up at him where he stood next to the bench, Darcy saw the set of her jaw and the glint in her eye. She sat straight before him, her shoulders squared, and her head held high. Why could she have not been more like her mother and less like him? A thought crossed his mind that she vexed him so because they were so much alike. He saw in her every flaw in himself amplified and thrown back in his face.

"Emma, your behavior of late is concerning to me." When he had rehearsed his speech, he thought to say her behavior was inexcusable. He had changed his mind and was glad for it. Even with this milder version, he could see by the flash in her eye she was ready to do battle.

"I do not see why. I have done nothing wrong." She broke his gaze and looked off into the distance.

Darcy took a deep breath and stood before her. "Look at me," he ordered.

When her eyes met his, they could not hold his gaze and flitted about from one side to the other. She was not as sure of herself as she tried to make others believe. He relaxed a bit and pressed his advantage.

"Your mother and I were concerned that you were out and about after darkness fell in a strange city with a young man you barely know."

"So, you do not trust Phillipe."

"I did not say that." He laid his hand on her shoulder. "And now you are calling him by his Christian name?"

Emma said nothing and turned her gaze from her father. He sat beside her and took her hand.

"Are you forming an attachment to him?" Again, she did not answer, and fidgeted so that her back was nearly turned.

"Oh, Emma. I do not know where to begin. The dangers that this city hold for a young girl who knows nothing of the world are immense. Anything could have happened to you last night. Even with all the trust in the world in Phillipe, there are things that may be beyond even his control."

Emma turned back to Darcy. "Phillipe can defend himself, and me, of that I can assure you." The instant those words were out of her mouth, she covered it with her hand and stood, turning her back on her father.

"What do you mean by that, my girl?" Darcy demanded, quite forgetting his promise to Elizabeth to hold his temper.

Emma turned back to face him. "It was nothing. No one was hurt except a few ruffians."

Darcy rubbed his forehead with the tips of his fingers and then ran his fingers through his hair. The situation was far worse than he had imagined. He stood, breathing hard, trying to think.

Finally, he stepped toward Emma, who backed away from him. She had a look on her face that he recognized from her childhood. The look of a little girl caught with her fingers in the jam. He extended his hands to her, palms up, and she placed her hands in his.

"Sit down. Please. Let us not quarrel."

As they took their places, Emma then began talking rapidly. "You do not understand, Father. This is the nineteenth century. Things are different now. I have learned so much since I have been here. I am not a little girl anymore that you have to hover over and protect."

Darcy shook his head. "There is a brutality in this world of which you know nothing."

"And you do, I suppose," she said haughtily.

He looked at her, forcibly holding her gaze, and his expression must have told her much, for she stopped talking and lowered her eyes.

Darcy ignored her impertinence and continued. "As a matter of fact, I do. And so does your mother."

Emma's head jerked up and her expression filled with horror. "What do you mean?" she squeaked.

Darcy sighed and look both of her hands in his. "I will let her tell you for it is her story to tell when she is ready to speak of it and you are ready to listen. Suffice it to say, your mother knows of the brutality of men who have no conscience. She was held prisoner during an uprising in Grenada and was powerless against..." He stopped talking lest his voice should betray his emotion. It was he, then, who turned his gaze from hers.

When he turned back to look at her, her eyes were glistening. She held his gaze. "And what of this attachment to Phillipe?" he asked.

She jumped up from her seat and turned from him. "I do not know, Papa. How does one know if one is in love?"

These subjects were what daughters and mothers discussed, not daughters and fathers, yet here he was, a prisoner of his own making. His thoughts were racing, and he knew he must gain control of them if he was to counsel and warn her. "If you are not sure, then perhaps you are not..." it was difficult for him to speak the words, "... in love." He rose and touched her shoulders to turn her to face him.

She threw her arms about his waist and buried her face in his chest for a moment. He gingerly patted her back. "There, there, now," he muttered feebly. He detested such scenes, but knew it was his duty to not only chastise, but comfort his daughter.

She looked up into his face, and her words came out all in a rush. "I know it is an impossible love. I am trying to keep my distance, but I find I cannot. Everyone keeps telling me in one way or another that there is no future for a man such as he and a woman such as myself. I am trying to fight against forming an attachment but feel powerless against it. Do you understand, Papa?"

Of all the questions she could have asked him, this one cut him to the quick. Of course, he understood her feelings. He understood only too well. Some part of him wanted to tell her to persevere, to ignore the naysayers, to follow her heart, yet he knew that her situation was not his, and that the obstacles that stood between her and Philippe were insurmountable, no matter what their efforts might be to overcome them.

He was lost in these thoughts for a moment and then peered down into Emma's lovely countenance, noticed her eyes were searching his. What was he to tell her? "You must do your best to guard your heart, Emma. This journey will not last much longer, and we will depart for England and resume our lives. You say yourself that you are not sure of your feelings. What of his? Has he declared himself to you?"

She released herself from her father's embrace and studying the ground at her feet, shook her head slowly. That gesture assuaged many of his fears. Perhaps this display of emotion was merely a young girl's fantasy and nothing more. He breathed a sigh of relief.

"Emma," he said, drawing her up then looping her arm through his. They began walking back toward the house. "Try to enjoy your time here and view it as part of your grand travels. Once we are back in England, what has happened here will become a fond memory. You will see."

She said nothing, and did not look up at him. He took that silence as assent and spoke no more as they entered the house.

Chapter 12

A few hours later, preparations commenced for the ball that evening. There were thousands of details to secure, especially for the two belles of the ball, Elizabeth Ann and Adele. As Poppy explained, this was a sort of introduction to society for the two of them. Their elder sisters had done the same and now it was their turn.

A young woman called Marie Laveau was summoned to arrange everyone's hair. Poppy had informed Elizabeth, the woman was well known in the city for not only her hairdressing skills, but also as a voodoo priestess.

"You will like her. She is a kind woman, and de bes' in arranging hair. Everyone go to her. We are lucky she come here today." She was smiling, and Elizabeth could see the excitement in her eyes.

"What is voodoo?" Elizabeth asked.

Poppy looked at her incredulously. "You do not know it?" Then she paused, and a thoughtful expression enveloped her face. "Of course, how would you know? It come from Africa and some t'ings from de Indians. It help me t'ink about the world we see and de worl' we don'."

"But I thought you and your family were Catholic."

"Oh, you can be a Catholic and follow de voodoo. It all good."

Elizabeth did not see how any of this could be possible, but there were many things that became clearer in time. There did not seem to be any harm in it, despite Benji's misgivings. She changed her tack.

"You are happy today." It was a statement rather than a question.

"I am. We about to settle t'ing for one daughter at leas'."

"What do you mean?"

"You'll see." Poppy had that impish smile on her face. "Dis a special ball we go to tonight."

***

With all the chaos of preparations, Elizabeth could not find a moment to confront her daughter about the events of the past evening. She suspected that Emma was avoiding her. When Marie Laveau arrived, Elizabeth had in mind the entrance of a head of state more than a hairdresser. Everyone from slave to master treated her with the utmost respect, and even awe.

The woman was strikingly beautiful with a honey-colored complexion and round, soulful eyes. Elizabeth guessed her age as near Emma's, but her inquiries about this strange woman were met with shrugs from Poppy. She remained a woman of mystery, and Elizabeth suspected that she cultivated this aura.

Her hair was done up in a tignon, as was the custom for the free women of colour in the city. The women of the household were seen to one by one for their hair arrangements. Poppy and her daughter Elizabeth Ann had their hair done by covering it in elaborately folded and decorated tignons, but Elizabeth, Emma, and Adele had theirs washed, trimmed, and shaped by Marie's deft ministrations. Elizabeth was the last of the family to be seen. As she sat for her session, she tried using her best French to draw out this enigmatic individual.

"You are quite skilled in dressing hair."

"I do my best. My mission on this earth, though, is to provide solace and hope. I try to provide counsel for those in need of it. I am a practitioner of voodoo, an ancient religion."

Elizabeth was fascinated by the mention of this religion. She said nothing in hopes that this young woman would enlighten her.

Marie continued. "I have learned much of the practice, and I do what I can to help and advise." Elizabeth pondered how a woman so young could advise anyone on anything. "Your daughter, for example…" she began, and then worked on twisting and twirling Elizabeth's hair and arranging it with pins. Elizabeth tried to remain patient, and then chastised herself for being drawn in by this woman's charisma and reputation. Still, did she know something about Emma?

"There," Marie said, and held a looking glass in front of Elizabeth. Her hair was exquisite. No one had ever made it look quite that striking before. "Are you pleased?"

"Indeed I am. You are a magician." Elizabeth wanted to let the matter of Emma drop, but she could not make herself do so. "You mentioned my daughter." She turned to look into Marie Laveau's face.

"Ah, yes. She has embarked upon a joyous yet terrible journey. You would do well to take her from this place before it is too late." Without another word, she began to arrange her things in her large cloth bag. Elizabeth stood and opened her mouth to speak, but then thought better of it. Perhaps this woman could read minds. She only confirmed what Elizabeth had feared.

Emma was falling in love with Phillipe Peschier.

***

Emma could barely contain her excitement. They were finally to attend a ball in New Orleans. Their time on the plantation was interesting enough, but Emma craved the life she lived in London. Admittedly, New Orleans was still a backwater town in a backward country, but she would make do. She would enter on Phillipe's arm, and they would dance and mingle with people of comparable social standing at last. It was a mystery to her how her parents, her father especially, eschewed these lavish and exhilarating social gatherings. She lived for them, and now she would be part of one again.

The Chevals owned a beautiful barouche, which could accommodate four of them. The Jordains, whose party they were attending, sent another so that they all might travel together.

Phillipe handed Emma into the carriage, and she could feel the heat of his hand even through her glove. She could also feel her father's gaze burning through the back of her head. He had not quite forgiven Phillipe for whisking her off to Congo Square, and their conversation that morning haunted her. Phillipe returned to his mother's carriage and helped her and his two inseparable sisters into it.

Once the carriage containing Poppy, the twins, and Monsieur Cheval left, Phillipe positioned himself beside the driver. The carriage was off, and Emma was of the distinct impression that he arranged to have her seated facing front so he could periodically turn and smile at her. Her father and mother were across from her, and therefore, did not notice this subtle ploy. She was sure that his sister, Manon, did, however. The expression on her face when he turned to look at Emma told her as much.

The Jourdain house was in the new extension of the city in the Fauborg St. Mary district, and one arrived on a circular drive that led to and away from the house, which was set well back from the street. Torches blazed along the drive that led to a spectacular Greek revival mansion complete with tall columns that rose to the second story. Emma felt that she had finally arrived in her element. These were the people she understood.

The Jordains were a mixed-race couple who stood by the door and welcomed each guest as they entered. Her father had taken her mother's arm, and offered his other to her, but she turned slightly from him to Phillipe, who motioned to her that she should enter with him. She turned and smiled at her father and then took Phillipe's arm.

Perhaps it was her imagination, but this small gesture seemed to create a great deal of consternation among the guests. Her attention, though, was drawn to the spectacular entry hall that contained a magnificent staircase that twirled in a spiral to the upper floors like the inside of a seashell. It nearly took her breath away.

Guests were milling about everywhere, and as soon as they were through the receiving line, Phillipe spirited her off to look at the gardens, which were as magnificent as the house. As they walked among the guests, Emma was struck by the fact that she, on Phillipe's arm, and her parents, were an anomaly among the guests.

"What is it?" Phillipe asked as they crossed a footbridge that led to a small pavilion where he invited her to sit. "You have the most peculiar look on your face."

"The people here…" she began to speak, and then felt that she did not know what to say. She had no intention of causing offence but was overcome with curiosity.

"This does not look like a ball that you would attend in England?" He smiled wickedly at her. Obviously, he knew she felt uncomfortable and he was teasing her. It gave her the courage to speak her mind.

"The couples, they are all white men with women of colour," she said, translating the term from the French.

"That is true. What you see here is *mariages de la main gauche,* the left-handed marriage. Many of these men fetched their wives from Rampart Street where they live with their children. Most do not live as the Jordains or my parents live. Many of these men have a white wife and children who live in these beautiful houses. Madam Jordain, who is a free woman of colour and whom you met at the entrance, is truly the mistress of this house. She is quite essential to her husband's business dealings. If you want to speak to him, you must first go to her."

"But in the eyes of the law, these women are not married to these men, is that not so?"

"In the eyes of the law, and even of the Church, that is so, but in the eyes of many of the people like my parents, they are indeed married to one another."

Emma shook her head. She could not imagine such a society in England or even speaking of it, for that matter. She said nothing for a long while, trying to reconcile all these conflicting facts in her head.

"You do not approve."

She thought for a moment. "I do not approve or disapprove. It is none of my concern, is it? I am here to enjoy myself and dance. Finally dance." She smiled at him, trying hard to be enticing.

"If you are so inclined then, Miss Darcy, let us dance." Whereupon he stood and offered her his arm. She inhaled a satisfying breath and took his arm gratefully.

***

Elizabeth watched her husband as he extended a gloved hand to dozens of new people to whom he was formally introduced. She also noticed his glance shoot from one side of the room to the other. Emma had disappeared with Phillipe almost the instant they arrived, and she knew Darcy was concerned. Being transported so far from home to a place where the standards of conduct and the society were so different from your own gave one a sense of boundless freedom. She knew from experience that the rules restraining one's behavior seemed to vanish in these foreign surroundings and were replaced with a kind of euphoria.

In Elizabeth's case, the lack of restraint had been tempered by the belief she had lost her beloved Darcy, and that grief kept her tethered to the ground while in Grenada. Her daughter, although having had her heart bruised by Edmund Montjoy, was not grief-stricken in the least, and she could almost see her younger self in her daughter's flouting of her former constraints. Her husband, however, was behaving like a father, and she could not fault him for that. Added to his burden was the thing he despised the most, small talk at a large social gathering. She would have to persuade him to dance with her, at least once.

"So kind of you to join us today, Monsieur and Madame Darcy," Monsieur Jordain said in French when he and his wife finally extricated themselves from the receiving line. "I do hope you enjoy yourselves. We are all friends now, are we not?"

"If you are speaking of the French and the English, then you are quite correct," Darcy replied. "But you are American now. In that case, I believe we may still be enemies."

This elicited a great guffaw from Jordain that Elizabeth had not expected. He slapped Darcy on the back. "I like you, Monsieur Darcy. Please, come, have some champagne, dance, enjoy yourselves." He led them to a long table set with champagne glasses that a liveried servant was filling with the bubbly liquid.

He handed one to her, to his wife, then one to Darcy and took one for himself. "A toast," he said in a rather loud voice. "To the best of enemies." And with that he downed the entire shallow glass in one gulp. She and Darcy drank from theirs and her husband made a slight bow to his host. Jordain laughed again, took up another glass, and left them to their devices. As soon as they were out of earshot, Darcy took Elizabeth by the hand and led her to one of the anterooms.

"Where is Emma?" he asked when they were quite alone.

"I have no idea, my dear," Elizabeth replied in her most soothing tone. "But I am sure she is safe with Phillipe."

"She is too easily swayed by a handsome face and clever banter." That dark scowl she knew so well clouded his countenance.

Elizabeth was sure he was again creating a catastrophe where there was none. "Is that what you think of Phillipe, my dear?" It would take effort to coax him out of his mood.

"No, of course not. I believe him to be a fine young man, possessed of a good mind, a faithful heart, and a sense of honor."

"What an awful scoundrel to have accompany our daughter." She gave him an arch look.

"Now, Lizzy, you know quite well what my concern is." He looked into her face. She hoped her smile would generate one in him.

"Do not think you can cajole me," he protested, yet a smile hinted on his lips.

"And why not? I have spent the last twenty years thus engaged." She laughed and ran a few steps from him to the window.

He began to laugh as well and caught her in mid-flight. "I do believe I will kiss you, Mrs. Darcy." He was still smiling, his eyes softening in their expression.

"Oh, do be quick about it, sir, my husband is in attendance."

He kissed her first quickly on the cheek, and then fully on the mouth, cupping her face in his hands. She could feel herself yield to him and wished that they were home and not in a stranger's house, surrounded by droves of people.

"Let us run away together," she whispered in his ear as he kissed her again and again.

"Would that we could," he said, finally pulling away from her. "First, though, we need to find our daughter."

She entwined her arm with his, and they entered the garden through the veranda.

***

The November weather was warm and fine, and their host had all of the large windows of the ballroom open to the garden. Emma and Phillipe took their places in the line of couples for a dance that looked somewhat like an English country dance of which Emma was familiar. A middle-aged man with a balding pate and a loud voice proclaimed something called the Virginia reel, and Emma was confident that she could follow the steps.

Phillipe insisted that they take the last place in the set in order for Emma to observe the steps. They set off with great gusto. The American dance was not sedate in the least and Emma enjoyed it immensely. By the time they arrived at the top of the set, she felt quite the expert and they acquitted themselves well. Upon finishing, she felt herself quite flushed, and Phillipe went off to bring her some refreshment. As she took a seat on the lawn, she noticed that some of the guests were looking over at her and whispering. How odd. Did she not acquit herself well?

Phillipe arrived with a glass of lemonade, of which she drank thirstily. She looked over at his handsome face and realized that she was filled with happiness.

"Thank you." She blushed in spite of herself and smiled. She hoped he would ask her to dance again. Before he had time to speak, another young gentleman, tall and blond, extended his hand.

"May I have this dance?" he asked, offering his hand. She looked over at Phillipe. His face was expressionless. If he would not object, she would dance with another.

"I would love to," she said, and entered the dance floor with her new partner. Phillipe stood aside for a moment, and then, to Emma's dismay, disappeared into the crowd. She turned to her new partner, and they entered the allemande.

***

"These English have no manners," Phillipe complained to his mother when he finally found her sitting at a table alone. "I see that Monsieur and Madam Darcy are no better than their daughter, leaving you alone here."

"Dey dancing, son," she said calmly. "You know your sisters. Dey do not dance and enjoy demselves. The Darcys persuade dem. I am grateful." She pointed into the lines of couples, and saw not only Emma, but her parents and his sisters partaking of the dance. "I do not know what to do wid' your sisters. Dey never fin' husbands if dey don' try a little bit." She sighed.

Phillipe was partially listening. He only had eyes for Emma, which he found disconcerting. It was obvious that the stares and whisperings of the assembled guests were directed at him and Emma. He knew these white men took umbrage at the fact that he was dancing with a white woman. In his heart of hearts, he knew what he was beginning to feel for this spoiled, outspoken English girl was forbidden in both his society and hers, but his heart and his desire would not listen to his brain. He wrenched his thoughts from his misery to focus on his mother. His sisters were beginning to present a problem, and he would try to focus on them.

"Perhaps you should ask the girls what they want."

His mother began to laugh. "I don' b'lieve dey know what dey want. Dey need to get married." She looked over at Phillipe. "You do too, my son."

He met her gaze only for a moment, and then looked back to the ensemble. The dance was concluding and the Darcys and his sisters joined them. The Chevals were nowhere to be seen, but Phillipe knew Manon would find them eventually. The orchestra struck up another tune, this one in three-quarter time.

Emma looked expectantly at him. That girl could dance every dance and never tire, but would she dance this one with him?

"Whatever sort of music is this?" Madame Darcy asked as couples arrived on the dance floor, but not in a circle or in two lines, but holding only each other, in a small orbit. They began to twirl.

"Ah, this is new. Lately come from France. It is called the waltz." Monsieur Darcy made an uncomfortable coughing sound, and Phillipe looked up at him.

"Oh, do teach me," said Emma enthusiastically. "It looks ever so intriguing."

Phillipe held Monsieur Darcy's gaze, and when he nodded his head ever so slightly, Phillipe assumed Monsieur Darcy had given his assent. Phillipe held out his arms to Emma, who flew into them as if no one was observing them. He held out his left hand, and Emma, glancing back at the couples that were already dancing, placed her right hand in his. Then, still looking at Emma's father, gingerly, Phillipe placed his right hand in the small of Emma's back.

"Put your left arm across my shoulder, *s'il vous plait*," he directed. Not seeing any strident objection from her father, he drew his attention back to Emma.

"Now, step together close, step together close. You step the opposite of me." At first, they were quite awkward.

"My dear," he heard Madame Darcy say, "let us try also." Phillipe did not dare look at Emma's father again but let go of Emma immediately as her parents joined them. He showed both of them the steps, and with gratitude, he watched Madame Darcy take Emma's hand and they practiced the women's part together. Monsieur Darcy stood obediently next to Phillipe and imitated the steps. Neither man looked at the other.

"Now, *monsieur*," Phillipe said to Darcy, "take your wife's hand so, and place your other hand so." He demonstrated this position with Emma, who looked at him with the most devilish grin he had ever seen on a woman. What was he to do with such a girl?

"Now, when I let go of you this way," Phillipe said, letting his hand release its grip from her back, "you move backwards, and if I do this," he increased the pressure on her back and drew her to him in an embrace of sorts, "you come toward me. Are you ready?" He looked over at the Darcys. "*Monsieur*, madame, would you like to try?"

"Out there?" Darcy asked incredulously. His wife bit her bottom lip, and did not smile outright, but her eyes were dancing with delight. Phillipe could see where Emma learnt her charmingly insolent ways.

"Oh, I do believe we can find ourselves a secluded place to practice," Madame Darcy said playfully to her husband. Emma was already tugging at Phillipe's hand. The orchestra struck up another waltz. Not waiting to see what his pupils would do, he joined Emma on the dance floor. Without hesitation, she placed her hand in his and rested her arm on his shoulder, her fingers brushing the back of his neck. Even such a light touch made him burn with desire for her. He forgot her father and mother, and his own, completely.

At first they moved in rather small and controlled swaying movements back and forth. Toes were trodden, but the awkwardness soon evaporated, and they moved in a more fluid manner. Taking a chance, he pushed slightly at the small of her back and she responded immediately, moving toward him. They began to whirl across the dance floor. He felt as though they were as light as air, as though they were flying.

As the music concluded, he looked into Emma's flushed and exuberant face. She wore an expression of absolute bliss and he wanted to kiss her here, before everyone.

Then he heard a voice he had not heard in a long time.

His eyes went from Emma's face toward the silvery laughter from the other side of the room. There she was—tall, proud, strikingly beautiful like a Senegalese goddess.

Rosaline Lacoste.

Chapter 13

Even though nothing around her had physically changed, Emma knew something had happened. She turned to look over her shoulder at whomever it was who so suddenly and entirely stole her partner's attention. Phillipe took her by the arm and led her from the dance floor, but not before her eyes fell upon one of the most extraordinarily stunning women she had ever seen. Phillipe's entire demeanor changed at the sight of her. She wanted to ask him about her, but the expression on his face, which had moments ago been alive with laughter and elation, now was a mask of anger, and perhaps even pain.

They rejoined the chattering group formed by their distinguished company and noticed that two young white men had joined them. Formal introductions were made, and at Poppy's insistence, they each took the arm of Phillipe's younger sisters and joined the quadrille. Phillipe seemed distracted and excused himself, barely looking at Emma. She watched as he disappeared into the crowd. Feeling abandoned and not a little vexed, she looked about, and there were another two Frenchmen at her elbows. They seemed unsure as to which one should speak to her first, and she smiled at both of them. She was soon, once again, partaking of the dance.

They were nearly to the *La Poule* of the quadrille when she espied them. There was Phillipe with that splendid woman as his partner. They did make a rather handsome couple, which infuriated her. She tried her best to concentrate on her partner, but her attention was drawn back to Phillipe. It seemed that she was not the only one to notice them. There were murmurs in the crowd and by the time the dance finished, a rather portly, extremely well-dressed white gentleman plucked the woman from Phillipe's grasp. From where she stood, she could not hear the words exchanged, but she could see from their faces that they were not pleasant. Phillipe clicked his heels and bowed, and the other man nodded his head. With that,

Phillipe retreated from the floor and disappeared through one of the many French doors to the veranda. Emma had another partner waiting for her and, not wanting to be rude, joined him in a dance.

The music again drifted into more familiar territory and her partner seized every moment they were together on the floor to talk with her. "I saw you come in with Monsieur Cheval. Are you related?"

Emma thought that a strange question. Surely everyone knew of the Darcys and their relationship with Phillipe's family. "No, we are newly arrived here."

"Ah, from Saint-Domingue, I suppose." With that they were again at opposite sides of the line and could no longer converse. Whatever was this young man on about? As they again took hands, he continued. "I thought I recognized the accent. You are exceptionally light-skinned for an octoroon." He smiled widely at her.

"Octoroon?" she said incredulously. This was a most vexing and confusing conversation.

"Oh, *excusez-moi*, perhaps you have even less Negro blood than that. I should have known looking at your mother."

Emma was so shocked by this statement she stumbled slightly in the dance, losing her place. Righting herself, she stared at her companion. Her eyes were drawn to her mother and father, who were engaged in conversation with Poppy. This fellow believed that her parents had a relationship like nearly all the other couples in the room. An arrangement not sanctified by marriage, but one that floated slightly above the law, in some sort of interracial miasma. How else could she and Phillipe be dancing together if she had no Negro blood in her? To this young man, and all present save her parents and Poppy, it would be a social aberration, perhaps even dangerous.

It was odd that one could be told such things in one way or another as she had and understand them, but one did not fully grasp a situation until one experienced it firsthand. No wonder the world made such slow progress. Every person, it seemed, needed to learn the same lesson as his or her forebearer through experience rather than being instructed through someone else's. Finally, she now understood the impossibility of her and Phillipe's situation, if it even was a situation.

As the dance ended, she looked up at this young man. "Thank you so much, sir, but I must find Monsieur Peschier."

He sighed. "Ah, that is unfortunate. He is a lucky man." Then, as she turned to go, he added, "You could do better for yourself, you know."

She stopped in mid-step. This poseur was infuriating. She looked into his face. "No, *monsieur*, I do not believe I could."

The veranda was now ablaze with torches, and long tables were being laid for supper. She stood upon the steps and looked out into the garden, searching in the growing, shadowy darkness. Most people had abandoned the garden for the house as the sun set, but there was enough light that she detected the agile movement of Phillipe as he made his way toward the bridge they had crossed earlier. She knew then where he was going. She found him moments later, leaning against the slatted sides of the gazebo, staring into the gloom.

"There you are, Monsieur Peschier." He turned suddenly as if startled.

"Go back to the ball. There are many men who would like to have you for a partner." She did not enjoy this commanding tone and decided to ignore it.

"I have danced enough." It surprised her that she actually meant what she said. She hoped that if she stayed here with him, he would confide in her.

"You, Miss Darcy, could never dance enough," he said ruefully. They stood in silence for a moment.

He had to make an insulting remark to her again. Abandoning her manners completely, Emma spoke directly. "Who was the beautiful woman with whom you were dancing?"

He turned to look at her and then sighed. "It is none of your concern. It does not matter. She is married now. She made her choice."

Emma had seen enough in her journeys though the endless suppers, salons, and ballrooms to recognize the hapless demeanor of a jilted lover. She would not press him. "You are quite right. It is none of my business. I will see you at supper then." She turned to go, and had only reached the step and began to descend when she felt his hand at her elbow. She turned to look into Phillipe's face, which was illuminated by the moonlight.

"Please," he said. "I apologize. Sit with me a while."

Emma acquiesced. They sat for a while in silence, and then, with the shadows cast by the gathering darkness obscuring their faces, Phillipe began. "Her name is Rosaline Lacoste. When I knew her, she was Rosaline Santiago Roche, born a free woman of a Spanish father and a free woman of Dominique. We met each other in church, like Manon and Monsieur Cheval."

"Your sister and Cheval met in church? I thought that perhaps a ball or some other social occasion."

Phillipe shook his head. "Many couples of *couleur libre*, free people of colour, meet our husbands or wives, or our partners in our *left-handed marriages,* in church. That is where I met Rosaline."

"She is quite beautiful."

Phillipe sighed again. He looked up at Emma. "Do you know how susceptible men are to beauty in a woman?"

"I do believe so, as women are susceptible to a handsome face and a flattering tongue. But I also know many of both sexes would forgo beauty for money, or even status." She suddenly thought of Edmund Montjoy as the words left her lips.

"That is true. Money and status are what came between Rosaline and myself. I have a small fortune in my own right, but I do not have the wealth of Monsieur Lacoste, Rosaline's protector. And even though I am a free man, I do not have the status of a white man."

"But she could never legally marry Monsieur Lacoste."

Phillipe laughed ruefully. "You are no longer in England, Emma. Such things are less important to a woman in Rosaline's position. What she and her children will eventually inherit is much more important. She does not suffer because she and Monsieur Lacoste never stood before a priest." Instinctively, Emma put her hand upon Phillipe's who snatched it away. "Do not pity me, Miss Darcy." His tone was angry, and he stood.

"I do not. I merely sympathize. You are not the only one who was passed over." She stood too and made her way to the steps of the gazebo.

He hesitated a moment and then ran and caught her. Seizing her by the shoulders, he twisted her round to face him. In one swift movement, he threw his arms about her and kissed her mouth.

At first, she yielded to him, and then suddenly, pushed him backward. "Do not think that you can use me as a poor substitute. I will not be treated thusly." She pulled herself away from him and ran back toward the house.

She could hear him calling her name through the fragrant blooms as she ran. Was she angry? Did he care for her? Did she care for him?

How different she felt on this night, as if she was moving through a dream.

***

As the hour approached eleven, they were called in to supper. Long tables were set up on the extensive veranda, which bordered the house on four sides. Unlike the English, whose host and hostess were each seated at the end of the table, the host and hostess in this house were seated in the center of the table facing each other. They led the conversation. Darcy felt himself fortunate that they were some distance from the center and not at the main table. No doubt, the more important guests were near the host and hostess, but he was wearying of speaking French constantly, and was content that they were all seated together. Emma and Phillipe were across from him, and their enthusiasm for each other's company seemed to have cooled somewhat from what he had observed before. Perhaps they had quarreled. No matter. He was relieved to observe it.

Their supper ran the gamut of heavily sauced French dishes to more native concoctions that Poppy called Creole cooking. Some of it was heavily spiced, and it made Darcy long for bread pudding and boiled mutton. Nonetheless, no expense had been spared, and the wine flowed freely. Dinner was a long, drawn-out affair, almost interminable, so after coffee and more French, he was about to suggest to his wife that they return home shortly. It was then he was accosted by a portly, well-dressed, rather pinkish gentleman who drew him aside.

"Is that your daughter, *monsieur*?" he asked, not waiting for an introduction. From the way he was pronouncing his words and his unsteady stance, Darcy concluded that this person had imbibed a bit too much wine at dinner.

"I beg your pardon," Darcy began, somewhat offended. "Do I know you?"

"My name is Lacoste, Monsieur. I would like to warn you against letting your daughter in any way connect herself with that young buck, Peschier."

Darcy knew enough of the expressions used by these Creole to know that the word *buck* was extremely insulting. "You overstep your bounds, *monsieur*, and I take offense at your remarks."

Lacoste backed up, wavering a bit, and tried to look Darcy in the eye. He smiled. "Ha," he exclaimed. "You do not understand our ways, *monsieur*, and that young buck does not know his place."

Phillipe must have observed them from afar, and now was standing at Darcy's side. How much of the conversation he heard was unknown, but the young man's eyes were aflame. The situation could easily degenerate into violence and Darcy had no desire to embroil himself in another duel.

"What did you say, *monsieur*?" Phillipe shouted as he confronted a bleary-eyed but still haughty Lacoste. Darcy watched in horror as the young man produced a blade from the top of his boot.

"Stay away from my wife," Lacoste blurted. Apparently, there was more to this convoluted story than Darcy knew. A crowd was gathering around them. Something had to be done to defuse the situation.

"How dare you?" Phillipe shouted. Darcy quickly stepped between the two men. The blade was still in Phillipe's hand, but he had yet to raise it.

"Please, *monsieur*," he said to Phillipe. "First, I must settle with the gentleman about the remarks he made about my daughter."

Lacoste jerked his head up and stared, confused, at Darcy. "What did I say about your daughter, *monsieur*?" Darcy shook his head then made a grandiose gesture to the crowd as if to say, *Can you believe what you are seeing?* He turned upon Lacoste. "You, sir, are drunk. I would demand satisfaction from you, if I believed you were in full control of your faculties, but obviously, you are not." The man stepped back, and without any action on Darcy's or Phillipe's part, tripped over his own feet and landed soundly on the floor with a great thump. The crowd erupted in laughter.

Lacoste scrambled to his feet, blinking. "You... you..." But before he could utter another word, Monsieur Jordain reached them. He made a deep bow to Darcy. "I am so sorry, *monsieur*, that this unfortunate encounter has happened in my house." Then, turning to

Lacoste, he handed him his hat, and said, "Take your woman and leave my house. Never darken my doorway again."

Lacoste began to grumble, and from out of the crowd, Rosaline appeared to take his arm. They made their way solemnly, if not a trifle unsteadily, to the doorway. Darcy, his blood pounding in his ears, watched as Phillipe surreptitiously secreted his dagger back into his boot.

Jordain invited his guests to partake of more champagne and pastries and the crowd dispersed.

Darcy found himself alone with Phillipe. The young man was scowling. "You should not have interfered."

Darcy was determined to remain calm. "It is you, sir, who interfered with me."

Phillipe seemed taken aback at this remark for a moment. "Then you should have challenged him to a duel."

"I have experience of duels, and they always end badly." By then, the rest of their party had reached them.

Elizabeth rushed to his side and had a look of great concern on her face. "What happened?"

"All is well, my dear," he said calmly. "Monsieur Peschier and I took care of the scoundrel. I will explain all later."

He knew her well. She was not convinced. "I believe it is time to take our leave. I have had enough excitement for one night."

"I will arrange for a carriage," Phillipe said with a slight bow. Darcy watched as Emma followed him with her gaze. It had been a strange and eventful night and Darcy, for one, was glad to see it end.

***

Another two days saw the Darcys take their leave of the Chevals and New Orleans. Benji and Gustave held each other by the shoulders and kissed each other on both cheeks at their parting. Elizabeth watched in her amusement as her husband beheld the new habits of his youngest child.

"We are raising a Frenchman," he grumbled when they were out of earshot of the others.

Emma was quieter than usual but denied that anything was amiss. Elizabeth suspected it had something to do with Phillipe. She did not press her. Perhaps it was for the best.

As soon as they were out of the city and engulfed again in the greenery surrounding the wide Mississippi, Darcy removed his hat and jacket. Elizabeth saw him draw the first easy breath since they arrived. "I will be glad to see our friend, Monsieur Peschier, once again." She knew that was not the whole of his sentiment. He was glad to be rid of the city and heading toward a more bucolic setting where he felt comfortable.

Poppy, however, looked uneasy. "I hope he all right. We get no word of him for almos' a week. Probably jus' know we comin' home soon." She did not look convinced of her own words, and Elizabeth put her concern down to missing her husband. "You all enjoy yourself at the ball?"

Emma and Phillipe looked away from each other almost simultaneously. Neither of them replied. Something definitely had happened between them.

Elizabeth broke the silence. "It was most enjoyable." It had not escaped her notice, however, that she and her husband were the only couple of European descent there and that there were murmurings from some quarters whenever Phillipe and Emma were together. She would not mention it unless Poppy did first.

Poppy, however, seemed wrapped in her concerns. "I was hopin' my twins fin' someone nice der. I pray for it every day and look for a nice man for placage w' Elizabeth Ann or even marriage like my Cecile wit' her Valentine. But no. Dey stuck togeder like two peas in a pod." She turned to her two youngest girls. "What we go'n' to do wid you?"

The two girls looked at each other and took each other's hands. "Mama, we wanted to wait until we saw Papa, but I think we will tell you now," Adele said. "We are not going to marry anyone you put before us, no matter how much money he has or no matter what a fine man he is."

Poppy looked confused. "I don' understan'."

Elizabeth Ann took up where her sister left off. "With your permission, and Papa's, we will join the Ursaline Order in the city. We will begin our novitiate at the convent next month if Papa gives his permission."

"But will dey take you? Bot' of you?" Poppy asked incredulously.

Adele looked over and smiled at her sister. "They will take me without hesitation, and I told them that I will not join the order without my sister. It is unusual, but they will make an exception."

"And you do dis all on your own? Never talkin' to me or your papa?"

The girls left their seats and went to sit next to their mother. "We received a calling from God," Adele said. "We are telling you now." Poppy put her head in her hand and shook it slowly.

"We could have save ourself a lot of trouble if you tol' us sooner." She patted the girls on the hands. "Wait 'til we tell your papa."

***

When they arrived back at the plantation, Phillipe was surprised that his father did not come out of the house to greet them. Ninon, who ran the household, met them on the veranda and told them that his father had taken ill. He excused himself from the Darcys and entering the bedroom closest to the parlour through the French doors, he and his mother found his father sitting up in bed, drinking tea.

Maman rushed to his father's bedside and took him by the hand. "What is wrong, *mon cher*?"

"It is nothing, *mon cher*."

"Why did you not send word that you were ill?" Phillipe asked. "We would have come at once."

"That is exactly what I did *not* want you to do. I knew you would be home soon. Besides, it is nothing. Only a fever. It will pass."

Phillipe watched his mother put her hand on his father's forehead. He shivered slightly.

"I t'ink you quite ill, my husban'. I send for Marie Laveau."

His father shook his head vigorously. "You are making a fuss for nothing. I will be fine. Ninon has made me some elderberry tea. The fever will soon break. Now leave me to rest." He slid down into the sheets and closed his eyes.

"Papa," Phillipe said. "About the twins." He felt his mother's hand upon his sleeve. Raising his eyes to her face, she gave a small shake of her head.

"Not now," she whispered. "Let him res'."

Phillipe and his mother waited, but it was obvious that his father was sleeping. This fever did not look like a trifle to him. Phillipe took his mother by the arm, and they left his father to his rest. He took both his mother's hands in his. "I will send for Marie Laveau. She will help him."

Poppy nodded and reentered his father's bedchamber. Although Phillipe was unsure about the validity of his words, he sent for Thomas to take the boat back down river and fetch the voodoo priestess.

***

Immediately upon disembarking, Benji ran past the house and back toward the kitchen and the slave quarters. Emma knew that he was looking for his friend, the slave boy, Toby. He chattered about it nearly all the way back upriver. She was grateful for his constant prattling as it afforded her an excuse not to engage in conversation with Phillipe. On such a small craft, it was difficult to avoid him.

She did not know if she was still angry with him. In fact, she might have to admit to herself that he hurt her by using her as substitute for the woman he really wanted. What he felt, or what she felt for him, should not matter in the slightest. From all that she had learned on this strange sojourn into this strange country, she knew that there could never be anything between them. Why, then, was she so upset? Did she love him? Could she even consider it?

Phillipe brought the news to the Darcys that the master of the house was ill. Emma's mother and father offered to help in any way possible, but there was little any of them could do. As soon as she refreshed herself from the long journey, they sat down to luncheon. Someone had recovered her errant brother, and again he was so animated, it saved them all from having to make much of a conversation.

He was telling them about finding Toby and playing carry the bucket, to which Emma rolled her eyes. Why her brother could not see that he was doing someone else's work was beyond her. To make matters all the more vexing, Benji now mixed French and English freely and sometimes it took her a moment or two to understand what he was saying. As he told his story, his mother interrupted him.

"You are not speaking English, dear heart," her mother told him.

"Oh, *pardon, Maman,* I did not realize," he began.

"There, you have done it again," Emma said. He stopped for a moment and screwed up his face in thought.

He looked again at his mother. "I am sorry, *maman*, that is the way the words come out of my mouth." Emma sighed and her mother and father merely smiled.

After luncheon, her parents disappeared, no doubt to find Poppy and receive news of Monsieur Peschier's condition. As she entered the veranda, she found Phillipe there. Wishing to avoid him, she turned, but he caught her by the sleeve.

"We must talk," he whispered close to her ear.

She turned to him haughtily. "All right. Talk to me."

"Not here. Not now." He turned his attention back to the house and the room in which his father lay. "When my father is better. I will find a place with more privacy."

She raised an eyebrow at him and gave small curtsey. "I am at your disposal, *monsieur*."

***

By the next morning, his father was out of bed and sitting on the veranda. Phillipe found him there drinking coffee and eating a beignet. He had a blanket across his lap.

"You are better, Papa," he said to his father, smiling.

"Yes, I believe we have sent for the Widow Paris for nothing. It seems that my strength is returning. Your *maman* was afraid it was the fever, but I have fooled you all."

"I am grateful, Papa, and relieved. We were worried. When Marie Laveau arrives, we will send her back to the city with our thanks."

His father patted the seat of the chair next to him. "Come, sit." One of the servants came out of the house and set some beignets on the small table next to Peschier.

"Bring coffee for Monsieur Phillipe." The woman disappeared back into the house. "So, tell me, son. Has your mother arranged something for your two sisters? She was so concerned for me yesterday that I could not get one word out her about your journey."

Phillipe cleared his throat and looked away for a moment. He dreaded telling his father the news.

"Elizabeth Ann and Adele do not wish to marry."

His father waved his hand dismissively. "Oh, they will change their minds. There is time yet."

"No, Papa. You do not understand. They want to join the convent," Phillipe blurted. "You were too ill, so we did not tell you when we arrived home."

Monsiuer Peschier began to laugh. "Oh, I expect that took your dear mother by surprise. I wish I could have been there to see her face."

"So, you do not mind, Papa?" Phillipe asked incredulously.

"Why should I mind? They will be together there and look after one another. So, with all your mother's efforts, they will become the brides of Christ." He shook his head and was still chuckling to himself.

"Your mother will arrange for their trousseaus. I am sure the... What order is taking them?"

"The Ursalines."

"I am sure the Ursalines expect that we will provide their habits and so forth and see to all their needs. You must arrange for a donation to the convent and the church on their behalf, Phillipe. We want to make sure that they are both treated with the respect they are due." He gave his son a knowing look.

"Surely you do not think that the church would ever treat them with anything but deference."

"The church, like anywhere else, is filled with people, and people can be petty, and cruel, and intolerant. You must take care of them, Phillipe, as if they were under your own roof."

"Papa, you talk as if I was master of this house."

"I am getting old, my son, and tired. Soon, you will be master of this house."

His mother came out of the French doors at that moment, with her hair done up in the red kerchief he had so often seen her when he was young. She was still in her nightclothes.

"Why did you not wake me, Phillipe? And why your father out of bed so soon after his illness? I don' know what I will do wid eider of you." He saw his father smile and roll his eyes.

"Oh, stop fussing, woman. I am taking the air."

Poppy began to arrange the blanket over his father's knees. Phillipe stood and took up his coffee and left his parents to their banter. Now that his father's illness had passed, he would speak to Emma.

Chapter 14

Now that he persuaded Emma to accompany him, he was unsure exactly what he would say to her. They were atop the farm wagon Phillipe commandeered from its regular duties. She sat next to him in the driving seat as he clucked the horse into motion. They drove out along a dirt road that connected the plantations all along the river. The road was set back from the water. They were quite alone, and she did not say a word to him. Soon they approached the neighboring plantation. It was built farther from the river than the Peschier house, and had a long drive lined with trees. The plantation house was clearly visible at the end of it. It was somewhat grander than his own house, but similar in its festive, multicolored decoration. He stopped the wagon and looked at it for a moment.

Finally, she deigned to speak to him. "Are we stopping to make a call on the neighbors?"

"No, we cannot call on them. They will not speak to us." He clucked the horse forward again. Emma craned her neck as they passed the grand house.

"Are you quarreling with them?"

"No, we have no quarrel with them. Not as such."

"I do not understand." He drove the wagon around a bend in the road where he led the horses down a small embankment and across a stretch of meadow. They were headed to a small thicket.

Finally, he spoke. "The Creoles will not associate with us. They are native born and have their ways. In any case, they would not consider us in their social circle because we have African blood. It is as simple as that." He looked over at her, and then focused his attention back on his driving. For good measure he added, "Some do not have such prejudices against the local Indians. One of the wives in that house has Choctaw blood." Emma craned her head to look back at the house.

By this time, they reached the grove of trees and he drove straight into it. Emma and he had to duck their heads in order not to be knocked to the ground by the branches.

"Where are you taking me?" The wagon ground to a halt and she swatted away the branches. Phillipe jumped down and held out his arms to help her from the wagon seat. She acquiesced and eased herself into his arms. As he lowered her to the ground, their faces were a breath away from each other. Quickly, she extricated herself and walked a few steps, putting her back to a tree. He moved to stand nearer when she spoke.

"Say what you have to say from here and then take me back." Her voice had that stern and haughty quality that drove him mad.

"Are you so angry that I kissed you, Miss High and Mighty Darcy? Are you so much above me?" His tone was angrier than he felt. He did not know how to disarm this young woman, and meeting her strength for strength might indeed be the best way.

"Paying your attentions to me to soothe you in your rejection. It is I who have been used. You have no reason to be angry with me." She turned her back on him. Now he really was angry. Taking great strides, he reached her and, taking her by the arm, turned her to him.

He did not know why that flushed and defiant face so filled him with desire. He wanted to kiss her again but knew he would probably only receive a slap for his efforts. Instead, he decided to take a different tact.

"You entirely misunderstood me at the gazebo. You were not a poor substitute."

She seemed unmoved by his meager explanation. She did not look convinced, or as if she was listening to him at all. He wanted to shake her.

"You did see fit to mention how beautiful she was. Do you think I enjoyed hearing that?" It was becoming clear to him now.

"So you are jealous of her? That is why you are angry with me." He knew the instant he spoke that he had made a mistake. Always the wrong thing came out of his mouth when he was with her. Perhaps it was the effort of speaking English that was thwarting his efforts. This was not what he wanted to tell her at all, but the conversation was veering off in a direction he had not intended.

Emma was standing, glaring at him as her hands balled into fists. He believed she might strike him. "You arrogant man," she shouted.

"What do I care who you long for? What is that to me?" She turned her back on him.

"Oh, for goodness sake, you silly girl. I am trying to tell you that I love you." Now he was shouting. It was the tenderest of human expressions set in the angriest of tones.

For a few moments, nothing happened. Then, Emma turned around slowly, her eyes wide as saucers, her eyebrows lifted. She blinked at him. "That is the most extraordinary declaration I have ever heard, and in such a tenor. And here I thought Frenchmen were so skilled at making love."

He was humiliated. He turned his back on her and marched off toward the wagon.

"Wait, wait," she called out and caught him by the coat before he mounted. "Stop."

He turned to her, his blood on fire. "If you think I will stand here and let you laugh in my face, you are sorely mistaken, Miss Darcy." He forced himself to look in her eyes. What he saw there was not mirth or taunting or hardness of any kind. She was standing close, holding the lapels of his jacket.

"You merely caught me by surprise." She hesitated for a moment as if gathering her thoughts. "No one has ever shouted their love for me with such anger."

He was not about to let his guard down. "I am not angry, but—"

She interrupted him. Again. "But we seem to understand one another for a time, and then fall to quarreling again. I feel you come close to me, and then withdraw."

The nearness of her body, the sound of her voice, the tiny wisp of a curl that had come loose from her perfectly coiffed hair, all labored to make him lose his train of thought and even made him forget his anger. They stood in silence for a few moments while he tried to gather his thoughts. "I know what I feel for you is impossible, yet I feel it nonetheless."

"You are not alone in your feelings." She did not drop her gaze from his but held it for a long time. "Dear Phillipe," she said, and then leaned in and boldly kissed him on the mouth.

He could feel the barriers between them crumble as he let the fullness of his desire return her kiss and her embrace. He lifted her off the ground and felt the heat radiate from his loins throughout his body. He let her go and turned from her, lest she see the rampant evidence of his longing. She, in her innocence, embraced him from the back, throwing her arms across his chest and leaning her head between his shoulders. She stood holding him in this manner for a few minutes, and then, releasing him, stepped back. He turned to face her.

"What shall we do?" he asked this question, even though in his heart he knew the answer.

"In this moment, there is only the two of us. Let us live for this moment at least, and not think of anything else." She touched his cheek and he kissed her gently on the lips, then again with more fury. She returned his passion, and he felt her press her body into his.

He kissed her neck, and she threw back her head, pressing his face into her breast. He was nearly delirious with hunger for her: his body awash in it. He wanted her now. In spite of all the differences in their social positions, despite their so often being at cross purposes: despite all, he wanted her. A war began to rage within him. His body and his heart tasting her sweetness, his mind calling to him that it must not be.

Suddenly, she stepped back, and looked like a startled woodland creature. "Do you hear it?"

"What?" He could feel the sweat drip down his back causing him to shiver slightly.

"Someone is calling your name."

At first, he thought she was trying to put him off. He held his breath a moment and then he heard it. It was one of his slaves, calling from the road. Emma was already straightening her hair, and she pushed a lock of his own off his forehead. Handing her up to the seat of the wagon, he climbed in beside her and took the reins. The voice was drifting off, and it occurred to him that he might drive the wagon onto the road without giving away their hiding place. He knew from experience as a child in the slave quarters, anything that happened in the big house was instantly known to all the slaves.

Clucking his tongue and driving straight through the thicket, he directed the wagon to a bend in the road and turned it back toward the plantation. There they spied one of the slaves, running away from them. Phillipe called out to him.

The man turned and began running back to them. "Master Phillipe, Master Phillipe," he panted as he caught up with them. "Your *maman* is looking for you. Your papa is much worse."

"Get in the back of the wagon," Phillipe commanded, and leaning on the seat, he turned back to watch the man jump aboard and sit at the back, his bare feet dangling. Phillipe felt Emma's fingers touch his hand, and then entwine with his.

"*Je t'aime,*" she whispered and then let him go as he took hold of the reins.

***

When Phillipe arrived home, he crossed the veranda and entered his father's room through the open doors. His mother was seated there, holding his father's hand and talking softly to him. "Oh, *mon chere, mon chere,*" she said soothingly. She was so fixated on his father that she did not hear Phillipe approach. He watched his father reach up, and with a shaking hand touch his mother's cheek and brush a tear away with his thumb.

"Do not weep for me, *mon amour*. We have had a good life together, no?"

His mother nodded silently and watched her wipe her own tears away and then take his father's hand again. "De Widow Paris be here soon. She help ease your pain."

He nodded. Phillipe had never thought before this moment about whether his parents loved each other or not. After all, there were many marriages wherein love was not a factor. He could see it now between them. It was something deep and abiding, not the fury of passion that engulfed him. It was something that grew as they lived their life together. Phillipe sat near his mother. His father closed his eyes and they sat listening to his shallow breathing.

"What has happened?" This was not the state in which he had left his father only hours before.

His mother rose and took him out of the doors onto the veranda. "He felt better and den de fever came back. He was retching and we put him to bed. He start talkin' off his head. It de yellow fever, son. I know it. Dis how it go."

Phillipe put his arm around his mother. "All right. All right. There is no need to panic. We will give him as much sweet tea as he can drink and wait for Marie Laveau." He was trying to remain calm, but he had seen this sickness before. What was happening now was not a good sign.

Hours later, Phillipe finally convinced his mother to go to the other room and get some rest. He would sit with his father. They all waited anxiously for Marie Laveau's arrival.

Although she made her living as a hairdresser, her reputation as a healer, despite her youth, was well known in New Orleans. Some said she was a sorceress, some a visiting angel. All knew her skills in worship and healing. Her intervention and perhaps the divine were their greatest hope. As he dabbed the damp cloth over his father's face, he noticed a stain on the fabric. He brought it closer to the oil lamp next to his father's bed. It was stained with blood. Phillipe knew it was a sign that his father's condition was worsening. They all did. He, his mother, and his sisters all were acclimatized to this wretched fever. They all had it years ago in Grenada, but his father never contracted the disease before now, and he was suffering for it.

"Papa, can you hear me?" His father was tossing about in his bed, moaning. Phillipe continued to dab the water on his brow, and down his neck. His father seemed to respond to his ministrations and opened his eyes.

"Oh, it is you, my son. Where is your mother?" His voice was weak.

"She is resting now. It took all three of us to get her to leave your side for one moment." His father closed his eyes and nodded. Phillipe took up a glass of water from the table next to the bed. Slipping his other hand behind his father's head, he brought the glass to his parched lips.

"Here, Papa, you must drink." Peschier made an attempt and then collapsed back onto the pillow. He clutched at Phillipe's sleeve.

"Listen to me, my son. My time is short." His father's voice was a mere whisper.

"No, Papa, you will get well."

"We both know that is not true, my boy. You will be man of the house. Take care of your mother and your sisters. Look out for them, especially Elizabeth Ann and Adele."

"Papa." Phillipe could feel a cold panic rising. His father clutched his abdomen, turned on his side, and squeezed his eyes shut, moaning in agony. In a few moments, he seemed to relax again, and lay back on his pillow. He patted his son's sleeve.

"Take care of them, my son. Find your own way in the world. Be careful. You feel your strength now, but some things may be beyond your grasp." Phillipe knew he was speaking of Emma. Were the two of them so obvious in their feelings for one another? His father spoke again, more quietly this time. "Remember that I love you all. Will you remember?" He turned his head and looked into his son's eyes. Phillipe blinked back the tears and nodded, unable to say anything. His father's eyes rolled back in his head and his body began to shake uncontrollably. Phillipe immediately held down his arms to steady him until the spasm passed. Phillipe leaned in closer and could hear his father's labored breath.

Where was Marie Laveau? She must come. She must.

***

"Mama," Benji called, as Elizabeth was laying out his clothing for the day. "Is Monsieur Peschier going to die?"

She watched him as he pulled on his breeches and began buttoning his shirt. How frank children can be, and how their words can pierce straight into one's heart.

"I do not know, dear heart. He is quite ill."

"I thought you were going to die, Mama. Papa said he did not think so, but I thought so."

"What are you talking about, Benji?"

"You know, Mama. Before. Before when we were home and the baby died. I thought you were going to die too."

Goodness, how far they had come. Her mind was so filled now with thoughts of Poppy and her family and all that had transpired since they left England, that the memory of why they had come was seated in the far recesses of her mind. He was right. She thought she would die as well, but she would never tell him so.

"There, you see, Benji. Sometimes people are ill, and they recover. You must keep that thought in your mind."

He put on his stockings and then took them off again. "My shoes and socks get in the way when I am working." He looked at her with a serious expression.

"Is that so?" She tried to suppress a smile. "Nevertheless, you will wear them."

He pouted a bit but did not argue. "May I have another shirt?"

"Why do you need two shirts? You may wear your coat if you are cold."

He looked up at her and sighed. "I am not cold, Mama. I want to give the shirt to Toby." He finished buckling his shoe.

"Did Toby ask you for a shirt?"

"No, Mama, it is a surprise if you say it is all right."

She opened his wardrobe that was filled with his clothing, more clothing than he possibly needed and soon would outgrow. She turned to him.

"You may choose a shirt for him. Perhaps he also needs a pair of breeches and some stockings."

Benji shook his head. "No, Mama. Only a shirt. It is my present for him. Is that all right?"

Elizabeth nodded her head and wanted to rush over and embrace her little son but refrained. He would not understand or probably appreciate such an outpouring of affection. He soon retrieved a shirt similar to his own and, folding it carefully, put it under his arm.

"Now we will look the same. Like brothers." He smiled broadly. She had misunderstood his charitable act. It was not charity at all. She followed him out of the wing they were occupying and came upon Poppy, who was sitting alone drinking coffee at the dining room table. Benji accosted her immediately.

"I am so sorry, madame, that Monsieur is so ill," Poppy looked up at him and then at Elizabeth. She looked nearly as ill as her husband.

"Thank you, chile," she said and patted him on his head. "We hope he can find the strength to be wit' us once again."

Then Benji did something he, no doubt, observed the men around him doing. He took Poppy's hand and kissed it. Elizabeth felt so touched by this gesture she blinked away a tear. Poppy looked up at her and managed a weak smile, then touched his cheek in return.

"You a good boy. Now run along an' play."

"*Oui, madame,*" he said and was off.

"He your chile, and that the truth of it." Elizabeth sat down next friend and took her hand.

***

Before the day was out, there was a great commotion on the river. How the slaves received the news before they did in the house, he did not know, but they were all gathered in the front of the house to greet their visitor. Marie Laveau had arrived.

She stepped from their boat onto the dock, and walked toward the house, her hair done in a tignon, her gait like that of a queen. A call went out from one of the slaves, and the rest answered in some of the most beautiful and spontaneous harmony that Emma had ever heard. It reminded her of what she had witnessed at Congo Square. The alien and exquisite melodies rang out from all gathered as they parted to make way for her entrance into the house. Phillipe and Poppy were there on the veranda and ushered her in to visit Monsieur Peschier. All of them suspected that he was not long for this world, as he had not been conscious for a least a day and his fever had not broken.

Emma barely exchanged a word with Phillipe since their time in the wood. His face was haggard, and a squeeze of her hand as he passed her was all the exchange they'd had during these last awful days.

It was nightfall before Poppy, Phillipe, and his sisters emerged from Monsieur's bedchamber. Marie Laveau was still inside. They ate dinner together, but no one had much to say to one another. Even Benji was quiet. As night fell, Phillipe insisted that his mother and sisters rest while he stayed with his father. Phillipe asked Emma to accompany him to his father's chamber.

"Come and sit with me a while." She looked over at her mother, who nodded her head. No one spoke further.

As they entered, Emma greeted Marie Laveau. The room smelled of lavender and sickness. There was an altar in the corner. She had seen statues when she visited St. Louis Cathedral in town, and here was one of the Virgin Mary, with candles lit all around. Unlike the church, however, there were also other things on the altar: a glass of wine, a painting of a bucolic scene, a silver spoon, and many other objects. Next to the emaciated and prone body of Francois Peschier was a cup of a brackish-looking liquid.

"When your father wakes, give him more tea," Marie instructed Phillipe. "Leave the doors open for the spirits and pray."

Marie rose from her seat and went out on the veranda. Emma wanted so much to hear the conversation that she might have with her parents, especially her father, but she would sit here. This must be what people called a death watch. Phillipe's father looked so pale and his skin was taut over his skull like a death's head on a pirate ship. She looked up at Phillipe, who was sitting, looking down at his father. His face was impassive.

Emma looked out of the French doors and saw Marie Laveau walking toward the river. "Do you think she can cure him?" Philippe looked up at her with such a sorrowful expression that she wanted to throw her arms around him.

"The altar has things to ease his passage. The tea is only to ease his pain." His voice held resignation. Emma had never heard from him before.

"Is that what she told you?"

"She told us that we should call a priest."

Chapter 15

Elizabeth lay her head down on the pillow. She had been through all of this suffering before when Darcy lay dying from his wounds after that ill-fated duel. She knew how Poppy felt, how hopelessness grips your heart. She wished she could do something, but what was to be done? Darcy was on his side, turned from her. "Are you awake?"

"I surely am now." Groggily, he turned to face her.

"I wish we could do something to ease their pain."

He sighed. "You are here to listen, to talk with your friend, to aid in any way that they request. There is nothing else to be done."

"Do you think that voodoo priestess will save him?" As soon as she asked the question, she felt herself ridiculous. She waited for him to scoff.

Instead, he drew her close into his arms. "Speaking as one who rose from the dead, I do not discount anything. Now, try to sleep."

How much did she love this man? This man whom she told at one time that she would never be prevailed upon to marry. The man who'd followed her halfway around the world, debased himself and his social position for her sake. She pulled his arm over her and nestled her body into his. There was nothing left to say.

Before the sun rose, Elizabeth woke to the padding of little feet. "Mama, are you awake?" Benji's voice sounded raspy, and when he laid his hand upon her cheek, she could feel the heat radiating from it. Instantly, she was awake.

"Benji." She sat up abruptly. Darcy stirred. She placed her hand on Benji's forehead and felt a fever raging inside.

"Darcy, dearest. Wake up." She swung her legs over the side of the bed, Benji's eyes rolled up into his head, and he collapsed on the floor. Elizabeth called to Darcy once again and in a moment, he had the small boy in his arms, and carried him to his room and put him back in bed.

"You do not think it is yellow fever." She made it more a statement than a question, hoping the declaration would make it fact.

"I pray it is not, but we have among us someone who knows much of these things." He left her there and came back seconds later in his dressing gown. "I will go and fetch The Widow."

He rushed down the hallway and Elizabeth followed. As he entered the parlour, he met Marie Laveau coming directly toward him.

Before he could speak Marie said, "It is the boy, is it not? He has the fever."

***

Darcy always prided himself as a student of the Enlightenment. He did what was required of him from the Church of England, maintained his chapel, saw to it that religion was taught in the village school he'd founded. However, he thought of himself as a rational man. At least he thought so up until that moment. How had the Widow Paris known of Bennet's illness the moment they knew? Perhaps she did possess supernatural powers. At that moment, it did not matter. She was here and they were dependent on her help.

He followed her to his son's room and watched as Lizzy made way for her to examine their son. The first signs of dawn were edging their way between the curtains of his room. The widow stood looking at Bennet for a moment, then drew back the curtains. His son contorted his face and threw his hands over his eyes. Marie nodded, and then sat down next to the boy. She turned him on his side and pressed her thumbs gently against his back.

"Does this hurt you, *mon poussin*?"

"Yes. It hurts."

"And here?" she asked, squeezing his knee. Bennet let out a groan.

"*Tire la langue*," she commanded, and Bennet stuck out his tongue. She shook her head slightly and covered the boy over with a sheet that she tucked in around him. Then, motioning to Elizabeth and Darcy, she exited the bedchamber.

"It is yellow fever." Elizabeth let out a cry and immediately covered her mouth. Darcy put his arm around her shoulder. "We will begin with yarrow tea, with elderflower and moringa."

170

"What is moringa?" Darcy asked.

"It is an herb for fever from Africa. The boy will undoubtedly begin vomiting. Make him drink as much as you can."

Darcy thought that was ridiculous. If they made the poor child drink, he would only vomit all the more. Still, they were putting their faith in this healer and he would acquiesce to her wishes. Elizabeth was already filling the washbasin with water. She soaked a cloth, then sponged Bennet's forehead, face, and arms. Darcy cursed himself for bringing them here. Try as he might, the same question began pounding over and over in his brain: What if they lost their little boy?

***

Now the Peschier home was a house under siege. Both families were battling something they could neither see nor take up arms against. There were many soft-spoken conferences in the parlour and many rosaries said by Adele and Elizabeth Ann. Elizabeth rarely left Benji's side and followed Marie Laveau's instructions to the letter. Poor Benji was subjected to cooling baths to reduce his fever, but he was so hot that he wept when put into the tepid water. Elizabeth felt like weeping as well, but she knew that all her strength was now required. There would be time for weeping later.

Benji was back in bed after one of his baths. Emma, to her credit, helped, and sat with him when Elizabeth was too weary to do so herself. She could not bear to have the servants attend Benji when he was so desperately ill. Darcy also was in attendance, and Elizabeth felt that he was as concerned for her as he was for their little boy.

"Let Emma sit with him a while," he said as he entered the room. Benji had fallen into a fitful slumber.

"I can manage a while longer." She could not take her gaze from Benji's dry and feverish face.

"Please, Mama, go and rest. I will call you if he worsens," Emma said. Darcy gently took Elizabeth by the arm. She rose, still looking at her little son, and had to use all her determination to look away for a moment.

"Come." Darcy pulled her gently from the bedchamber. "We will be in the next room. There is tea and something to eat."

"Call me, Emma, if there is any change. Even if I sleep? You will, will you not?"

"Of course, Mama. Of course." Emma wrung the water from the rag in washbasin and placed it upon her brother's brow.

As Elizabeth sat down heavily on the tufted armchair in their room, her husband lifted the teapot. "Shall I be mother?" he asked, smiling at her. She dissolved into tears. Putting the teacup down with a clatter, he ran to her side. He knelt next to her and took her in his arms.

"Hush now, dearest, all will be well."

She pulled herself from his embrace. "You do not know that. I will not be comforted while my precious little one hovers at death's door."

Darcy stood and handed her the teacup. "You do not know that he is at death's door. The Widow Paris was here from the start and has poured gallons of her noxious potions into him. He will recover." His voice had that firm, confident tone on which she had so often relied. He handed the cup to her. "Now, do not make yourself ill so that you cannot help him. Drink your tea and eat something."

She suspected that tone of voice was for her benefit alone. He was as worried as she but would not show his concern. Everyone was trying to be brave, from Poppy to Emma, but the shadow of death hovered over them all. She took the tea with shaking hands and sipped a little.

"There now. That's better." She finally looked up at his face. His expression was cheerful until she looked into his eyes. They could not lie to her. There she read his true thoughts.

"This is all my fault," she said and put the teacup down.

"Whatever are you talking about, Lizzy?"

"If I had been in a fit state after I lost our last baby, you would not have brought us here. It is my fault we are here, and it is my fault my little boy is dying in the next room." She brought her hand to her mouth to silence her sobs. He approached, but she turned from him.

"There you are wrong, Lizzy. If it is anyone's fault, it is mine. I brought us here without consulting you. I let him go about playing God knows where. I subjected him and all of us to this miasma of a climate. If anyone is to blame, it is me."

She looked up at him and this time it was he who turned his face from her. She rose immediately and, taking his face in her hands, turned it until their eyes met. His were brimming with unshed tears. She wound her arms about his waist and leaned her head on his chest.

"Whatever are we doing?" she asked, when she finally gained control of herself. His arm moved up toward his face, and although she did not see it, she knew he quickly wiped the tears from his eyes. "It does not matter who or what is to blame. It does us no good now." She looked up at him, and he kissed her. She smiled weakly at him.

"You are quite right, I do no one any good if I make myself ill. Here, sit with me and we will drink tea and eat our... What time is it? Breakfast? Luncheon?"

Darcy fetched his pocket watch from his waistcoat. "It is two in the afternoon. Teatime, perhaps?"

Elizabeth looked down at the delicacies before her. She realized she was famished. When had she eaten last? Darcy reached over and squeezed her hand. Then he began filling his plate. He took a bite, and then looked over at his wife.

"After this repast, you will sleep."

"Yes, dear," she replied, and shared a meal with her husband.

Her darling Benji, though, was ever on her mind.

***

The Widow Paris departed the next day, but without all the fanfare of her arrival. She left her herbs and potions with complete instructions for both families and left them to their devices. Since their boat was returning Marie Laveau to New Orleans, Phillipe sent for his sisters in town. Although he tried to put a brave face upon the situation, he had little hope for his father's recovery. Now he had the additional worry of the Darcys' little boy. How distant his assignation with Emma seemed. The weight of his family fell upon his shoulders now. He had not time to think of impossible romance.

Early in the evening he had woken his mother to sit watch. He did not know how many hours he spent in that sick room. There was no sign of his father in that broken body now. He had not spoken or opened his eyes in days. His skin had yellowed, and the spasms

Phillipe witnessed before had become more frequent. How grateful he was that they had a house full of servants to empty chamber pots and clean linen and look after meals for his family and their guests. His only duties now were to sit with his father and to oversee the plantation. He was grateful for those mundane tasks that took him from his father's bedside. They also took his thoughts away from his family's sorrows.

He walked out onto the veranda and stretched his arms. The evening was falling, and it did him good to breathe the fresh air coming in a breeze from the river. He could hear the soft singing from the slave quarters and realized he was hungry. When he reached the dining room, he saw Emma. Her eyes had none of the sparkle they held only a few days before. When she saw him, she bit her upper lip and blinked her eyes.

"You may weep, you know, English girl. It is a time for weeping." He did not wait for a reply from her but opened his arms. She pushed her chair aside and flew to him. He held her close and patted her back.

"How is your brother?" If he could talk about the boy, perhaps he could stem his own tears for his father.

"I do not know. He looks so small and weak. I try to speak to him, but he rarely opens his eyes."

"Is he taking any of the tea Marie Laveau left for him?"

"Yes, when we can wake him. He drinks, then it all comes back up again. Oh, Phillipe, I will not be able to bear it if he dies." She sobbed into his shoulder.

This was not the arrogant, argumentative girl he first encountered. Death was the great equalizer for it came to them all. "I have seen those herbs of hers do much good. Do not despair. Come, we will visit your brother together. I have seen yellow fever many times. I also had it as a child, and you see, I am still here."

"Yes, but many die."

He nodded. "But some recover. I will look at him, with your permission."

She took him by the hand, and they entered the wing of the house the Darcys occupied. She pushed open Benji's door and found her father there. Benji's eyes were closed, but Darcy was reading to him, nonetheless. The book was the story of the hero Ulysses. Mr. Darcy looked up as they entered. He held out his hand to Phillipe.

"How fares your father?" he asked, grasping Phillipe's hand in both of his.

"I am afraid he worsens every day. I thank you for your concern."

"And how do you fare, *monsieur*?"

Phillipe was quite moved by Darcy's words. "Please, call me Phillipe. I am feeling the burden of my family descend upon my shoulders."

Darcy nodded. "I well know the feeling."

"Phillipe has come to look at Benji, Papa. He knows yellow fever well."

"If I may, *monsieur*." Darcy gave a nod of his head. Bringing the candle close to Benji's face, Phillipe raised each eyelid. He examined the little boy's arms, and then felt his forehead. "The fever is still quite strong."

"You should not talk about me. I can hear you," Benji said in his small voice.

Emma immediately fell to her knees beside the bed. She took her brother's hand. "How are you feeling, Benji?"

"Thirsty." Darcy immediately took up the tea that was left to them by Marie Laveau. Emma raised Benji's head and he drank thirstily. As she laid his head back on the pillow, he looked directly into Emma's eyes. "That is the worst tea I ever drank." He closed his eyes again. Without opening them, he turned his head toward his father. "Read me the story, Papa."

Darcy did he as he was bidden, and Emma and Phillipe slipped from the bedchamber. When they were out in the hall, Emma reached for Phillipe's hand.

"What do you think? Will he live?"

Phillipe touched her cheek. "That I cannot tell you. That he still can speak to you should give you hope, but the sickness is treacherous. It can turn at any time." Emma turned her head away from his and quickly wiped her eyes. "Come. We will light a candle for him at the altar in my father's room."

She looked at him. "And one for your father as well."

***

Time seemed to stand still. There was only Benji, shaking with fever, retching and groaning. Elizabeth thought back to her own suffering at the hands of the rebels in Fedon's camp. She had suffered much then, but somehow, it was easier to bear than her child's suffering. Emma proved to be a competent and uncomplaining nurse, which greatly surprised Elizabeth. That self-centered, spoilt girl disappeared, at least for a time. Why was it that tragedy brought families closer together?

Elizabeth had taken to sleeping on a pallet near Benji's bed. Darcy, Emma, and herself took turns sitting with him. The morning sun had begun to insinuate its rays through the curtains of Benji's room when there was a soft knocking at his door. The door was open, and anyone could enter, so Elizabeth was surprised at the sound and turned to see Toby standing there. He was looking down at the floor and wearing the shirt Benji had given him. It was clean and looked as if someone had pressed it. The boy was holding something in his hand that Elizabeth could not fully see.

"Hello, Antoine. Have you come to see Benji?" she asked in French. The boy nodded. "Come closer. I will try to wake him."

Toby walked in softly and stood by Benji's bed. Elizabeth put a cool cloth on her son's forehead and gave him a little shake. Benji moaned.

"Benji, darling, your friend is here to see you." Benji tossed his head back and forth and then opened his eyes. They came to rest on his friend.

"Hello, Toby," he said, and then continued in French. "I cannot play today. I am very sick."

"I know. I can see your face is red."

Benji smiled. "I feel hot." Then he sighed.

"I brought you something. I made it myself. I will teach you how to make one when you are better." He placed a small wooden duck into Benji's hand.

The boy raised it up close to his face and examined it. "You made this all by yourself?"

"I did. With a knife. My father taught me." Toby straightened his shoulders as he spoke. "I can make other things too."

Benji turned the toy over and over in his hand. "And you can teach me?" His voice faltered and then he closed his eyes and began breathing hard.

"Perhaps that is enough visiting for now," Elizabeth said.

"No… wait. Wait, Mama," he said in English. Elizabeth dabbed his forehead with the damp cloth again.

"Here, sweetheart, drink something. Antoine will wait." Benji nodded and let his mother raise him up to drink more of the concoction they had now been brewing for him for days.

Benji drank and then asked Toby to describe how he made the duck. Her son lay back for a few moments. Elizabeth was afraid that this visit was taxing what little strength the child had left.

Toby stood, shuffling his feet and looking about. Finally, he said, "My brother and my grandmother died of the yellow fever."

"Oh, I am sorry," Elizabeth said and hoped that the boy would not continue to try to make conversation. This news was not what Benji needed to hear. It was not what she needed to hear. Finally, Benji turned his head, and opened and closed his eyes with effort and spoke.

"When I get well, you will teach me to make a duck, all right?" Then, as if the effort to speak was too much for him, Benji closed his eyes again, his little hand clutching the toy.

"I will." Toby bowed slightly to Elizabeth. "Thank you for letting me see Benji, madame."

"Thank you for coming, Antoine."

"You may call me Toby," he said and then turned and ran from the room.

Chapter 16

The next morning Manon and Cecile arrived accompanied only by their servants. The men, it seemed, could not leave their businesses in town. The two families exchanged perfunctory greetings, and Poppy's daughters disappeared into the front wing of the house where they went to see their dying father. There was no doubt of it now. The priest had come to give the last rites and chastise them for their voodoo shrine. Poppy refused to take it down. She told the good father in a voice that would wake the dead that she would go to confession later, but the shrine would stay where it was.

Elizabeth always admired her friend's strength and pragmatism. She wondered if she could bear herself in such dignity if she were to lose her little Benji. She had been tested in such a situation as a younger woman when Darcy lay wounded, and felt that she could bear up under the crisis, but what does one do after it has passed, and all hope is gone? She tried to shake those thoughts from her mind and finished her morning ablutions. Darcy was with Benji, both of them asleep.

She bent down and kissed Darcy on the cheek. He stirred and then opened his eyes, blinking in the early morning sunlight. He did not speak, but he grasped her hand and did not let it go for a long while.

"How is he?" Elizabeth asked.

"I expect he is the same as he was a few moments ago when you left." He rose and stretched out his arms. He had abandoned his waistcoat and jacket and sat only in his shirt and trousers. Reaching his arms above his head, he took a deep breath and then furrowed his brow. "I believe I should have a wash."

"And a rest. You look done in." She patted his stubbly cheek.

"Then I will say good night," he told her wearily. "Or good day." He bent down first to pat his son on the forehead. Touching the boy's brow, Elizabeth saw him look at his hand as if he had seen it for the first time.

"Lizzy, come here. Touch him," he entreated. A cold fear ran through her. Her little boy cannot be dead. He cannot.

"What is it?" She covered her mouth with her hand.

"I believe the fever has broken,"

She rushed past him, sat beside her son, and took him in her arms. His nightshirt was soaked with sweat. She held Benji in her arms swaying him back and forth. "Oh, thank God. Thank God." Finally, she laid him back on the bed. She began smoothing back Benji's wet hair. Turning to her husband, she asked, "Do you think the danger has passed?"

Before Darcy could answer, Benji croaked, "I am hungry."

***

Elizabeth ran in the direction of the dining room to find a servant who could bring her some broth. As she entered, she saw Poppy sitting alone in the parlour, her face in her hands.

"Poppy." As Poppy looked up, Elizabeth could see that something was terribly wrong. She sat down next to her friend and waited for her to speak.

"He is gone, Elizabet'. My Francois is gone," she said. Elizabeth took her by the hand and they sat in silence for a moment. "His sufferin' is over."

"I am so sorry, Poppy."

"At leas' he have de las' rites." Then she stood and turned toward the back stairs. "I go tell Thomas to get de slave to make a coffin."

Elizabeth shook her head and took Poppy by the elbow. "No, you will do no such thing. I will send Darcy to do it."

"But he wid your Benji."

Elizabeth could not help herself and her expression broke into a broad grin. "Benji's fever broke this morning. I will send Darcy to the carpenters. He will be glad to do it."

Poppy patted Elizabeth's hand and sighed. "I am glad we not havin' two funeral." She stood up. "Come, we find Noni and get de boy some broth. He need to build up his streng' now. He be weak as a newborn after dat fight."

Poppy turned to go, but Elizabeth stopped her and embraced her. She held her friend for a few moments. Poppy released her. "You let me go now, Elizabet', or I'll take to cryin' all over again."

Elizabeth let her friend go and watched her disappear into the recesses of the house.

Chapter 17

Phillipe saw to it that the arrangements for Monsieur Peschier's interment were made swiftly. His mother seemed adrift, so he and his sisters dressed the body. The coffin was being constructed on the grounds by the slaves who did all the carpentry work at the plantation. Stepping onto the veranda, he heard the pounding and sawing of the coffin work and walked to the dining room to look out to observe from the window. He was surprised to see Mr. Darcy there.

"I am so sorry for your loss," Darcy said as soon as he noticed Phillipe's presence.

"I thank you, sir. I am happy to hear that your son is recovering."

"Yes, yes, thank you." Darcy's eyes drifted back to the men constructing the coffin in the yard. He seemed riveted on their work.

"Are you quite all right, sir? You seem distracted."

For a moment Darcy said nothing. "I am sorry." Darcy looked up briefly and then focused his attention back outside. "It has been a difficult time for all of us." Darcy then shook his head slightly and then looked at Phillipe. He changed the subject. "Your slaves seem genuinely saddened by your father's death."

"He was a good master, if one has to have a master. There were never beatings on our land, and families stayed together." There was a pause in the conversation as the two men stared out the window. Phillipe broke the silence. "You may have noticed, *monsieur*, that my father was not happy when you mentioned that the Americans burned Barataria."

Darcy thought a moment. "Yes. I did find that peculiar."

Phillipe smiled. "My father spent time there, at the pirates' slave market. Slaves could be obtained for a good price since they were stolen from other slave ships. Many who attended these markets would resell these people at the slave market in town, but not my father. He would allow the slave to buy his freedom for the price he paid. Many of our slaves bought their freedom thusly."

Darcy shook his head.

"You find our ways difficult to understand, no? Emma says that you have been trying to abolish the slave trade in your parliament."

"That is true. Your mother was the impetus behind my standing for parliament at all."

Phillipe looked surprised. "My mother?"

"Your mother. And also my wife." Phillipe smiled at this revelation, and then he turned, his expression serious.

"Now I am the master of this house. A former slave who is now a master of slaves." He again turned his attention out the window. He felt Darcy's hand on his shoulder and in a moment, he was gone.

***

A few minutes later, Darcy joined Elizabeth in Bennet's room. He was sitting up in bed but looked like a rag doll bereft of his usual liveliness. Elizabeth rose and greeted Darcy at the door. "How is he faring?"

"The fever is gone, but he is weak. He has eaten some porridge and broth, so I am hopeful that we are on our way to convalescence."

Emma was reading to her brother but stopped and looked at his face. She began to whisper. "I believe he is asleep."

"No, I am not," Benji said, his eyes still closed. He yawned and looked up at his parents. Darcy smiled and took the book from Emma.

"I will sit with him for a while, now. Perhaps you can be of some assistance to Poppy."

"Can I go too?" Benji asked, his eyes opening slightly. He yawned again.

"No, you will sleep and become well again." Elizabeth kissed him on the forehead.

"No fever," she said softly to Darcy.

Benji spoke again, this time opening his eyes. "Kiss Papa. See if he has a fever."

"Oh, Benji," his sister said, rising.

Elizabeth smiled and kissed Darcy on the forehead. "No fever," she said, and then she and Emma went to join the Peschiers, whose fate they had so narrowly avoided.

Chapter 18

Well past midnight, Emma awoke. At first, she thought she heard something, but then settled back to listen to the sounds of the insects and the rustling of the leaves in the night breeze. Dinner had been a solemn affair and they had all sat vigil with the Peschier family into the night. With Benji still needing care, the Darcys excused themselves as the sun set, and they retired to their rooms.

Emma turned in bed and then she heard it again. Was someone speaking? Lighting a candle, she rose, put on her dressing gown, and looked into her brother's room. He was sleeping peacefully. Her parents' door was closed and she listened but heard nothing there.

Barefoot, she crept along the hallway in their wing of the house and stood in the doorway of the second parlour and looked furtively around the opening to the main parlour, where Monsieur Peschier lay. Candles cast a soft light into the room, and Phillipe was standing over his father's coffin, his hand resting on the edge. The rest of the room was empty. Not wanting to be discovered, Emma blew out her candle and secreted herself against the doorjamb. Phillipe would not see her there, even if he looked.

"Papa, how could you do this to me?" he asked. He was not whispering, and sounded angry and argumentative. "What am I to do now, eh?" He walked on the planking. "Mother and all of us were born slaves, except for Adele. How could you have kept slaves, eh Papa, knowing what life was like for us?" The walking stopped, but Emma dared not look lest he see her there. "Now I have become the slave owner. How do I reconcile myself with that? And what do I do now? I am responsible for our family and must safeguard our fortune. I know you provided for us and recognized us as your own. I love you for that, Papa." The anger had drained from Phillipe's voice and he was gulping air in stifled sobs. "You know that I will miss you, don't you, Papa?" Emma stood perfectly still and dared not breathe. Phillipe would never understand her intruding on him in such a way, but she had no choice now. She wanted to run to him, to take him in her arms and let him weep upon her breast, but she dared not. Philippe did not speak again, but stifled sobs

After what seemed an age, she heard other voices. Poppy had come to sit with her husband's body and Emma peeked through the doorway that led to the parlour. Phillipe was gone, and she breathed a sigh of relief. Carefully she crept back to her room and lay in her bed, thinking of Phillipe.

***

Darcy stood in the parlour of the house as the slaves brought in the coffin lid. Each member of the family said their good-byes, and Darcy stood, holding Benji, whose blond curls nestled in the crook of his neck. Their little son insisted on dressing and attending the burial. Elizabeth had protested, but Darcy felt it was a good idea. Life was often quixotic and cruel, and he did not want to instill a fear of death in Benji by making it something mysterious and therefore terrifying. He, though, felt a certain terror as he watched the men cover Peschier's body and then begin pounding each nail into the coffin lid. He remembered that sound, that pounding, as he lay inside just such a coffin, unable to move or cry out. Unable to tell anyone that he still lived.

The service took only an hour or so, and they laid the coffin in a small mausoleum that was constructed on the grounds. The family retreated to the house, but Darcy could not help looking back over his shoulder at the slaves bricking up the entrance to the tomb.

A meal was served, and even some laughter began to bubble up from the mourners as they recalled incidents from their childhoods. Manon, her husband, and their children, and Cecile and Valentine took their leave soon after as they needed to get back to their lives in New Orleans.

All of these events passed before Darcy as if in a dream. He was filled with a horrible, gnawing feeling that they had buried Peschier alive, and at this moment he was gasping for air in that walled-up tomb. He knew he was being irrational. He had touched Peschier's lifeless body and felt the cold stiffness that was only possible in a corpse. Yet...

The day ended and Elizabeth was occupied with Benji. He did not know where Emma was. His agitation grew and he dared not speak of it with his wife, lest he betray his weakness. She would understand, no doubt, for she understood everything, but he felt humiliated. Long after everyone in the household retired, he lay wide awake, staring at the ceiling, wondering if they had made a terrible mistake. Finally, he could stand it no longer and he dressed quietly in only his boots, pantaloons, and shirt, and made his way out of doors.

The moon shone brightly that night, and he took neither torch nor candle with him to light his way. Soon, he came upon the silent tomb in the darkness. The slaves had finished bricking up the entrance. There was no iron gate to be opened, but a wall to be torn down. Darcy had not expected this turn of events. Opening a gate, pushing away a heavy stone, and opening a coffin lid were well within his capabilities. He could satisfy his unreasonable anxiety without anyone being the wiser, but a brick wall? That was another matter. How could he explain himself in the morning if he knocked down the entrance to their beloved father's tomb? He sat down heavily, his head in his hands. Now he knew what it felt like to go mad.

He sat for a time until he could bear it no longer. Looking up, he searched for something with which to break down the sealed entrance. Finding a tree limb that had fallen, he stood before the sealed tomb. Breathing hard, he raised it above his head.

"Darcy," Elizabeth's voice called out of the darkness. "Whatever are you doing?" He turned to her, his heart pounding, still holding the tree limb above his head. Seeing her approach, he lowered it and then dropped it onto the ground. "My God, whatever are you about?" She ran to him. He turned his face from her, overwhelmed by embarrassment and guilt.

"I...I..." he began but did not know how to continue. The madness seemed to seep out of him the minute she called his name. How would he explain any of his actions to her?

"He no longer lives, my darling. Peschier is gone. Come away."

He knew she spoke the truth, but still, something inside him churned with unease. She looked at him, the moonlight illuminating her face. He did not move. She took his hand.

"Stand here with me," she bade him. "Stand here and breathe deeply." He did, and at first all that assailed him was the scent of newly laid brick and mortar. But then, then a foul odor greeted his senses. It was the smell of death.

He looked at her and then quickly looked away. "I do not know what came over me." And then loosening his grip on her hand, he walked away from her. "I feel I must be going mad." He ran his fingers through his hair.

"You are no more mad than I." He felt her touch his arm. "You nearly lost your son. You have been a tower of strength for both our family and Poppy's. And," she hesitated walking back to him, then she took him by the hand again, "you nearly lost your life by being buried alive. You may be excused for one irrational act."

He turned to her. "So, you excuse me then?" It was not so bright that he could see her face clearly, but he thought she might be smiling.

"There is nothing for which you need to beg pardon. I will follow you into madness if that is where you choose to go, my love." She wound her arms around his waist, leaning her head upon his shoulder. He kissed the top of her head and rested his cheek there. What did men do who did not have a helpmeet such as his dear Lizzy?

They stood still in each other's arms for a while. "Perhaps, rather than a descent into madness, we walk along the river so I can clear my head."

"I would prefer a walk along the river." She took his arm.

They walked together in in the silent moonlight.

***

During the days following his father's funeral, Phillipe rode out before breakfast. Emma saw little of him. Even during evening meals when they were all together, he directed his comments generally, but never to her. She felt she had become invisible.

Everyone knew the lawyer would arrive soon with his father's will, and she assumed that contributed to his aloofness. He appeared to her as a man alone, but sorely wished he would confide in her.

They were seated at breakfast together, again without Phillipe, and her father brought up the subject that she dreaded.

"Soon I will need to travel down river to make arrangements for our passage home," Darcy said.

"Will you stay with us for Christmas at leas'?" Poppy asked. "With my Francois gone…" She left off speaking.

"Oh, of course. I was thinking perhaps soon after the new year, but I must make arrangements now."

Poppy looked up at him and smiled. "After new year is a good time. De storms have gone. You will have a peaceful passage. But…" she hesitated a moment, "I hate to see you go." She then looked over at Benji and said mischievously, "Maybe you leave your Benji here to keep me company."

Benji, who was making a rapid recovery from his illness, piped up. "Oh, may I, Mama? That would be ever so jolly." Poppy was smiling at his mother. Her father shook his head but said nothing.

"And you would have us go home without you? Would you not miss your father, me, and Emma?" Elizabeth asked.

He looked at each one. "Yes, I did not think of that," he said seriously. "I was only thinking about staying here with Toby." He ate another mouthful of egg, and then stated, "I know. Let us take Toby with us."

This time her father intervened. "Do you think his mother and father would let him go?" Benji sighed.

Emma was silent during this exchange. She knew they were all teasing and making light of their departure, but she could not. Nothing had been settled between herself and Phillipe. She had to know what was in his heart.

Determined to speak with him, she spent the later part of the afternoon outdoors. She knew from observation, he often rode his mare into the barn, and sometimes saw to her care himself. Therefore, when the sun was low in the sky, she could see him coming from the fields. Walking swiftly to the barn, she found it deserted and waited there for him.

As he rode in and dismounted, he began speaking softly to his horse. She revealed herself from her hiding place in the shadows.

"I have been waiting for you."

He seemed taken aback and did not speak. "You mean to ambush me then."

"No, I mean to have to you speak plainly to me. My father is going to town soon to arrange our passage back to England."

He turned back to his horse and started to brush her flanks. This infuriated Emma.

"Do you have nothing to say?" she asked stridently.

He turned to her. "What would you have me say?"

"Oh, for goodness sake, Phillipe. I thought, after all that we… that you said…" Then, screwing up her courage she said, "I thought you would declare yourself to my father."

He looked at her as if she had sprouted another head. "And what do you suppose he would say, hm?" Phillipe stepped away from the mare and stood before one of the posts holding the roof of the barn. He looked at it, clicked his heels and bowed to it, and then addressed it.

"Sir, I am asking you for your daughter's hand in marriage." Then, turning to take the part of her father, he continued, "Oh really, sir? Will you be married in the Catholic Church then? I do not think I approve of that."

He again changed places and became himself again. "Oh no, sir, we cannot be married in the church, it is illegal."

He became Emma's father again. "Oh, then you will be married in town by a magistrate."

He then turned and looked directly at Emma. "No, sir, that is also illegal. You see, a man with Negro blood may not marry a white woman. She would have to live with me here, on this plantation, in what we call common law, without benefit of marriage." He then stepped a bit closer to Emma and said vehemently, "Then your father would take out a sword," he motioned as if he himself was engaged in such a deed, and then flung his crossways in front of him, "and cut off my head." With that, he turned from her and picked up the brush, and began to minister to his horse.

"Oh, do not be ridiculous, Phillipe. My father would not cut off your head or do you any harm whatsoever."

He turned to her again. "Then he is not much of a father, for if I was a proper Englishman from a good family and it was my daughter, I would not let any young man propose anything so indecent."

Emma did not know if he had insulted her father, the English, or himself. Whatever he had done, she knew he was suffering as much as she. Emma stepped forward and placed her hands on his shoulders. He turned to face her.

"Do you love me or do you not?" she asked softly. He was breathing heavily as if he had come from a great exertion.

"I should tell you that I do not, and that, perhaps, would make it easier on all of us. You would then return to the land of your birth and marry a rich Englishman who would suit everybody. I will find a suitable woman, a pious woman of my own kind, and marry her. You and I would remember these moments fondly from a great distance."

She did not let go of him but studied his face. She was not convinced. "Is that what you want?"

"It is not a matter of what I want, but what has to be." He would not look at her, so she was not convinced.

"We will find a way."

Slowly, he shook his head and she stopped him by taking his face in both her hands. The flow of words between them stopped and he kissed her gently, and then again, more passionately, wrapping his arms about her. He covered her face with a flurry of kisses and then kissed her down her neck. Pulling away to look into her face, he brought her hand to his lips, and he kissed her wrist and down the length of her arm.

She never felt sensations like this before. Her skin tingled down the length of her back, and she felt a sweet ache between her legs. Her mother had told her of the communion of a man and a woman, and she wanted to join herself thusly with her beloved Phillipe. She could hear his breath coming in short bursts and she wondered if he could feel the beating of her heart as she pressed herself ever closer to him.

He broke their embrace and stepped back. "We must not, Emma. We must not."

"I want to have your child," she blurted.

"And I would like to give you such a gift, believe me." He looked at her intently. She stepped toward him, but he held out his hand.

"No. It would not be fair to you, me, or to the child. You would take my child away to England where he or she would live a sheltered life at best, the symbol of our disgrace."

She opened her mouth to speak but held up his finger to silence her. "He would never know me, his father. I could not bear it. I never knew my father. He shunned me. Francois Peschier gave me that father back. I do not want another man raising my child. No, it

190

cannot be." He turned his back on her and went back to brushing his mare. "Go back to the house."

"I will go back when I have a mind to," she said firmly to his back, but she did turn and walk out of the darkness of the barn into the last rays of the day's sun.

Walking back to the plantation house, she pondered his words. There must be some way this dilemma could be resolved. She had only a few weeks to think of something, but she was determined to find a way.

Chapter 19

The entire family sat assembled for the reading of Francois Peschier's will. The Darcys were present at Phillipe's request. He felt since they had shared life and death together, they were entitled to attend. The lawyer read in a monotone of many small things his father left to each of them. A painting to Manon, a pistol to her husband Gustave, his favorite horse, Antoinette, to Phillipe. He sat listening, dreading what would come at the end of the reading. The full weight of the Peschier Plantation would fall upon his shoulders, and, more importantly, he would now own his father's slaves.

"And to my daughters, Manon, Cecile, Elizabeth Ann, and Adele, I leave $50,000 in gold doubloons to be distributed equally among them. Half to Manon and Cecile now, and the other half equally to the twins upon their marriage."

Elizabeth Ann suddenly spoke up, "Oh, we cannot take that money. We will be the brides of Christ, of course, but I do not think that is what Father meant."

"And we are about to take a vow of poverty," Adele said, nodded her head toward her sister in agreement.

Phillipe interrupted. "We will discuss this matter later. You will need your habits and such things, and I am sure the convent would appreciate donations from time to time."

This seemed to satisfy his sisters. The lawyer continued, "To my wife, Poppy, and my son, Phillipe Peschier, I leave the bulk of my estate, the plantation, the house, the outbuildings, animals, and machinery. I leave all to them to divide in half, expense and profit. My son, Phillipe, will be the owner of the business. I leave all to them, save the slaves."

The lawyer, a white man with a balding pate, cleared his throat and then continued. "At Philippe Peschier's discretion, but within a year of my death, I hereby grant freedom to all my slaves and indentured servants. Each adult slave will be given thirty dollars and each child ten dollars upon their manumission."

Phillipe looked about the room to his mother, his sisters, and then to the Darcys. Emma was gazing at him, her eyes wide with surprise. He was in shock. The lawyer cleared his throat again and then waved a paper sealed with his father's crest toward Phillipe and spoke. "Your father left you this letter as well, *monsieur*."

Phillipe approached the man as if in a daze, He held out his hand and took the letter. Looking up, he saw that the entire room was riveted on him. He began to read aloud,

My dear son, Phillipe,

If you are reading this letter, I have passed on to a better place. I left you the plantation and everything you need to continue our business, except the slaves. I knew that keeping these people was a torment to you, so I have relieved you of the burden and the guilt of keeping them, but now, I fear, I leave you with a dilemma. If you wish to continue with our sugar business, you will find it is a challenge to find workers who willingly go into the fields. Your profits will not be as great if you can find anyone at all to do the work for wages. You may come to the same conclusion as I and choose to continue on as I have done.

I will not be there to judge your actions. You have only your own conscience to follow but remember this: you have a duty to your mother and your two unmarried sisters, and they are now your responsibility. If you decide to sell the plantation, consider this: it is the only real home your mother and your sisters have known, so you need to consider their wishes.

Make your own way in the world, my son. You now belong to a new age and a new country. I hope you will be happy.

Your Loving Father,
Francois Peschier

Phillipe looked to his mother, who smiled at him with shining eyes. "Well," she said. "Dat is dat. You are now master of dis house." She rose and kissed him on the cheek. He looked about him, and no one spoke.

"I believe I will take the air," he said and walked out onto the veranda. He needed time alone to think.

***

After nearly an hour, Elizabeth walked onto the veranda to find Phillipe still there, sitting in a chair near the open French doors that led to the room where his father had lain. He was staring into it, unmoving.

"I am sorry to disturb you, *monsieur*," she said softly, and she turned to go. He looked up at her with a haunted expression.

"No, please, sit with me a while." She drew up a chair and sat next to him. For some time, he said nothing, but then looked up at her, his eyes bright. "May I speak freely?"

"By all means."

"I truly do not know what to do. I know what is right, what I have always fought for with my father, and then again, I know what is right for my family. It seems an impossible situation."

"You must speak with your mother, Phillipe. She is not such a delicate flower that she will break at the first wind. She has endured a great deal in her lifetime. That you know well."

He looked up at her, silently, shaking his head. "I do not want to cause her pain in any way."

"After all she has suffered, I do not think that moving house would break her. Do you?"

"But my father said—"

"Your father spoke as your mother's husband and protector. Your mother wants only what is best for her children. She wants you to be happy, Phillipe. Go. Speak to her. Do not carry this burden alone. After all, she is half owner of the plantation now."

"But it is so soon. I need time to think."

"Come with me," she said and held out her hand, and then led him through the parlour to the dining room at the back of the house to the windows overlooking the back courtyard and the kitchen. There, between the kitchen and the house, the slaves were going about their various chores, but would look up toward the house or even stop and stare.

"They know."

He looked down on them and saw several look up to him with expectant faces. He looked back at Elizabeth. "You are right. I need to know my mother's wishes." He turned and left her standing there.

***

Phillipe did not find his mother in the house but sitting on a small bench near his father's tomb. A lump rose to his throat. She smiled as she watched him approach. "I been talkin' wid your father."

Phillipe smiled and sat next to her. "What did he have to say?"

"Been pretty quiet dese days." She sighed and was silent for a time. Then she took his hand and he looked into her eyes. "I know you want to sell de plantation, my son."

He felt like a traitor. How could he think of his own happiness before hers? If he decided to stay, they would be starting anew. He would have to, in all likelihood, betray his own moral code and go himself to the slave market to obtain labor enough to keep the plantation going. He said nothing, but looked away from her into the distance.

She continued. "I don' wan' to leave my Francois here all alone. I cannot do it." He looked back at her and she was quickly wiping a tear from her eyes as she looked away from him. "I also don' want to buy no more slaves. It not right."

He felt a sudden sense of relief, but it lasted only a moment. Now they really were in a quandary. They could not stay here without the profit from the plantation, and they could not run it without the slaves.

"So, *maman*, what are we to do?" As he said those words, the answer suddenly came to him. "What if we were to stay and bring in the harvest, then we can move Papa to the St. Louis Cemetery in town?" His mother looked at him again. She was not smiling. "Perhaps it is not only Papa that you do not want to leave. Perhaps it is this house and all its memories." He was trying to read her expression but failed miserably.

"You right. I hate to leave my house."

Phillipe felt a fist tighten around his heart. He would not, could not, force his mother to leave her home.

She again fell silent. Then, finally she spoke. "But it would be nice to be in town near Manon an' the chil'ren and Cecile an' Valentine. De convent w' de twins dere too. I did not t'ink of it before." She patted Phillipe's hand. "Your papa give de business to you, not me. You want to sell, you sell. We take your papa w' us an' we move to town." She smiled at him now. "If you like, we wait 'til after de harves'." With that she rose and walked back toward the house.

Elizabeth had been correct. His mother was more resilient than he thought.

***

The news of their manumission had indeed reached the slave quarters with lightning speed, but Phillipe needed time to consider the full import of his next actions. His mother reassured him that she would abide by any decision he made. She would be wealthy in her own right, and could do as she liked. Manon and Gustave would welcome her, as would Cecile and Valentine. As they walked back to the house together, Phillipe told her that he could buy a house in the *Vieux Carre* for both of them or she could even live in a house by herself. She made a face at that suggestion. "What good is money and property if you cannot share it with someone?" she asked. He thought her needs simple, and that, perhaps, was the secret of her resilience.

For the next few days, whenever he was out walking the grounds of the plantation or visiting the cane fields, he could feel every eye upon him. None of the slaves dared speak to him of the rumors they heard of their emancipation, but he knew he would have to address them soon. The lawyer had been helpful in instructing him on the various documents that would have to be filed for each of his slaves in order for them to carry the proper papers attesting to their new status as *les gens de couleur*. Even free, they would need to show these papers if they wanted to travel outside the city. They were free as he was free—free, but not free.

Except for mealtimes with his family and the Darcys, he spent much of his time alone, brooding over the decisions that he would soon have to make. With his youngest sisters with the Ursalines, and his other sisters settled, there really was only himself and his mother to consider. And Emma. Could he now consider Emma? Could they make a life for themselves somewhere in this vast, new country among these ruffian Americans?

On the evening of the third day after the will had put his life and his brain in such an uproar, he felt himself ready to speak of his plans. First, he sought out Poppy and his sisters, from whom he expected some kind of resistance or at least opinion. All sat looking at him inscrutably, so much so that he had to ask them what they thought.

"Only you know such things, Phillipe," Elizabeth Ann told him.

Adele nodded. "We told you, dear brother, that we only need our habits and our prayer books. You may do as you see fit."

Phillipe looked at his mother. "You say nothing, *maman*. You must tell me if you are unhappy."

Poppy smiled and patted his hand. "I will miss dis place. I don' deny it, but I can be happy if I know my chil'ren are happy."

"All right then. I will go and speak to the slaves." It was the first time since his father died that he felt at peace.

By the time Phillipe walked out to speak with them, the slaves all were gathered outside the kitchen, waiting for him. As soon as he descended the back stairs, Thomas shouted over the throng. "Is it true, *monsieur*? Have we all been set free?"

"That is so," he answered. Moving to the rear steps of the house, he climbed to the top of them and spoke in a loud voice.

"My father, Monsieur Peschier, has made arrangements for all of you in his will. As soon as we have obtained your papers, you all will be free men." He spoke slowly, loudly enough for all of them to hear. "Your wives, your children, slave and indentured servant, all will be free, owing no debt to my family or to me. He also provided some money for you and your families." He could hear them murmuring, so he raised his voice again. "Any of you who would like to stay and work for wages to bring in the sugar next autumn will share in the profit from the crop." There was a murmuring among the crowd, and a look of great optimism on many of the faces.

He continued to speak to them, answering their questions, for they had many. By the time he finished, the sun had set, and torches were lit on the small courtyard behind the house. He could hear some walking away talking of buying property in Treme, outside the

Vieux Carre. Smiling to himself, he entered the house with a light heart.

***

Christmas was fast approaching, and one morning Elizabeth noticed Phillipe hanging a mistletoe directly in the path between the front parlour and the dining room so that they all had to pass it several times a day. At first, Darcy thought it most unsuitable, since it appeared two days before Christmas. But there had been so much sorrow in this house, this holiday was a welcome relief for all of them. They did not make much of Christmas at home, but the customs here were different and not unwelcome. It was time to set aside their sorrows. Now, with her dear friend and her family, there would be only joy.

Of course, Elizabeth had her motherly concerns. One morning, as she entered the second parlour on her way to the dining room, she spied Emma and Phillipe beneath that very mistletoe. They thought themselves unobserved as it was early in the morning and the rest of the family had not yet risen. Rather than a discreet and familial kiss on the cheek, she found them lip-to-lip and lost to the world. Walking back down the hallway, she called in a rather loud voice to Benji, whose clattering footsteps would alert the young lovers of their approach. Chastising herself for not paying closer attention to her daughter during Benji's illness, she resolved to speak with her soon. She comforted herself with the thought that they were leaving in a fortnight for home and therefore, all would be resolved, if not by prudence then by geography.

"When we finish here," Benji said to Toby, "we can have a game of battledore and shuttlecock." He was tying a ribbon on the branch of small loblolly pine that Phillipe and Benji spent hours looking for the day before. Coming back triumphant, their German cook clapped her hands with glee. "It is our Christmas tree," Benji had said proudly.

"*Ausgezeichnet*," she cried.

This German custom of bringing a tree into the house at yuletide had been making its way to English shores. Here in this new country, many cultures mingled together, and Elizabeth marveled at it. Not that there was no conflict. She knew the Creoles did not like the

Americans and thought them crude as they committed the unpardonable sin of not speaking French and had no deference to French customs. And, of course, there was warfare with the native peoples of this land, and the continuation of the cardinal sin of slavery.

The tree was being dressed in candles and sweets and small presents tied with ribbons. Toby was invited to the house to help Benji with the decorations and, frankly, to keep Benji occupied. The holiday had so filled him with excitement that Elizabeth could hardly get him to close his eyes at night.

Phillipe lifted Benji up so that he could tie something on the higher branches of the tree. "Whatever is battledore and shuffle-something?" he asked the child.

"You know very well, battledore and shuttlecock," he repeated and looked at Phillipe as if he most certainly had to be pulling his leg.

"*Jouer de volant*, you call it, with a paddle and a cork with feathers?" Emma suggested.

Poppy laughed. "He know it very well. He make his sisters play all de time when dey younger."

"Oh, I do believe we may have some of the racquets still in my workshop. Unfortunately, I am sure that the feathers and corks have dissolved into the earth by now." Benji looked crestfallen. Phillipe lifted his chin and said, "But if your father will help me drink a bottle of wine, we may have a cork again. Cook will give us feathers I am sure. I believe she is plucking a wild turkey for our Christmas dinner." He turned to Darcy, who stood apart observing the festivities.

"Monsieur, may I interest you in a glass of wine?" He smiled roguishly at Darcy. Elizabeth could see why Emma was enamored of him.

"Please, Papa," begged Benji.

Darcy sighed. "It will be a sacrifice, but if you insist."

"Hoorah," Benji called out.

Toby repeated, "Hoorah," but Elizabeth could see by his expression that he did not know what he was cheering for.

The cork was promptly removed and placed in Benji's hand. Through a mixture of English and French, the two boys resolved to visit the kitchen in search of feathers. Phillipe and Emma excused themselves and went to find the errant racquets for the game. It was not without a little trepidation that Elizabeth watched them go off by themselves. How many times had they done so already? They were both sensible people and knew the impediments that stood between them, surely.

"This evening we shall sing," Poppy announced. "One carol in French, then one carol in English until we cannot think of any more."

Elizabeth reached around her friend's waist and squeezed for a moment. "In a few days' time, we will have a marvelous Christmas."

***

The Peschiers had a square pianoforte that had been imported from England many years prior and sounded as if it had not been tuned since. Emma, however, proved that her lessons with her Aunt Georgiana had not been in vain, and the family sang both French and English carols and even something called "Oh Tannenbaum" because the cook had come into the house and begun humming it from the dining room. Emma was beginning to feel quite sentimental about this house even though it had only been her home for slightly under three months.

When everyone stopped to have refreshments, she excused herself for a moment and went straight to her room to sit in the dark. Perhaps it was the Christmas season or the emotional turmoil of Monsieur Peschier's death and Benji's illness, or perhaps it was the rush of feeling she had every time she looked at Phillipe that led her to feeling overwhelmed and in need of a quiet sit-down.

When she was finally alone, she had to face herself and her new circumstances. What if Phillipe asked her to marry him? What if they left New Orleans and went north into this vast, new country to some American city? What if he asked her to follow him into the wilderness? What if they stayed here and she was alone and isolated on a plantation on the river, never to attend a ball again, or play cards, or speak English or see her family? Would her parents be able to receive her at home for a visit, her and her half-caste husband? Was her attraction to Phillipe one of forbidden fruit, or did she really love him?

There was a knock on the door. "Are you all right in there, darling?" Her mother.

"Quite all right, Mama." The door opened.

"Whatever are you doing sitting in the dark? Come and join us. We are in need of your expertise on the piano." Her mother's cheerful voice sounded in the darkness.

Emma did not move. Her mother walked to the small table near her bed and struck a match, lighting a candle. She sat down next to Emma and peered into her face.

"Would you like to talk a bit?" That soothing tone of her mother's always undid her most robust defenses.

"Oh yes, Mama," Emma said emphatically, nearly bursting into tears.

"Is it Phillipe that worries you, darling?"

Emma turned her head and blinked back the tears. "Yes, Mama, how did you know?"

Her mother shook her head and smiled. "A mother knows these things. So, tell me what is troubling you."

"I love him, Mama. Did you know that? I do, but I am afraid I am not suited to being reviled and cast out."

"Has he asked you to marry him?"

"Oh no. He says it is impossible, but now that he is not tied to the plantation, perhaps it is possible. What if I have to live in New York?" She was horrified at the thought.

Instead of commiserating with her distress, her mother laughed softly. "Would that be so terrible?"

"You and Father could not receive us, could you? He would have to disown me due to his social position."

Elizabeth stood up. "Is that what you think of your father? He certainly would do no such thing, but," she hesitated, and Emma looked up at her searchingly, "I cannot speak for the rest of society. If you decide to marry, and decide to reside in England, you may find yourself isolated. Not from us, but from the gay society you so enjoy."

"I am not such a child that I do not know that. Phillipe is strong-willed and would not consider living such a life. He feels there is no future for us."

"And how do you feel?" Her mother's tone was gentle.

"I do not know. Sometimes I feel that I cannot live with him, and then other times I feel that I cannot live without him."

Her mother eased herself down again next to her daughter and took her hand. "Come home with us." Before she could speak further, Emma withdrew her hand and stood up. "Emma, listen…" her mother said sternly, "I have not finished. Come home with us. If in six months you feel the same about him, and he feels the same about you, the two of you can decide what to do."

"You think I will forget him, do you not?" Emma asked, arching her brow in exactly the same manner as Darcy's late Aunt Catherine.

"I think some time apart might clear the air. You—" Before she could finish, there was a knock on the door.

"May I come in?" Phillipe.

Emma felt herself light up inside. "Please do," Elizabeth said, rising and opening the door.

"Come see the Christmas tree. We have lit all the candles," he said, smiling. Offering an arm to each of the ladies, they entered the parlour. There was the tree, ablaze with light.

***

Their dinner was quite a change from the solemnity that had engulfed them in the past fortnight. Emma gave herself over to the delights of the evening, her previous dismay evaporating like a morning mist. The meal was a mixture of French and Creole dishes, and when the fish course arrived, Benji squealed and began clapping his hands.

The servants brought in great platters piled high with what looked like spiders coated with breading. She looked over at Phillipe in dismay.

"Whatever are these monstrous things?" she asked.

Poppy began to laugh. "They are blue crabs. You must see something like them in England, no? You live by the sea."

Emma had not seen these things before. She looked askance at them, and Benji said, "I want to eat the spider."

"They are not spiders, son. They are crabs," her father corrected.

"They look like spiders to me."

"Observe." Phillipe took two of them from the platter. He placed one upon her plate and one upon his. He then squeezed a lemon over both, and with his knife and fork, began to dismember it, and proceeded to place the spider-like legs into his mouth. Emma squeezed her eyes shut for a moment.

She could hear her mother laugh. "Do you eat them in the shell? I have never heard of such a thing."

"The shells are soft when the crabs are young," he said, directing his comments to Elizabeth. He then turned again to Emma. "Please. Try." He then lifted her knife and fork, and cutting away at the crispy creature, he held a portion of it outside her lips. He nodded his head slightly and gave her that disarming smile. She took a deep breath, closed her eyes, nodded her head, and opened her mouth. The crispy shellfish was now inside. She forced herself to chew, but then was pleasantly surprised by its taste and texture.

"Oh, that really is quite delicious."

"Ha. You should learn to trust me to tell you the truth."

"I have no doubt that you will always do that, *monsieur*." She commenced dismantling her spider with enthusiasm.

Benji picked one up with his fingers and dangled it over his mouth. "Watch, Mama." He bit the creature in half, still holding its remains in his hand.

"Benji, your manners," Elizabeth said, and Poppy laughed. "Put that down on your plate immediately and use your knife and fork."

"*Oui, maman*," Benji said through a mouthful. Darcy rolled his eyes and Poppy laughed again. She reached for Elizabeth's hand and squeezed it. "I am glad that you are here."

Phillipe then held up his hand to silence the assembly.

"What is it?" Emma asked.

"Shhh. I hear someone on the river. *Excusez-moi*." He got up and crossed from the dining room into the parlour and opened the French doors that lead to the front stairway.

In moments, his brother-in-law Valentine was inside. Phillipe kissed him on both cheeks and bade him welcome, but Emma could see he was greatly agitated. Poppy rose from her seat and asked him to join them.

"I have not come for a social call," Valentine said rapidly. "I have news."

"Please, sit, tell us, Valentine." Phillipe poured the man a glass of wine, from which he took a hearty swig, and then addressed himself to Phillipe.

"You must arm yourself, brother, and come with me. The British are on our doorstep. They are about to attack New Orleans."

Chapter 20

"That cannot be," Darcy said, standing to face Valentine.

"It most assuredly is, sir. General Jackson has declared martial law in the city. I found a way to hire a boat and came to warn you." Looking intensely at Phillipe, Valentine continued, "And to enlist your help."

Phillipe shook his head. "What do I care for these Americans, eh?"

"You are an American whether you like it or not. Have you not petitioned the government yourself, with us, to grant us our voting rights?"

"And have we received them?" Then answering his own question, he said, "No. And if the British come, we can surrender to them."

"They will burn your house and your farm."

"They most certainly will not," Darcy said vehemently.

Phillipe looked up at him. "*Pardon, monsieur*, but he is right. They most certainly will."

"I do not understand. When we left, there was already a delegation on their way to Brussels to negotiate a treaty to end this blasted conflict."

"Perhaps they never agreed, or the British fleet never received word," Valentine continued. "None of that matters now. They are on our doorstep and many have already been killed. We are vastly outnumbered. There are more than fifty ships from the Gulf all the way to the Villere plantation. You must come and fight for your country and for your family."

"Fight for my country, ha," Phillipe said disdainfully. "They have repeatedly ignored our petitions. We must carry papers wherever we go to prove that we are freemen. We are second-class citizens at best."

"But all that has changed now. Look, look at this." Valentine produced a newspaper from inside his waistcoat and handed it to Phillipe. "It is a speech General Jackson gave to all the free people of colour in the city. He enlists our help, as Americans."

Phillipe took the paper gingerly and began to read. "He says that their policy has been mistaken and we should participate with full rights."

"See." Hope shone in Valentine's face.

"Listen," Phillipe said, and began to read:

As sons of freedom, you are now called upon to defend your most inestimable blessing. As Americans, your country looks with confidence to her adopted children for a valorous support as a faithful return for the advantages enjoyed under her mild and equitable government.

"Hmm. Not so equitable, but…"

"Read on," Valentine urged.

In the sincerity of a soldier and the language of truth I address you, he says, *to every noble-hearted, generous freeman—men of color, volunteering to serve during the present contest with Great Britain and no longer, there will be paid the same bounty in money and lands now received by the white soldiers of the United States viz.: $124 in money and 160 acres in land.*

"This would be a great boon to all your father's slaves whom he has freed," Valentine suggested. "And the British are promising emancipation to all slaves who join their cause, but it matters not to your slaves. They are already free. It is said the British even tried to enlist the help of Lafitte, the pirate."

Valentine and Phillipe looked up at Darcy, who threw up his hands. "Gentlemen, I have nothing to do with the policy, or even with this war."

Phillipe said nothing but continued to read silently, paraphrasing as he went. "This Jackson says that he has told all these things to the governor of Louisiana." He put the paper down and looked over at Valentine. "I do not see how we have a choice. I would like to believe that this new country will honor us as full citizens as it should. I will join you, Valentine."

Before he could continue, he heard his mother say, "You cannot. I will not lose my son so soon after losing my husban'."

Phillipe looked over at his mother. "I have to defend my family, my property, and my honor, and even the promise of these United States. You will not lose me, *maman*. I am a good shot." Poppy got up from the table and ran into the recesses of the house.

"Is there no other way?" Emma asked. She could feel each thump of her heart.

"I am afraid not. I will assemble all the men of the plantation tomorrow and let them choose to fight or to stay here. Either way, they will gain their freedom, my father and I have promised it. But if this *Général* Jackson is to be believed, they will have much to gain by defending America. We will prepare ourselves in the morning. For now, please, everyone, let us enjoy our Christmas meal together and forget on this night that we have become enemies."

Phillipe raised his glass and drank, but Emma had lost her appetite.

***

Phillipe's imminent departure spurred Emma's mind to become clear. She lay awake, thinking that he would be killed, and she would never see him again. This new country and its new possibilities may hold promise for them both, or it could shatter any hope they had for happiness. Either way, she could not let him go without telling him she loved him one more time.

His father's room had remained empty since his death, the bedding and the mattress ticking burned to keep the fever from spreading. His mother did not want to return to that room without her Francois, so Phillipe accepted it as his, keeping the small altar that the Widow Paris had assembled. The house was dark, but a fire burned low in the parlour. The candles had been extinguished on the tree. Slowly, she opened the door to Phillipe's room.

"Who is it?"

"So, you cannot sleep either," she said as she crossed the room to his bed. Candles were lit on the altar, casting a dim light across the room.

"You should not be here." Quickly, he got out of bed. He did not sleep in a nightshirt but bare-chested, only in his undergarments. She bit her lip at the sight of his half-naked body.

"I want to be here. I want to give myself to you before you go off to war."

He took her by the arms and looked into her face. "Oh, *mon cher,* you do not know what you are doing. You know that we can never be together."

"Do you love me, Phillipe?"

"It is because I love you that I say these things to you."

"But everything is different now. You will be a full citizen of the United States when this war is won."

"Or the British will win, and we will be back where we started."

"I do not care. I will not give you up. We will live in New York or somewhere."

"No matter where we go, even New York, it will be difficult. A man with Negro blood and a white woman?"

"You told me once that even a drop of African blood makes a man or a woman black, is that not so?"

"That is so."

"Well, then." She walked to the altar. There were many small trinkets upon it; some were Monsieur Peschier's, others belonged to other members of the family. Emma found a hatpin and gestured for Phillipe to join her. She pricked her finger with the pin and then, taking Phillipe's finger, pricked his also. Small drops of blood began to ooze from the wounds. She rubbed her finger on his and said, "There, now your blood is mine and mine is yours. Since I carry a drop of Negro blood, we can forever be together."

"Were it that simple," he said. He looked at her for a long time, searching her face. Then, taking a small stick of wood from the altar, lit it, and handed it to her. Covering her hand in his, they lit a votive on the altar. "To you, Emma Darcy, I plight my troth."

Emma moved to the next votive and together they lit another. "And to you, Phillipe Peschier, I plight my troth."

"Until I can speak to your father and get his blessing, this will have to do." With those words, he plunged the lighted stick into a small cup of sand. He then took her in his arms, and they fell to the bed.

***

Emma knew something of what to expect when a man and a woman consummated their marriage, but she was still filled with trepidation. No one save her mother and her maid had ever seen her without her clothing, and now she was about to expose everything to a man. Granted, it was the man she loved, but still, it was far beyond anything she had ever done before.

Phillipe was gentle with her, pulling down the neck of her nightdress to expose her shoulder and kissing it from her collarbone to her arm. It was odd that touching her in this manner made the most private parts of her ache with desire.

Since this was the first time she had ever been intimate with a man, she felt herself half participant-half observer in this act of love. She felt his hands move to the hem of her nightdress and then, to her delight and dismay, he placed them upon her thighs and then slid them up the length of her body to her breasts. She nearly cried out with both pleasure and surprise but knew that the house was filled with sleeping relatives, and their discovery would be unthinkable, so she contained her outburst.

He cupped her breasts with his hand and then whispered sweet French endearments in her ear. Her body tingled with anticipation. Running his thumbs over the nipples of her breasts made her nearly swoon with delight. He then did something she did not anticipate. Taking hold of her hand, he guided it first to the hard muscles of his abdomen, but then lower, into his undergarments, where it met with a muscular appendage covered in the softest skin her hand had ever touched. Under his wordless tutelage, he instructed her to touch his member in such a way as to make him moan into the crook of her neck. Both his breathing and hers were coming more rapidly.

Letting go of her hand, he pulled off the little clothing he had covering him, and wordlessly bade her to do the same. She complied willingly and he threw back the bedclothes and revealed both himself and her in the soft candlelight. They both stared, their breathing coming in short gasps. The secrets of the male anatomy were now revealed to her. She reached out and touched not only his rampant member but all that lay below. His eyes rolled up into his head and he bit his lower lip.

Falling upon her, he kissed her most passionately. Their mouths opened to one another; his tongue entered her mouth. Then, moving his hand down the length of her body to her most intimate place, he gently opened her legs and teased open the lips of her mound of Venus. There he touched something that made her body shudder. He ministered to her there while kissing her breasts. She touched his cheek and had him look into her face. She felt as though she had nearly dissolved in his arms.

"Are you ready, *mon couer*?" he whispered. She nodded but was not really sure. "One moment." He left the bed and opened a small box on the bureau. There he removed something that looked like a piece of parchment.

"What is that?"

"It is called an English letter. It will help us not to create a child tonight."

"But—"

"Do you trust me, Emma?"

How could she say no to him now? They were alone together, in only the skin in which they were born. He had touched her in ways that made her blush even now in thinking about them. And she had touched him. He took this parchment and slipped it over his standing member. With a tender but decisive movement, parted her legs and slid himself between them.

"Guide me," he said, placing his throbbing manhood in her hand. She guided him to her opening and felt him push himself forward with his hips. She thought she must be terribly small, for his entrance felt somewhat painful. She began to breathe rapidly.

"Am I hurting you, Emma?" His face was close to hers.

"Perhaps a little, but please do not stop." He thrust his body forward and she felt him seated inside her.

At first, he did not move, but kissed her face, and down her collarbone. Then, grasping her legs, he pulled them over his back, wrapping her around him. Grasping her shoulders, he slowly began to drive himself in and out of her. There was some pain in this activity, but nothing that she could not bear. In a short while, she began to feel the pleasure of this union of the bodies and allowed herself to rock into him at each thrust. Soon his movements became more rapid. She could hear his breath quicken and suddenly, his body stiffened, and he let out a soft groan and collapsed upon her.

She pulled him into her using muscles she did not know she possessed. He rocked his body forward twice more and then rolled off her. She kissed him again and then noticed that there was a stain of blood upon the sheet.

"Oh." At first, she was alarmed, and then remembered what her mother had told her. "Oh, it is all right."

He was covered in beads of perspiration, and she touched his face. "I love you, Phillipe." He leaned over and kissed her. "And I love you. We have embarked on a perilous journey together."

"I am not afraid." She leaned over to kiss him. Then she gathered her nightdress, pulled it over her head, and left him alone to await the dawn.

***

Darcy did not sleep well that night. By the time the dawn reached his window, he was fully dressed. He stepped out into the hallway and, upon entering the parlour, found Phillipe and Valentine assembling their kits.

"*Bonjour*," he said as he entered and startled the two men. Weapons of all sorts lay upon the sofas and settees in stark contrast to the lonely Christmas tree in the corner.

Both men looked at Darcy suspiciously. Phillipe spoke first. "It seems, sir, that we are at war."

"We were at war when we arrived, *monsieur*, and at that time it seemed to make no difference." Darcy could almost feel the ground shifting beneath his feet.

"Your forces are here to bombard our city and threaten our families. That is different, *monsieur*," Valentine said in French.

"Yes, I know," Darcy replied wretchedly. "What do you propose we do?"

Phillipe picked up a rather fearsome-looking dagger with a long blade and a crossbar and pointed the tip toward Darcy. "I could take you as a prisoner of war." Darcy noticed Valentine looking over at his brother-in-law in shock.

"You could, indeed, but then who would stay behind and protect the women?"

At this juncture, Elizabeth entered the room, still clad in her nightclothes and dressing gown. Darcy heard her voice behind him. "What is going on? Phillipe!"

Darcy turned to her and smiled. "We are having a diplomatic discussion." But from the expression on his wife's face, he could see she was in no mood to be cajoled.

"Would you betray your country for the sake of my family?" Philippe asked stridently.

"I have no intention of betraying my country, nor do I have any intention of letting any harm come to your family. I will put them all under my protection if the British forces ever come this far up the river. I will not leave them under any circumstances. My family's fate is inexorably tied with yours."

Phillipe stood still a moment, then lowered the dagger and walked toward Darcy with it still in his hand. Darcy then heard another cry, but the voice was that of his daughter. "What is happening?" she asked, rushing into the room.

"Your father and I were discussing how best to protect everyone in my absence." Phillipe held Emma's gaze. He then handed the dagger to Darcy. "I will also leave you a rifle and some ammunition, but I will need to take the rest of our weapons downriver. You understand."

"Perfectly." Darcy turned and extended his arm to Elizabeth, who rushed to his side. Emma stood, her mouth open, and looked from her father to Phillipe and back again.

Darcy spoke directly to Lizzy and Emma. "Dress quickly. There is much to prepare this morning."

Elizabeth reached her hand out to her daughter and they disappeared into the second parlour and toward their rooms.

"Valentine," Phillipe ordered, "go out to the stable and get some of the slaves to help you bring in anything that General Jackson might find useful. Shovels, axes, whatever you can find." Valentine nodded and disappeared down the back stairs. Darcy and Phillipe were alone. "I want to apologize for my behavior just now."

Darcy shook his head. "No need. If I were in your shoes, I would want to assess the intentions of my guest who had suddenly become my enemy."

"I am glad you understand, Monsieur Darcy, for there is another matter that I most urgently need to discuss with you."

Darcy could feel a lump in the pit of his stomach. He knew the young man wanted to discuss his Emma.

Phillipe motioned for Darcy to join him on the veranda. They went through the doors to be greeted by the damp winter air. Darcy drank in a lungful and prepared himself. Phillipe looked directly into his eyes.

"I love your daughter, *monsieur*. I want to ask you for her hand in marriage."

There it was. What Darcy had been dreading. He said nothing for what seemed like an eternity. Phillipe waited patiently, never dropping his gaze.

"How can you ask for her hand when you know that a marriage between you is not allowed by law?"

"But do you not see, *monsieur*, that now everything has changed. This is a brave new country that recognizes a freeman such as myself. This General Jackson asks us to fight beside the white soldiers like brothers. Begging your pardon, sir, but when we expel the British once and for all, everything will change. Everything."

Darcy shook his head. He remembered the idealism of his youth, but understanding what he knew of British politics at least, he had no faith in the fairness of governments.

"Do you truly believe that everything will change?"

"I have to believe it."

"Let us say that you are right, and that all will change on the basis of this battle. Let us say that you return, unscathed. I am loath to leave my daughter thousands of miles away in a country that may or may not treat her kindly."

Phillipe's expression suddenly hardened and when he spoke again, his speech was tinged with anger. "It is the colour of my skin that you really object to, is it not?"

Darcy looked at him and tried to choose his words carefully. "Not the colour of your skin, per se."

"Ha. I knew it. For all your fine words and your egalitarian attitudes and even your fight against slavery in your parliament, you draw the line at a half-caste black man marrying your daughter."

Darcy clenched his fists, the ire rising in him. "You did not let me finish." He strode up to Phillipe and touched his shoulder. Phillipe whirled around, his eyes flashing.

"Sit down and hear me out." Darcy was trying mightily to control his own temper. Phillipe said nothing but sat on a bench against the wall. Darcy sat down in a chair across from him and muted his tone. "I think you a fine man of excellent character." Phillipe was not meeting his eye. "You have the means to support my daughter and any children you may have, but—"

"Aha."

"Will you let me finish or not?" Phillipe said nothing. "I do not have the faith in politics that you have."

"But you are a member of Parliament."

Darcy noticed the look of disbelief on Phillipe's face. "That is exactly why I do not have your faith. I have seen time after time expediency triumphing over truth, wealth over the best interests of the people."

"But that is in the old country, not so here in the new."

"We can discuss these finer points of your country versus mine when you return, but let me tell you this. The hearts of the people are not so easily changed. In your heart of hearts, do you really think that you and my daughter will be accepted in American society?"

Phillipe sighed, sat back and looked Darcy in the eye again. "We could go north, to New York. There are many people there. Things could be better." Darcy cocked an eyebrow at him. "And Emma could have her social engagements." Phillipe smiled and that made Darcy smile with him.

Darcy shook his head. "New York society may not be much different from English society."

"We would never be accepted in England."

"No," Darcy said immediately. "Even with me as her father, even with all my wealth, even with my social position, and even as a member of Parliament, I can tell you frankly that people would make you unhappy."

"I am used to being unhappy."

"But do you wish it for Emma?"

Darcy heard the clank of metal and realized that Valentine and a good many of the men of the plantation were moving implements and weapons of all sorts toward the small dock. The time to join the fight was fast approaching.

"I must go now," Phillipe said, standing, "and I must have your answer." Philippe stood, meeting Darcy's gaze.

Darcy sighed. "If you can find a way to make her happy, I give you my blessing."

Phillipe's eyes grew wide and he embraced Darcy, kissing him on both cheeks.

"I will never get used to that."

Phillipe's face broke into a grin and he flew into the house to find Emma.

Chapter 21

Emma dressed quickly, and as she entered the parlour, she saw her father in deep discussion with Phillipe. Had he confessed their liaison from the night before? Were they going to leave and try to cross the American lines of battle to join the British? A thousand thoughts whirled through her head. She retreated back to the wing she shared with her family and found Benji, his face pressed to the window, watching the activity outside. He looked up at her with his usual beatific expression.

"I think we are moving house. Look. The men are taking all kinds of things out of the barn and walking toward the river. Where do you think we are going?"

She knelt down and hugged him to her. "We are not going anywhere. The British fleet is here. They mean to attack New Orleans."

Benji looked up at her with a confused expression. "Why would they do that? We are friends, aren't we?"

"I truly do not know, Benji. Get dressed and then go ask Papa." She did not want to discuss anything more with her brother. She wanted to speak to Phillipe before he left.

As if on command, Phillipe came striding down the hallway. "Quickly, Emma, we must speak." His expression, which so often was a scowl, was lit up by an internal fire.

Her mother came from her chamber and saw the two of them together. "You have come to say good-bye?" Phillipe nodded. She extended her hand to Phillipe and he took it. "Godspeed and come home to us." Phillipe swallowed hard and nodded. "I will see to Benji now." Emma was grateful that her mother was so perceptive.

When they were quite alone, Phillipe took Emma in his arms. She threw her arms around his back and held him tightly. She whispered, "Do not go."

His voice was a whisper too. "I must, you know that." Then, he held her out at arm's length. "I have something important to tell you."

Good God, what a man. What could be more important than the fact that he was leaving to risk his life, and perhaps never to return to her? She studied his face. He seemed about to burst with excitement.

"Your father has given us his blessing."

"His blessing for what?" she asked, not letting herself believe the impossible. With that, he got down on one knee and took her hand. "Emma Darcy, would you consent to be my wife?"

It was as if a large bell began clanging in her ears. She could not think. Had he really spoken with her father? How were they to marry in this place that did not allow them to marry? *How?* It did not matter. She looked down into his beaming, happy face. "Yes, yes. Of course, I will marry you." He leapt to his feet and embraced her. "But how?" Before she could finish, Valentine stepped into the hallway.

"We are ready, Phillipe. Come."

Phillipe touched her face and she kissed him fiercely, then embraced him so that he had to pry her arms from around his back.

"Come back. Please come back to me."

"I will, *mon cher*. Do not worry."

He turned and she called after him. "Wait." She disappeared into her room and emerged with a muffler that she gently wrapped around his neck. "It is cold."

He kissed her again quickly and was gone.

***

Phillipe was full of hope that morning: four craft from his plantation, including the one provided by Valentine, embarked on their crusade. As they neared the city, more boats joined them heading down river, many filled with what he judged from their manner of dress to be *homme de couleur* like himself, and also many white men and slaves. He could hear them talking and shouting at one another, some in French, some English, some even Spanish from St. Domingue. They were all there together to fight a common enemy and save their city. Phillipe felt buoyed with optimism. If he survived, he would return to Emma and they would be married. He was sure that anything was possible now.

There were so many small vessels they had no choice but to come near one another even though the river was wide. When they were close enough, Valentine called out to a craft captained by a friend from the city. "Where are we bound?"

"There has been fighting at Villere and Bayou Bienvenue. Many have been killed," his friend shouted back. "They say Jean Lafitte and his buccaneers have joined us."

Phillipe turned to his brother-in-law. "If these stupid Americans had not attacked Barataria, the pirates might have stopped the British and we could all be at home."

Valentine looked at him askance. "You are now a stupid American, my brother."

Yes, he had made an impassioned speech to Mr. Darcy this morning about his allegiance to this fledgling country. He must, in a day, shed his French attitude and become one with his American brothers.

They had traveled about five miles from the city when Phillipe saw the boats alongside his pull ashore at the Plantation Chalmette. He signaled his men to pull ashore and immediately all his tools were commandeered and his men set to digging. It looked as if they were throwing up a rampart from the river to what Phillipe knew was a cypress swamp on the east side on the plantation. As soon as he stepped ashore, he was accosted by a white man covered in dirt who looked as if he had seen battle.

"You," he called, pointing at Phillipe. "Yes, you. Do you speak English? *Parlez vous anglais?*"

"Yes, I speak English, why?" Before Phillipe could inquire further, he was whisked away. "Come with us. We have a job for you." They began wending their way through the mud and the bustle of men setting up a line of battle. There was every manner of men all working together. The slaves, however, were set to the digging. He heard the rough sort of English of the Cajuns and Creole French.

Men with kerchiefs wrapped around their heads with many scars worked beside men such as himself, in what looked like a regiment all their own. Finally, he was brought through a group of men in blue uniforms, which he surmised was the regular American army, though there did not seem to be many of those.

In a clearing, behind the hubbub, he was brought to a tent. There was a line of men standing before it, and he was deposited there beside them. Many had the look of Lafitte's pirates. The flaps of the tent were thrown open and inside, leaning over a table covered with crudely drawn charts, was a tall, gaunt man with steel-gray hair in a blue uniform, black boots to his knees, and gold epaulets on his shoulders. Phillipe was sure this was General Jackson.

"They're ready for you, sir."

"Thank you, you are dismissed." The general stood silently, still studying the map. Finally, he looked up and exited the tent. Walking up and down in front of them. "So, you speak English, do you?"

There was a general murmur of assent. "If I asked you to go behind enemy lines and report on troop movements, do you think you could do so?"

Phillipe stole a glance at his compatriots. None of them seemed to understand well, or at least none of them spoke. "I believe I could do so, sir." Jackson turned his head toward him.

"Know much of tactics, do you?"

"No, sir, but I do know the territory and I believe I could find out what you need to learn."

Jackson eyed him suspiciously. "From St. Domingue, are you?"

"Originally, sir. Now I am an American." He did not know if he actually felt that way but thought it may be the correct thing to say at the time. It seemed to have its desired effect.

Jackson smiled. He turned to his adjunct. "Get him a lobster uniform and put him behind the lines. And you, you are now a Jamaican. See if you can infiltrate and report back. We need troop strength, positions, battle plans—anything you can get." The general then turned his attention back to the rest of the line.

The man who had brought him here took him away from the front line, and before he knew it, he was dressed in a red British uniform that was covered with mud and a dark stain that Phillipe assumed was blood. Apparently, the original owner did not need his coat anymore. He retained his gift from Emma and secreted it within the garment.

Phillipe was taken back to the river to a canoe with a Choctaw warrior at either end. He lay in the bottom as they began to paddle down river. Phillipe heard shouting and the sound of horses from shore and of other craft close by. But their canoe slipped by unmolested. As night fell, they pulled into shore and Phillipe was roughly deposited at the mouth of what he assumed was Villere's Canal at the foot of the levee. Between his limited Choctaw and their limited French, he was instructed to find out what he could and they would rendezvous with him in this same spot in two days. The two Indians pushed off back into the river, and Phillipe was cast ashore well behind enemy lines. He climbed the levee and dropped over the other side. He took cover and waited until dawn.

***

Darcy disappeared into the plantation soon after Phillipe and the other men's departure. Elizabeth knew from his deliberately impassive countenance that he was anxious for their safety and would do his best to assemble whomever he had left to him on the plantation into some sort of defense. The old caretaker did not follow Phillipe, nor did the overseer, saying that he would never be an American, and the fight was not his.

Darcy always assumed that mask of indifference when the situation was its most dire. It seemed as though they were surrounded by enemies. The French planters, who hated the English as a matter of course, but held no love for the Americans either. They also faced danger from their own kind, who, in their desire to capture the port of New Orleans, might attack them peremptorily, not realizing their allegiance.

Elizabeth had been in this situation before in Grenada where every day they waited for what was certain death for most of them. She had survived all her trials there, and she was determined to survive this one. Her fear was not for herself or even for Darcy, but for her children, whom she hoped would never have to endure what she had endured.

Poppy had sequestered herself in her bedchamber as soon as Phillipe left, and did not emerge until midmorning. There were only a few house servants left, as many of the slave women accompanied their husbands, hoping to aid the cause any way they knew how, as cooks or as nurses for the wounded. Elizabeth knew full well the horror of gunshot wounds and their aftermath. She hoped and prayed Phillipe would be kept from harm for his mother's sake, and for Emma's.

220

Their rations had been much reduced by the men heading off to battle, but there was plenty of firewood, so a good blaze was kept up in the parlour. It was bitterly cold, which surprised Elizabeth. She always felt that New Orleans was a southern clime, like Grenada, but in truth it was much farther north, where winter spread its dank and icy chill.

Benji followed his father everywhere on the plantation, with Toby in tow. As they returned to the house for luncheon, Elizabeth observed the worry on her husband's face.

"Have you not been successful in your endeavors, my love?"

He tried to again look unconcerned, but she knew him too well. "We have some weapons, and a great deal of wood to create a barrier if need be, but we are decidedly short of manpower."

"I will help you, Papa. I can fight the British." Benji was speaking French again.

Emma looked at her brother, her mouth agape. "Bennet Fitzwilliam, you ARE British."

He looked at her a moment, confused. "Oh, I do believe I am. So, who are we going to fight, then?"

Emma brought her hand to her mouth and suddenly left the table. Elizabeth looked up at her husband.

"I will go to her," she said, standing suddenly. "Excuse me."

Before Elizabeth reached her rooms, Poppy caught her by the sleeve. "Wait a moment," she said. "Der is somet'ing I need to show you."

"Can it not wait?"

"No, it cannot." Poppy led Elizabeth across the parlours to the room once occupied by Poppy and Francois. It was the bedchamber that was recently vacated by Phillipe. As they entered, Poppy shut the door. She seemed uncomfortable and reticent to talk, so Elizabeth waited until she spoke again. "I hear dat Phillipe ask for your daughter's hand."

"He did. Darcy gave his permission for them to marry, but I cannot imagine how they will accomplish it. I fear for them both."

"You got good reason to worry." Poppy then pulled off the blanket covering Phillipe's bed. There were a few small bloodstains from the night before. "I t'ink dey already marry." Elizabeth stood motionless and stared at the telltale sheets. A myriad of thoughts and emotions ran through her. Foremost, she was angry with Phillipe.

Poppy must have read her expression, for she shook her head. "I don' know what come over him. He know better."

Elizabeth sat down heavily in the nearby chair. "The lure of forbidden love is impossibly strong. They have been thrown together for weeks, and with his leaving to fight—"

"Still."

The anger that flared in Elizabeth soon was banked by the knowledge she had of her daughter's headstrong ways. "I will talk to Emma." She turned, but before she left the room, the muffled report of cannon fire echoed in her ears.

***

Phillipe awoke shivering in a small thicket near the British encampment. As he got to his feet, he could see dozens of small ships, most of them canoes, delivering men to the shoreline. Downriver, he could hear bombardment, but did not know if the Americans were shelling the British or vice versa. A sudden explosion rent the air, and Phillipe could see all manner of debris flying from the direction of the river, and then flames erupted. Some ship had exploded, and the booming sound of the shelling stopped.

A column of British soldiers was advancing along the canal, and he thought best to join them. He determined that he could find out what happened on the river, and also the strength of their numbers. Waiting in vegetation until he spied a larger contingent of men, he joined them. They marched along in silence. As the sun reached its zenith, the men were set to creating their bivouac downriver from Jackson's rampart at Chalmette. One of the men accosted him.

"Oy, you, Jamaican." At first Phillipe did not know to whom he was referring. Another soldier shoved him, and he turned toward the voice. "Wha'cher doin' 'ere? Yer troops is over there to the east."

Phillipe attempted what was left of his Grenadan accent. He hoped it would do. "I got separate from my company during de fight."

The man eyed him suspiciously, and more men closed around him. "And where'd ya get that uniform, eh? It ain't Jamaican."

Phillipe's mind was whirring. "De dead don' need a uniform. Mine was too col'."

"Can't blame a man for that." Some of the men grumbled, but the matter was dropped. Phillipe tried not to let the relief show in his face.

"Come 'ere and 'elp w' the tents," someone said, and he did what he was told. Then the men began to speak freely as they set up the rear line.

In this manner, Phillipe wandered from camp to camp, on the pretext of rejoining his Jamaican troop, and gathered a great deal of information. The explosion he heard was the *Carolina*. It had been harassing the British landing for days and delaying the troop movements from Pea Island. Both the British and the Americans had suffered losses at the Villere plantation, but they were of the mistaken opinion that Jackson had amassed an army far greater in number than he had. The British, however, had thousands of men and more than fifty ships; many of them had come from recently defeating Napoleon. A new general, someone called Packenham, had taken command.

When night fell, Phillipe made his way through the British encampment more easily for they could not discern his features as well in the firelight, and he merely had to say he was carrying a message to the troops at the river. When he reached the levee, he climbed to the top and took the risk of standing atop to survey the length and breadth of the British encampment. Satisfied that he had accomplished his mission, he dropped over the side to find a spot to take cover and wait for the Choctaws.

The river side of the levee was deserted, so he crept into a small space between a live oak and the levee and waited until dawn. Although he tried to stay awake, he slept fitfully, and as the first light began to dapple the muddy river, he was wide awake. His muscles were cramped so he allowed himself to stand and shake loose his arms and legs. Not long after, he heard voices from the other side of the levee. The troops had moved all the way to the river. Another bit of information that he could report to Jackson. This furtive deception was not what he imagined his contribution to the battle would be, but if it helped secure their victory, he would do what he could.

The lapping water changed its tune slightly and he spied the canoe coming toward him. Coming out from behind a tree, he gave his signal, and they signaled back. Looking about, he saw no one, and waded into the water, to meet the canoe. This time, it held a swarthy fellow, who, despite his rather ragged shirt, sported a gold chain about his neck and rings on his fingers.

"*Salut, frere*," he said as Phillipe helped drag the canoe ashore. "What have you learned?" he asked. Phillipe told him all he knew, and the man listened carefully. He smiled and Phillipe could see a gold tooth sparkling in his mouth. "You have done well, my friend. You would have made a good pirate, I t'ink."

Their friendly discourse was interrupted by the ping of shot that rang out between Phillipe and the canoe and made a splash in the water on the far side of the boat. The pirate gave Phillipe a shove and he lost his balance and fell backward into the water. As he recovered himself, he watched the canoe paddle straight into the middle of the river. He could hear his pirate friend shout from the water, "All's fair in love and war, my friend."

Within seconds, British troopers pulled him from the water and a bayonet was pointed at his throat. "Traitor," one of them said.

"Prisoner of war," replied Phillipe.

***

"Is there anything you would like to tell me?" Elizabeth asked as she sat at the end of Emma's bed where she lay prostrate, weeping.

"No, Mama," came the muffled reply, but Elizabeth knew better. There were so many things she could say to her daughter now, things her mother would have said to her if she had found her in a similar circumstance, but what was the use? The damage, as they say, was done.

"Are you worried about Phillipe?" She asked this question already knowing the answer. She recalled her own paralyzing fear the morning Darcy went off with her father to that ill-fated duel.

Emma lifted her head, her face puffy and flushed from crying. "Of course, I am, Mama. How can you ask that?" She sat up on the bed, and wiping her eyes, she looked at her mother furtively.

"Is there something else you want to tell me?" Emma's face had the look of a small, trapped animal.

"Whatever do you mean?" She turned from her mother and walked to the window.

"Emma, we have been to Phillipe's room. We know what happened between the two of you last night."

Emma turned to her, her eyes wide with shock and possibly fear. "You and Papa? Oh no." She covered her mouth with her hand. "Papa will kill him. He will. He will cut off his head."

"Do not be ridiculous. Your father will not cut off his head. He does not even know. Poppy made the discovery."

The girl seemed to visibly relax, but then looked at her mother, her eyes narrowing.

"What are you going to do?"

"What can be done? We cannot go back in time and caution the two of you."

"You cannot blame him. It was I who came to him. I could not let him go without telling him that I loved him."

"You did more than that, my dear girl." Elizabeth sighed. "Did you not think of the consequences of your actions, how this one night would shadow your entire life?"

"It will not be a shadow, Mama. He will return and we will find a place in the world where we can be married. You will see. Papa gave his consent."

Elizabeth pondered a moment. She knew that these rules of society had their purpose, but as a young woman, she railed against them as Emma was doing at this moment. Her daughter, however, had taken matters far beyond anything Elizabeth could ever conceive.

"And what if he does not return?" Elizabeth paused for a moment. "And what if your liaison yesterday produces a child?"

"Will Papa put me out of the house and disown me?"

Elizabeth sighed. "You know your father better than that."

She knew her Darcy. He could never disown his children, no matter what foolish thing they did, although she knew it would be a great blow to him. It would cost him his place in parliament and all their places in society. Still, if all were said and done, Darcy would be perfectly content to live on the *island* of Pemberley for the rest of his days and would rejoice in never having to attend another ball or social function.

"You know, you would be shunned by society, you and your child. No more elegant dances and balls, no more dinner parties. If we received you, all that would be forbidden to us too. In fact, to preserve themselves, you may never see your Aunt Jane or cousin Charlie again." As the words came out of her mouth, she instantly regretted them as Emma, once again, dissolved into tears. Uncharitably, she wondered to herself if these tears were for her cousin Charlie and her family at Longbourn, or if it was for the glittering social life of which she was so fond. "Oh, Emma," she said and moved to comfort her daughter.

Instead, Emma turned to face her. "If Phillipe and I go to New York and live, then I doubt we would see anyone ever again anyway." Her tone was decidedly cross, and she ceased her crying immediately. "And if I do carry his child and he does not return, I could live with Poppy on Rampart Street here in New Orleans." She leveled her gaze at her mother in what looked like defiance. Elizabeth had to smile.

"Bold words, Emma, but do you really mean them?" Elizabeth asked.

Emma looked at her mother, her expression softening. "I have to mean them, Mama. I have no other choice."

Chapter 22

As Phillipe was being dragged behind the lines, his hands bound before him, he tried working out what he would do when they began to interrogate him. Perhaps they would not bother and simply shoot him, or, as he had said to Emma in jest, they could cut off his head. He fell to his knees several times as they dragged him behind a horse, but each time quickly he scrambled to his feet. He would not allow himself to be dragged if he could help it.

At last, they brought him to an old barn that the British were using as some sort of meeting point or headquarters. The men there all had epaulets on the shoulders and medals on their chests and clean uniforms, so Phillipe surmised that they must be officers. He was dragged to an underground area that he recognized from his own plantation. The barn was built on stilts, aboveground to prepare for the Mississippi's regular flooding. He was cast into the area under the barn. It was tall enough for a man to stand upright, with a floor made of stone. The sides, too, were stone walls, so it made for a good makeshift prison. It was damp and cold, and he shivered in his wet clothing.

There were other men there; most looked like his pirate friend from the river. He could see that he was in the company of many of Lafitte's men who, like him, were recruited to slip behind enemy lines. There were faces there, as dark and swarthy as his. At least they would all die together.

After about an hour, one of the officers entered with soldiers carrying rifles fixed with bayonets. Roughly, they took a man out who appeared to be chosen indiscriminately. This went on throughout the day. From time to time, Phillipe heard shots being fired. None of the men returned.

When his time came, he got to his feet and straightened his shoulders. If he were to die, he decided, he would do so with dignity as a free man of colour and citizen of the United States. He was marched to another outbuilding he had not noticed before. It looked like an overseer's or gardener's cottage and was set back from the river. The first thing he noticed when he entered was the warmth of a roaring fire. There was a small table in the room, with two chairs set across from each other along the width. A British officer of about forty years of age or older sat in one, and Phillipe was pushed roughly into the other by the two guards. These two soldiers then stood on either side of the door at attention.

"I hear that you are traitor to the British Empire," the officer said sardonically. Phillipe looked down at his uniform.

"There you are wrong, sir," he said in English. "I am a spy." This made the officer roar with laughter. Phillipe felt almost detached from his body, and his senses were keenly aware of everything around him. This officer had the haunted look of a man who had seen much and had shed blood. His hands and face were scarred, and Phillipe guessed that he had fought many campaigns against Napoleon.

"You are not a pirate then, but one of those free men of colour that we have heard of, I expect."

"I am."

Suddenly the jovial demeanor of this officer changed. He lunged across the table at Phillipe, slapping his hands down hard on the surface. Phillipe jerked back, startled.

"How many men does Jackson have?" Phillipe said nothing. He was determined to give this man false information but could not do so right away. That would create suspicion. He would have to take his punishment first. It was amazing how calm one could feel when staring death in the face.

"How many men?" This time swung his arm and backhanded Phillipe across the face. Phillipe tasted blood.

"This could go on and on, *monsieur*. We could even roast you alive like your red men do, if you like." His face was close to Phillipe's now and he had the eyes of a dead man.

Phillipe swallowed. "Even if you beat me and burn me, you will only get the information I choose to give you." He spoke boldly, although he did not feel bold at that moment.

The officer laughed again. "I like this one." He turned to the two officers at the door, who did not move, but stared straight ahead.

He leveled his gaze on Phillipe once again. "You are quite right. In any case, I already know you have more than a thousand men, so there is no need to burn you alive." He peered into Phillipe's face, and it took all of Phillipe's self-control not to react. This man was clever. He did not need to torture him. He would get what he needed by guile and wit.

"I would like to play cards with you, my friend. It would be a good match. You give nothing away. Unfortunately," he resumed his seat, "I am afraid that you will be taken out forthwith and shot." He motioned to the sentries at the door and they moved to take him in hand again.

"Wait, sir, if you please."

"Yes, what is it?" The officer was already studying the papers on his desk. He began writing.

"I do get a last request, do I not?" The officer looked up at him. The sentries had already taken him by the arms.

"I suppose that is customary, if it does not take too long and it is in my power to grant it."

"You are truly a gentleman."

That remark elicited another guffaw from the officer. "No one has ever accused me of that. State your request."

"I would like to write a letter to my intended, telling her—" Phillipe stopped abruptly.

"Yes, yes, all right. You may write it and if it is in my power, I will have it delivered to," he made a vague gesture with his hand, "to wherever it is she lives. After we capture the city."

Phillipe held out his hands, which were still bound, and the officer gestured with his head toward the sentries. They untied him and the officer motioned for him to sit and gave him a paper and handed him the quill. Phillipe began.

My dearest Emma,

    I write to you to tell you that I have been captured by the British and am soon to lose my life. I bear no grudge to my captors, for we all must do our duty for our country. I believe, though, that I have not been fair to you. The dreams I had for us were doomed from the beginning and I had no right to seek your affections.

Phillipe looked up at the officer who was observing him. "You know I will have to read it to make sure it contains no contraband."

Phillipe nodded and continued writing.

If it comes to pass that a child is born, my family in New Orleans, especially my mother, will welcome you, I am sure. Please tell her and my sisters that I love them, and with all my heart, I tell you that I love you, my sweet Emma. I go to my death, thinking only of you.

Yours,

Phillipe

Phillipe handed the letter to the officer without looking him in the face, and summarily it was returned to him. He shook a bit of sand over the ink, and then, shaking it off, folded the letter in three.

"Would you like to seal it? It would be sealed with the emblem of the British Empire."

"As long as it is sealed." He then wrote "Emma Darcy" and "Peschier Plantation" on the outside, handed the letter to the officer, and rose. The officer looked down at the letter, staring at it a long time. His eyebrows went up, and a broad grin crossed his weathered countenance.

Phillipe looked up at the officer. "You do not have to bind my hands. I will go willingly." The officer looked at him with a look Phillipe had not seen before. Was it respect? Sympathy? Amusement?

He turned to his two sentries and gave them an order. "Bring me another one." The two men looked at each other in confusion, but neither of them spoke. They hesitated a moment, and the officer barked at them. "Are you deaf?" The two sentries left in haste. Then the officer turned to Phillipe.

"The fates have smiled upon you today, my boy." He was flipping Phillipe's letter over and over. "Take off that coat," he commanded. Phillipe did as he was told. Turning to the shelving behind him, he threw Phillipe a rough wool blanket. "I do not think you will be needing this missive after all." With that he tore the letter in half and threw it in the fire. He then took out a piece of parchment, wrote a quick missive upon it, folded it, wrote something on the front and sealed it. He handed it to Phillipe. As he took it from the officer, he saw that it was addressed to Emma's father, Fitzwilliam Darcy. Phillipe stood there, his mouth agape.

"You know him, do you not?" The officer was grinning. Phillipe nodded mutely. "Put it somewhere safe and deliver it for me. Now come, quickly."

By this time, the sun was setting, and the officer led Phillipe away from the cottage and pointed to the cypress swamp. "Go in that direction. The river will be watched. Go." He shoved Phillipe.

He ran for all he was worth, back across the field, keeping as low as he could so as not to attract attention. Within a half an hour, he reached the morass of the cypress swamp and, picking his way carefully, managed to secrete himself within. There was no one in sight.

How he had escaped death, and why that officer took pity on him, he did not know. All he knew was that he had to make his way to the American line.

**

Elizabeth held her peace in regard to Emma's rash behavior and did not inform her husband of what had transpired between his daughter and Poppy's son. There would be time enough for that if the consequences of their act came to fruition. Besides, she could see Darcy's agitation grow with each passing day.

As they reached New Year's Day, no word came from Phillipe, or anyone else on the river. The sound of cannon fire could be heard almost constantly, and as they looked to the southeast at night, the flickering light of flames could be seen.

By nightfall, the bombardment stopped, and an uneasy silence enveloped them. Elizabeth found her husband standing at the window of the dining room, looking toward the distant mouth of the river.

When she joined him, gently, she took his arm. He did not look at her, but his gaze remained fixed on the distance. "I remember seeing those flames as we approached Grenville. I did not know if you were alive or dead."

"And I knew that you were dead."

He looked into her face. "And here we are again embroiled in yet another war. We have come a long distance to find ourselves where we started." His tone was wistful.

"No, not where we started, but perhaps..." She did not know quite how to put it. "Perhaps watching history repeat itself."

Darcy sighed. "I truly hope that that is not so. I will do whatever I can to protect you and the children, and Poppy and her daughters."

"I know you will move heaven and earth if need be." She rested her head on his shoulder.

He sighed. "It may not be enough. I believe that my name and my position will protect us from the British forces if they stop long enough to enquire. They could, however, stay well into the river and continue to bombard us assuming that we are Americans."

Elizabeth let go of his arm and turned to look at him. "Do you think that is possible?"

"You know as well as I that anything is possible in war."

She was silent for a moment. "Perhaps the Americans will stop them before they reach the city."

He huffed a bit. "How could they possibly? They must be vastly outnumbered and the men the British government sent here have defeated Napoleon. They are crack troops. How can a small army and a ragtag militia stop the greatest fighting force on earth?"

"Are you hoping for an American defeat?"

He answered immediately. "I am hoping that whatever happens, we will all survive."

***

Even though the distance between the back of the British line and beginning of the American one was only a few miles, it took Phillipe two days to reach them. It was easy to get lost in the swamp, and he found himself turned in the wrong direction more than once. He admired Jackson's strategy of trapping the British between this treacherous quagmire and the river. How they would hold their own against so many well-trained men, though, was a mystery to him. He escaped death once, but would he escape it again? The crashing explosions of the last day had ceased, and it allowed him to listen for the sound of voices and a thousand shovels from the American embankment. By the third day of the year, he emerged from the west to the surprise of the men on the far rampart.

Phillipe had witnessed the beginning of this barrier when he was summarily thrust into his ill-fated spy mission, but now it was a formidable bastion. The western side was not well manned, but from what he learned as spoke with his compatriots, they were hoping for reinforcements. Ordinarily, Phillipe would scoff at such a hope, but from his plan to marry the woman he loved to his continued survival, all he lived upon now was hope. He sought out one of General Jackson's attachés and was told that his message did indeed get through. Not long after, he found a hot meal and some warm clothing, but was far from the battalion of the freemen of colour.

The next day proved to be one of great encouragement to the American side. Barge after barge of rough-looking men from the Kentucky wilderness landed on the shore and took their places on the left flank of the rampart. Guesses were that they numbered nearly two thousand. The men were clad in caps of animal fur that ended in a tail that hung down the back. The clothing was similar to that of the natives Phillipe had seen, soft buckskin shirts and trousers.

Unfortunately, they were not well-armed, but rumors flew that many were sharpshooters and could shoot the wings off a fly at one hundred yards. Perhaps now, they stood a chance against the British forces. All they could do now was wait for the attack.

It came four days later as dawn was breaking. From where Phillipe was crouched behind the earthen work, he saw the infantry marching toward them in the mist—a sea of endless red. Every man, French, Kentuckian, freeman, and slave, held their breath and waited for the command to fire. The British came closer and closer, never breaking rank, never faltering. It reminded Phillipe of one of the machines in his workshop—unthinking, automatic, and relentless.

To his credit, General Jackson stood on the highest mound behind the rampart for all his men to see, tall, gaunt, his steely eyes fixed on the approaching enemy. The British seemed too close, the glint of their fixed bayonets flashing in the rays of the morning sun. When the first rows of oncoming infantry knelt and took aim, Jackson shouted, "Fire."

A volley of shots erupted from the American line and dozens of redcoats went down. Phillipe had no idea if he had killed anyone but did not have time to consider it. The British commander, mounted on a white steed, emerged from the infantry and, raising his sword, led a charge toward the Americans. They were met with volley after volley of gunfire from the American side and the mounted man went down along with dozens of his underlings. The English soldiers who reached the ramparts were hampered by the lack of any means of climbing them, so were shot or bayonetted for their trouble.

The battle raged on, and Phillipe could think of nothing but reloading and shooting. From time to time, he felt for the dagger at his side and would employ it handily if any of the British breached their fortification. He did not know how much time had passed, but the British seemed in disarray. Many of them lay wounded or dead on the field, their comrades stepping over them to join the fray. To his surprise, this low, makeshift, earthen fortress gave the Americans enough high ground to have the advantage over the British.

Time seemed to stand still in his effort to keep this endless onslaught of redcoats from breaching their line. Suddenly, the British were scaling the rampart with a great deal more ease than they had formerly. Phillipe did not have a bayonet on his rifle, but quickly produced his dagger when he felt the sharp pain of a bayonet blade slice his shoulder. Infuriated with bloodlust, he plunged the dagger into the chest of his assailant, who collapsed on top of him. The man breathed his last breath into Phillipe's face, and died in his arms. Phillipe pushed him off quickly and stared at the corpse. He had never killed a man before, at least not with his bare hands, and he felt suddenly sick.

A yowl roused him, and another redcoat lunged at him, but Phillipe rolled to the side and the man stumbled, falling over the rampart onto the American side. At least three knives entered his body, and he lay still. Phillipe retrieved his rifle and began loading it when a loud, deafened sound assailed his ears. He flew backward, and time nearly stood still. Earth and men erupted slowly from the ground and flew in every direction. He his only thought was *cannon*.

Everything then went black.

***

Emma, Poppy, Benji, and Toby were on the veranda the morning a sailboat made its way up the Mississippi. There were men aboard who were whooping and calling out. Before Emma could stop them,

Benji and Toby ran to the dock. Poppy called after them, but they did not heed her. By the time Emma and Poppy reached the dock, they could hear the men shouting.

They were calling out in French, "We won. We won. New Orleans is safe. The British have been defeated." They waved to Poppy and the children and made their way farther up the river to spread the news.

"I am going to tell Papa," Benji said.

"*Moi oci,*" Toby agreed. "*Papa va rentrer a la maison.*"

Poppy took his face in her hand. "That's right, *mon chou*, your papa will soon be coming home."

"And so will Phillipe," Emma said.

"If God wills it," Poppy replied, for they both knew they had received no word as to Phillipe's fate.

Chapter 23

Within a day of the boat bringing the news of the British defeat, a message from Valentine was brought upriver to the Peschier Plantation. It told of the victory of the Americans despite all odds, but Valentine knew not what had befallen Phillipe. The fighting had been fierce, and many were wounded on both sides.

Darcy was holding the letter, and he looked up at Emma, who stood twisting a handkerchief in her hand as her father read.

"Valentine requests that I come to town to help look for Phillipe." He handed the letter to Poppy, who began reading it in earnest. "He thinks I might be of some assistance if Phillipe has been taken prisoner by the British."

"Then he is alive," Emma said, more as a question than a statement.

Poppy, who finished reading, looked up at her. "Valentine don' know. He las' saw Phillipe when dey landed. Not since."

Darcy laid his hand on his daughter's arm. "They took many of the wounded to nearby plantations and to the city. Valentine can only spend part of his day searching. He cannot leave his shop unattended as many of the men who are not still harassing the British downriver have come into town."

"You must go, Papa. He could be wounded, or a prisoner." Emma was nearly in tears, and Elizabeth put her arm around her daughter, never taking her eyes from Darcy.

"I do not want to leave you here unprotected," he said.

"Don' you worry 'bout dat. Almos' all the men back again. De overseer and de foreman here. All de slaves wan' Phillipe back to sign de papers. You go. You go fine my son."

Darcy nodded. "Very well, then. I will leave immediately."

"I am going with you," Emma said.

"You most certainly are not."

"Yes, I am, and you cannot stop me." She looked at him defiantly.

"Emma, your father is right," Elizabeth interjected. "New Orleans now is no place for a young woman."

Emma turned to her mother. "You did not listen to your family when Father was lying wounded."

Darcy looked at his wife in surprise. He did not know how much of their early troubles Elizabeth had intimated to their daughter. More than he expected, to be sure. "But she did not enter a town, flush with victory, filled with every kind of backwoodsman, pirate, soldier, and God knows what sort of—"

"Riffraff," Emma said, finishing his sentence for him.

Darcy knew the set of her mouth and the glint in her eye quite well by now. He would have to take another tack to convince her to stay at home. She was baiting him, but he would not bite. He would try to appeal to her reason. "There are more than a thousand men, all drunk with victory and not a little wine, who would make my mission impossible if you were with me. I would spend my time fighting them off, and we would never find Phillipe. Do you understand?"

Her previously fierce expression softened a bit. She paused for a time to ponder his words. "I am not a child, Papa. I see the logic in what you say." She sat down with a pensive expression. Darcy looked at Elizabeth and she gave him a knowing look. At last, Emma spoke. "At least let me help you pack some medicine and bandages and food for him. May I do that, Papa?"

"I would welcome it." He smiled and extended his hands to her. She took both of them in hers and then stood and hugged her father round the neck.

"I am sorry, Papa. I am so worried and sitting and waiting is driving me mad." He pulled away and nodded. She ran off to make her preparations.

Within hours, Darcy was ready to set off. Little by little, more of the men from the plantation arrived from town, greeted by their wives and children. They brought tales of the British offering them freedom if they would cross the American line and gather round the British flag. Some, no doubt, did just that, but most returned as their freedom was nearly at hand, and as free men they would be entitled to not only the money left by Monsieur Peschier, but also the pay and land promised by Andrew Jackson.

Darcy had to admit that he felt better that the plantation was no longer deserted and bade his wife and daughter good-bye. As he was climbing into the flatboat at the dock, Bennet came running toward him, waving a paper over his head. "Papa, Papa, wait." The oarsman waited as the child reached them. "Here, Papa." Bennet bent over to hand his father the paper. "Give this to Phillipe." When Darcy looked at it, he saw it was a childish drawing of people of various sizes and shapes, all gathered in front of the plantation house. "It is a picture of us, to cheer him up. Give it to him, all right, Papa?"

"Yes, Bennet. As soon as I find him." He motioned to the oarsman who cast them off. Bennet shouted from the dock. "I put Monsieur Peschier in the picture too because he was here with us."

Darcy smiled at his son and waved, watching him as he faded from view in the bend of the river. He did not know what awaited him in town, or if that childish portrait would ever be delivered.

***

Darcy was correct in his assertion that the newly rescued town of New Orleans was no place for a young, highborn, English woman. Every public house was bursting with every manner of man, from those frontiersmen in buckskin to leathery pirates with a gold earring and a cutlass. Being an Englishman of means in a town nearly captured by the English armed forces put him at a disadvantage. He was accused of spying, of being a traitor, and even accosted at sword-point once, but persisted. Spreading about some money and drink did him a world of good in convincing the celebratory Americans that he meant no harm.

He soon found that churches, including the St. Louis Cathedral, were places in which large numbers of the wounded were being held, and went to visit each in turn. On the morning of the second day, he walked into such a place. It housed about fifty wounded men, who were laid out on the floors or benches, being attended by women of colour. As happened in all the other places he visited, a woman came forward who greeted him and asked his business. A small donation to their cause never went amiss, and soon he was walking up and down the aisles and in the vestibule, looking at every man who bore any resemblance to Phillipe. On the far right of the sanctuary he found him. His breath was shallow, and he seemed delirious, a large, filthy bandage covering his leg from the ankle to the knee, another wound around his shoulder. Darcy bent down and shook Phillipe gently.

The young man groaned a little and opened his eyes. He could barely keep them open, but he focused as best he could and croaked out, "Monsieur Darcy?" and then shut his eyes again. Darcy felt his forehead and he was burning with fever. Due to the thoroughness of Emma's preparations, he carried with him water from the plantation.

Holding the young man up, Darcy called out his name again and brought the container to Phillipe's parched lips. He drank thirstily and opened his eyes again. "Are you badly hurt?"

"My leg and my shoulder," he replied, and Darcy lay him down again. He began to undo the bandage on his shoulder and found the wound superficial and healing nicely. The wound on his leg, however, was another matter. There was a large gash that ran the length of Phillipe's leg. Already the edges were septic, and Darcy smelled the telltale stench of gangrene. He then unwrapped the entire leg, and while doing so was accosted by one of the women nursing the wounded.

"What'chu doin', sir?" the matronly woman asked, eyeing him suspiciously.

"It is better for the wound to breathe."

"De flies be all over it if'n you do dat."

"So much the better."

She shook her head. "You know dis boy?"

"Yes. He is a friend of the family."

The woman sighed and looked down upon Phillipe. "De surgeon comin' tomorrow to take off dat leg."

Darcy shook his head. "I do not believe that will be necessary."

"You a doctor, sir?"

"No." He looked up into her kindly face. "Simply one who has been wounded before."

She looked at him and then her mouth curved into a slight smile. "I bring you somet'ing to keep his head cool. Can you stay wid him 'til mornin'?"

Darcy nodded. The woman turned to leave when he asked, "Is there somewhere I can make a cup of tea?"

She looked at him askance. "You not from aroun' here nor Kentucky neither." He shook his head. "De hot water over der. We boilin' everyt'ing. Gonna be cholera wid all dem dead redcoats in dat fiel'."

Yes, the dead redcoats. His countrymen. He could not, however, ruminate the terrible waste of war or that he was among those who consider him an enemy. Now there was work to be done.

Darcy made his way to the large kettle simmering over the fire and made yarrow and elderberry tea for Phillipe to try to break his fever, and some good, English tea for himself. By the time he returned to Phillipe's pallet, there was a washbasin filled with water and a rag set next to him.

Darcy wet the rag and put it on Phillipe's head. After a few minutes, the woman returned to him. "Oh, I almos' forgot. He was carryin' somethin' when they brought him in." She handed him what looked like a letter. Darcy took it and looked it over. It was addressed to him, of all people. The handwriting looked familiar, but it could not be. It could not. Darcy tore the seal.

Darcy,
*   For good or ill, I return your soldier boy to you. Either I now owe you nothing, or perhaps you would like to double my debt.*
*   Your obedient servant,*
*   George Wickham*

By thunder. George Wickham. How he always managed to meet him at the crossroads of his life must be written somewhere in The Book of Fates. And Wickham always had a flare for the dramatic. Phillipe would have to tell him the tale of how he met Wickham when he was recovered. Obviously, his brother-in-law had spared Phillipe's life, and by doing so, changed forever the lives of the Darcys.

***

The surgeon, indeed, did come the following day, but did not seem to be much concerned with Phillipe and did not argue with Darcy when he insisted that the leg was healing. Darcy did not like the look of him in any case. He smelled of brandy and looked with disdain upon Phillipe. It was just as well, for the maggots were doing their work well, and much of the necrotic flesh was disappearing. Marie Laveau's potions also seemed to be having their effect, for Phillipe was conscious more often now, and his fever, though not gone completely, seemed to have abated. Darcy delivered Benji's gift to Philippe as soon as the young man showed signs of improvement. He caught Philippe looking at it more than once with a smile creasing his countenance.

Darcy arranged for a cart to carry Phillipe to the river, so that they might make their way homeward. The journey would be painful, but Darcy felt Phillipe would be better in his own bed. He also had worried women to answer to, and no way of communicating with them.

Darcy had taken to speaking French for the most part, as his stature as an Englishman of high rank and esteem garnered him no garlands in this town. The hatred and disdain for the English was palpable, and Darcy could see no purpose in antagonizing an entire populace. Thus, he and Phillipe slipped out of New Orleans on a flatboat heading upriver.

***

Phillipe was improving day by day due to the ministrations of both his mother and Emma. Elizabeth remembered clearly what a scandal she created in standing by Darcy in his wounded state. Here her daughter attended to Phillipe without so much as a murmur. Of course, they were not in the center of London with wagging tongues about, but isolated on a plantation in America. Emma also had the added benefit of parents to supervise her ministrations.

Darcy not only brought back their wounded warrior, but also news that the British fleet would be withdrawing soon. He shared with her the idea that they could book passage on a ship that, in essence, would be escorted by the retreating British fleet. In such a scenario, they would be much less vulnerable to pirates. She knew Darcy was more than ready to return home. Parliament was already in session and he was anxious to be ensconced in his beloved Pemberley. She shared this desire for home, and she felt now that

Phillipe had returned, he and Poppy would go about the labour of freeing their slaves and selling their property.

She went in search of her friend and, not finding her in any of the public rooms, knocked upon Phillipe's door. She heard Emma's voice within who bade her enter. There she found Poppy. Phillipe was sitting up in bed, holding a cup of what smelled like beef broth.

"He will not let me feed him, Mama." Emma's tone was querulous.

He lowered the cup and looked at Elizabeth. "I am tired of being treated like an invalid. Tomorrow I will stand and walk."

Emma folded her arms and glared at him. "You will do no such thing."

"And you will aid me."

She scowled at him and then turned to her mother. "Tell him that it is too soon."

Elizabeth smiled at their banter. Poppy looked up at her and smiled too. "Emma, may I speak to you a moment?"

"Of course, Mama." She took the cup from Phillipe's hands.

"In private, if you please." Emma excused herself and followed her mother to the second parlour, where her father and Benji were waiting.

"We are leaving in a fortnight." Emma looked from one of them to the other. She shook her head vigorously.

"No, no we cannot. I cannot."

"Your father needs to get back to Parliament, and we will be arriving in the middle of the Season. I thought you would be happy."

She knitted her brows and looked from her mother to her father. "My place is here with Phillipe."

"You will not stay here without benefit of marriage. Once he is well, he can send for you, or better yet, come for you."

Elizabeth expected an explosion of emotion, but instead, Emma took her by the hand and sat on the settee between her parents.

"Mama, Papa, we have already decided what is to be done. We will travel north and be married, perhaps in New York. Phillipe believes he can find employment there as an engineer. And even if he is not employed, he has wealth enough for both of us. The society is freer there and we can build a life for ourselves." She looked from one of them to the other.

"Are you not coming home with us?" Benji asked, running to his sister and throwing his arms around her neck.

"No, Benji, not this time."

Benji's eyes began to fill with tears and Elizabeth offered her hand to him. He took it and wiped his eyes on her shoulder, turning away from Emma.

Her father, who had been silent until now, finally spoke. "I will not allow it."

"Begging your pardon, Father," she never used the term *father* unless she was mightily vexed, "but you have nothing to say in the matter. Phillipe and I have decided."

"And what of his mother?" Elizabeth asked.

"She will buy a small house near the Ursaline convent so that she may be near all her daughters."

Darcy stood and walked to the other side of the room. "What if I told you that if you persist in this course of action, you will not receive any of your inheritance?"

Emma sighed. "Phillipe does not want or need my money. He is wealthy in his own right and has an education. We have the means to make a life together." Emma stood and crossed the room to her father. "Can you not be happy for us, Papa?"

Darcy turned to her, the anger disappearing from his face, leaving only sadness. He did not speak for a moment. "I will not leave you in this godforsaken country."

Emma laughed. "You are not leaving me here, Papa. I am staying."

***

Elizabeth knew from the look on her husband's face that the discussion was not over. Emma left the room to return to her nursing, and Elizabeth sent Benji off to play. They needed time to speak frankly. She knew she had to tell him of the extent of Emma and Phillipe's attachment.

The minute they were alone, Darcy turned to her, his eyes ablaze. "How can you be so calm? We cannot leave Emma here without benefit of marriage in a country that is hostile to her with a man whose social standing will never equal hers. We cannot."

She knew that Phillipe's inferior position in society was galling Darcy. Even after all he had suffered and all he had learned, his pride in his birthright was still very much a part of him. "So, it is the colour of his skin and his illegitimate birth that worries you so." Perhaps this was pouring salt into the wound, but she needed to ascertain exactly what he was thinking. "Be honest with me, my husband. After all, you were honest with me the day you proposed marriage. Honest about my *inferior connections*."

His eyes narrowed. "You will never let me forget those words as long as I live, will you?"

He was angry with her now. She had pushed him too far, and this was not her design, only to elucidate his true feelings. She crossed the few steps between them and took his arm. "It was unfair of me to bring up old history. I am sorry."

His expressions softened somewhat, but he turned from her. "You may be right in your assertion. Perhaps I am not being honest with myself about my own prejudices. I long to tell you what I am sure you do not want to hear." He turned and looked at her again.

Elizabeth took a deep breath. She wanted to know his true feelings on the matter of his daughter and Poppy's son, and yet she was afraid of what she might hear. But if he could not tell her of his true feelings, who then could he tell? "Speak your mind, Darcy. All must be open between us."

He sat down on the edge of the bed and ran his fingers through his hair. "Phillipe looks a great deal like your Edward, does he not?"

A chill ran over Elizabeth's body and her heart began to race. Was this his concern? Not Poppy's part in Phillipe's parentage, but Edward's? She paused for a moment. "He is not *my* Edward, Darcy. He never was *my* Edward." Was this some old jealousy come to rear its ugly head? She could scarcely believe it. Or was it something worse—the belief that the sins of the father are visited upon the generations? He was looking to her for an answer. "He does resemble Edward in his features and even in his manner sometimes, but he cannot be faulted for that. All of us arrive in this life by an accident of birth. We have no say in who our parents are and into what condition we are born."

"Yes, yes, of course I know all of which you speak, and I am not such a dullard that I have escaped learning from my own experience." He was not looking at her as he spoke.

She moved to him and sat on the bed, taking his hand. "What is it then?"

He turned his face from her but held her hand. "It is not how I envisioned our daughter's future."

"Nor is the situation one that I could have imagined in my wildest dreams, but it is one we are now facing."

Darcy stood and began to pace the room. "Philippe is a fine young man by all standards, honest, brave, loyal to his family, responsible, and well-educated."

"And yet he falls short of the ideal you had in mind for your daughter."

Darcy turned to look at her. His mouth was set hard. "You misjudge me again, Miss Bennet."

Was he joking with her, or throwing back in her face what she had thrown at him? It did not matter. "I am not judging you at all, I am merely trying to understand."

"What will become of them with this talk of New York? It is true that they abolished the slave trade in the New England states, but slavery still exists there. Anything could happen to them if they made their home in such a place. And to which society would they belong? I fear they would find themselves an anomaly there as much as here, neither part of the free black society nor of the white. Is no one thinking this through save myself?"

"Phillipe has mentioned to me that if they are not accepted in New York, they could possibly move westward to Philadelphia or even to the frontier." She spoke in a soft and soothing tone, for she knew there would be a strong reaction to her words.

"The frontier? Oh, good lord, Lizzy. Could you see our Emma as a frontierswoman, beating rugs and fighting off the natives?" He began to laugh ruefully. "Every scenario becomes more and more absurd."

A question was nagging her, and it kept popping into her brain. She dared not ask him, and yet she must. "Why, then, did you give him your consent to marry her?"

He did not speak for a moment. Finally, he said, "I gave my consent because I did not want Phillipe to go to war without hope for a future. Such an attitude would have doomed him from the start. I also hoped that, in the interim, we could talk some sense into our daughter, or that she would realize herself the impossibility of the situation."

Elizabeth scrutinized her husband. She wanted to ask him one more question but withheld it momentarily. He searched her face.

"What is it, Lizzy? You do not seem satisfied with my reply."

She closed her eyes and steeled herself. When she opened them, she gazed into her husband's face. "Did it cross your mind that he might never return, therefore solving all our dilemmas?" She thought perhaps he would react in anger, but a great heaviness seemed instead, to descend upon him.

"One cannot help what crosses one's mind." He paused for a moment. "Truly, I wished him no harm, you must believe that. But you have to admit, a few ragtag American troops thrown together to fight the greatest warriors on earth. What chance did they have?" He sighed and looked off into the distance. "These Americans proved more resourceful than we anticipated yet again." He sat down heavily. "I still cannot leave her here. They cannot be married. They cannot live in peace anywhere. It is an impossible situation."

Elizabeth had no more arguments save one. She would have to betray Emma and Phillipe's secret. "I am afraid she must stay."

"Whatever do you mean, she must? Have I not convinced you of the impossibility of such a connection between your daughter and this young man?"

"However sound your arguments, my love, I am afraid it is a *fait accompli.*"

Darcy did not move for a moment, and she could see him contemplating the full import of her words. He stood, his fury barely contained. "I will kill him, the vile seducer." Darcy strode toward the door, Elizabeth catching him before he reached it.

"No, you misunderstand, Darcy. Please, hear me out."

He stopped before the door but would move no farther. "It was she who went to him the night before he left to fight. I know that this is not what is acceptable to you or to me, but they made a pledge to one another. They will be married, whatever the consequences. There is nothing you or I can do now."

The wrath he was so filled with a moment before seemed to drain away from him. He did not speak for a time but stood unmoving. Finally, he turned to her. "I will book passage for Bennet, you, and myself." He left the room and Elizabeth followed him as he went out of the house. She stood on the veranda and watched him walk toward the river.

Chapter 24

Phillipe was hobbling about with a cane by the time the day of departure arrived. Nothing would dissuade Emma from her path, which Darcy was sure would lead straight to disaster. Poppy was happy that her son had finally found a woman who suited him but was as afraid for the two of them as were the Darcys. Phillipe assured them that once the sugar harvest was in, his slaves were manumitted, and the plantation sold, he and Emma would book passage by boat to New York. They would not attempt to cross overland through the wilderness and through the states in the south where there were no free *homme de coloure*, only slaves.

"You will write often to me, promise me," Elizabeth said into Poppy's ubiquitous kerchief as they embraced.

"I will tell you all that dese two get up to." She cocked her head toward Emma and Phillipe. Poppy held her friend to her as if she would never let her go. "You come back again. Firs' New York, den come see me here."

Elizabeth pulled back and quickly wiped the tears from her eyes. She nodded and turned to her daughter and her betrothed. "Take care of her," she said to Phillipe, embracing him. "And you, my girl. I do not know where you get your stubbornness." She embraced her daughter, who held her tight.

Darcy held out his hand to Phillipe, who took it and then covered it with his other hand. Darcy noticed that he was wearing half of a gimmel ring, its signature open hand facing right. Phillipe watched Darcy's eyes go to the ring and then to his daughter's hand. She also wore such a ring, its open hand facing left. When the two rings were joined together on one hand, they formed two hands clasping. It was a popular sign of betrothal on the continent and Darcy recognized it. "They belonged to my parents," Phillipe said, as if he was reading Darcy's thoughts. "Until such time as we can make it official."

Darcy nodded, and then did something remarkable. He kissed Phillipe on one cheek and then the other.

Darcy turned then to his daughter, who threw her arms around his neck. "You do not hate me, Papa, do you?" Elizabeth could see Darcy struggling. She knew he disliked displays of emotion and there was pathos to spare on this day. He pulled from her embrace and kissed Emma on the cheek.

"There is nothing you could ever do to make me hate you, Emma." He patted her on the cheek and then added, "Write often to your mother. You know how she worries."

"I will, Papa."

Benji threw his arms around his sister's legs. "Will you miss me, Emma?" He looked up into her face. "I will miss you very much." Emma bent down and Benji squeezed her tightly. She struggled to speak, her pretty face contorted with tears. "Be a good boy," was all she seemed able to say.

They all walked to the dock and stood there a moment, looking at the flatboat that held their luggage. Poppy walked up to Darcy and took his hands. "Thank you for bringing Miss Lizbet back to me." He kissed her hand wordlessly, and she caught him by surprise by throwing her arms around him in an embrace that he returned. He pulled away finally, and they began to board the boat.

When they were about to cast off, Elizabeth heard a cry coming from the direction of the house. It was Toby, his shirttails flying. "Benji, Benji." He arrived breathlessly on the dock. *"Merci beaucoup, mon ami."* He was waving his hand above his head holding a small wooden toy in his hand. Benji scrambled over his mother and out of the boat. He threw his arms around his friend and they kissed each other on both cheeks.

Elizabeth watched her son jump back in the boat, wipe his eyes quickly on his sleeve, and take his seat. The two boys waved to one another until the dock disappeared from sight. When they could see him no longer, Benji said, "I made him a duck."

***

Darcy was now in the company of the two most unhappy people on earth. He could count himself among them but tried not to give in to melancholy. They settled aboard the small frigate, which afforded them only one cabin for the return voyage. Elizabeth was making an effort at being cheerful, more for Bennet's sake than her own, but he found her more than once quickly wiping tears from her cheeks as she smiled.

Darcy began to regret allowing Emma to remain. He could think of a thousand arguments against their daughter's marriage, not the least of which was the fact that he had no faith whatsoever that they would be accepted in American society, even in New York. The northern states were somewhat better than the southern in that they voted to abolish slavery ten years before. To his mind, this did not mean that they viewed all men as equal. They also had no great love for the English, so Emma's dreams of a life in New York society was only that, a dream. He felt as though he had acted against his better judgment.

There were, surprisingly, other passengers aboard their vessel, and he was thankful for the distraction. He knew that he had a tendency to brood, and after a week at sea, Elizabeth found him in exactly that state standing at the railing.

She wound her arm through his. "It is beautiful here on the sea."

"Yes, I suppose so." He sighed and looked out over the water. She wound her fingers through his and raised the back of his hand to her lips, kissing it.

"She will be all right. She will. You and I have to believe it."

Before he could reply, he felt a thump, and Elizabeth pushed into him slightly. It was Bennet, who ran full tilt against his mother.

"Bennet, do be careful," Darcy scolded. He noticed that the boy was never far from their sight. The separation from his sister, and all at the plantation, had thrown him off his pins.

"I am sorry, Papa. I thought you were lost."

"How can we be lost on this tiny ship?" Darcy then spied the men at the stern engaged in their ubiquitous occupation of mending the sails. He looked down at Benji. "Perhaps the men need some help with their work." He pointed in the direction of the crew.

Benji craned his neck around his mother's skirts to look. "Do you think so?"

"If you like, you may go and ask them." Benji looked up at his father and smiled. Darcy watched as he spoke to one of the swabs and saw the man look up in his direction. Darcy gave a nod, and Benji settled in among the sailors, a needle in his hand.

Elizabeth sighed and watched her son for a time. "He is having a time letting go of his sister."

"It is inevitable that she should marry and leave us. It had to happen sometime. We must not let him brood." Darcy sighed and watched his son. "I suppose none of us should brood." Another family group made their way to the stern to watch, and their son also joined the sailors. He could hear laughter from both the children and the men.

Elizabeth turned to look at her husband. She whispered to him. "Dare we retreat to our cabin for time?"

The suggestion caught him by surprise, and immediately filled him with such desire for her that he was helpless against it. She looked up at him with shining eyes.

"I do so love you, Lizzy." Her eyes radiated tenderness. He took her arm and they passed a now smiling Benji as they entered the hatchway.

***

After the sugar harvest, the Peschier plantation sold quickly. Phillipe made arrangements with the new owners to exhume his father's body and transfer his remains to the St. Louis Cemetery, where Phillipe was having a tomb built. There would be room for all of them if they chose to make it their final resting place.

On the final day in the only real home he had ever known, Emma found him sitting on the dock looking out on the river. His mother was already settled in her house on Chatres Street, near the Ursaline convent.

"There you are." She sat beside him. He put his arm around her shoulder and kissed her on the cheek.

His countenance bore a wistful expression. "It is so quiet now with everyone gone."

"You have regrets then. It is understandable."

He turned to her. "I regret nothing. This place had its time. Now we shall start a new life, no?"

She leaned her head against his shoulder. "Yes," she replied.

He looked off into the river. "And you. Do you miss the life you left behind? All the parties, and balls, the theatre and all the other *divertissment*?"

She sighed and did not answer him quickly. "Perhaps a little. What I do not like is to be whispered about in the street."

"Ah. That is to be expected." He sat upright and looked her in the eye. "You will be pleased to know I have booked passage for us to New York in ten days' time."

She searched his countenance. "You are so good to me."

"Your happiness is my happiness." He kissed her on the forehead. Picking up the walking stick she'd bought for him in town, he leaned heavily against it and rose.

"Come, walk the place with me, one last time."

"With pleasure, *monsieur*." She took his arm and they slowly made their way through the plantation. It had been nearly a year since she first laid eyes on Phillipe Peschier.

***

The Season was well over and Darcy and Elizabeth were firmly ensconced in their life at Pemberley. The mill was operating, and Darcy was gratified that it provided not only extra income for the estate but employed several men from the village. The house felt peculiar without Emma in it, but he knew this was natural. It had been inevitable that the day would come when she would marry and establish a household of her own. Little did he expect that when he held her in his arms on her first day of life that she would be living far away, across the sea.

To her credit, she wrote often, and as the leaves began to turn, they received yet another missive from her. This one was postmarked, not in New Orleans, but New York.

Dear Mama, Papa, and Benji,

Phillipe and I are married. The laws in this region have no restrictions on the race of the bride and groom, so we were married before a magistrate on the 5th of October. I am sure that is a great relief to Father. We have settled in a place called The Bronx, and Phillipe is convinced that he can find a position as an engineer. He claims that the city is growing rapidly, and engineers will be essential to that growth.

I have not found my place in society as yet, but we are newly arrived, and I am sure that will come. I am not sure if the coldness of attitude from the people of our class is due to our "mixed" marriage (what the magistrate called it) or my British citizenship, the newness of our arrival, or the standoffishness that I have been told is a character trait of the people of New England. There is a decided difference between what people will tolerate and what they will welcome. I am prepared to soldier on, for what else can I do?

We left Phillipe's family well and thriving, although the promises of General Jackson to the free men of colour did not materialize after all. No money was paid to those who fought, and no one received any land. The money from Phillipe's father did go to his former slaves, and we know for certain that Joseph—Toby's father—and his family have a house now in a part of the city called Treme. I believe they are doing well.

I think Phillipe's mother is relieved to be living in the town where she can be close to her daughters. We did not see Elizabeth Ann or Adele before we left. They have entered their novitiate and will be closed off to the world for a time.

Give my love to Benji and Aunt Jane and Uncle Charles and Charlie. My greetings to Foster and his family. I miss you all.

With great affection,
Emma Peschier

"She tells us her news but does not sound happy," Elizabeth remarked, as Darcy finished reading the letter aloud.

"They have arrived in a strange place, and it will be an adjustment." Darcy was trying to be optimistic, although he did not know if he believed what he said. His fears that the young couple would not be accepted even in the more liberal north were apparently being realized. He had tried to spare his child this suffering, but began to believe that one does not learn from anything but one's own experience.

"She should come home to Pemberley."

"Her husband will not consent to that. He is a proud man, determined to make his own way." He looked over the top of the letter at his wife. "We both have to understand that she is married now, and no longer under our care and protection."

"I will always be her mother," Elizabeth said defiantly. It made Darcy smile. He crossed the room and took her hand.

"Of course, my dear. That gives you the right to worry and agonize, but nothing more."

Elizabeth sighed. "I must hold my tongue then." Darcy merely smiled at her and waited for her to speak again. "Have you nothing to say?"

He began to laugh. "I have been married to you for twenty years, my love. I also know when to hold my tongue." He was teasing her.

She narrowed her eyes and glared at him. "You are most vexing, sir." He leaned over and kissed her.

"We will be here if she needs us. But we must let them make their own way in the world as we made ours."

***

As winter approached, Darcy sat has his desk, poring over the accounts, looking up from time to time at the ever-growing documents that were accruing prior to the next session of Parliament. By February, they would be in London again. There was a short knock at the door.

"Enter." It was John.

"Mr. Foster to see you, sir."

"Show him in." The butler did not leave, causing Darcy to look up.

"Is madam here, sir?"

Darcy looked confused. "No, she is not. Why is that important?" With that Foster entered.

"What in heaven's name is this about, Foster?" John discreetly closed the door behind him.

"I brought a letter for ye, Squire. Came from New York."

Darcy took the letter in his hands. It was marked for his eyes only and sent to Foster's cottage. Darcy tore it open and read the contents. He then looked up at Foster.

"Not one word of this to Mrs. Darcy." Foster gave him a questioning look, nodded, and Darcy showed him out.

***

It was nearing Christmas, but Elizabeth was not really feeling the joy of the season as she missed her daughter. She put on a brave face for the rest of the household. Jane and Charles were coming with the whole of their family after the new year, the weather permitting. Benji insisted on a Christmas tree. When her husband suggested that he would send one of the servants onto the property to collect one, Benji folded his arms and pouted.

"Now what is the matter?" Darcy asked impatiently.

"We should go and choose it, Papa. That is what Phillipe and I did last year."

Elizabeth was peering out of one of the large windows that overlooked the front garden. It was her favorite spot of late. She could stand there for an hour or more, looking into the winter gloom, fretting over her daughter. Elizabeth found herself there again. "It is snowing, dear heart," she said to Benji, hoping that he would relent.

"That is the best time."

Darcy sighed and shook his head. "Go to nanny and have her get your coat."

"Hoorah, hoorah, hoorah." Benji disappeared into the house.

When he was gone, Elizabeth, never taking her gaze from the soft and falling whiteness, felt her husband standing behind her. "I will go and find some mistletoe as well," he said.

She leaned into him. "I do not believe we will need it, but if you insist." She turned and smiled at him. At that moment, she could not find the words to tell him how much she loved him. It was as if her heart was full to overflowing in small moments like these. He seemed to read her thoughts, or perhaps the expression on her face betrayed her. He took her in his arms and kissed her like a young lover.

She heard discreet clearing of the throat but did not care if the butler was witness to their intimate moment. They were married after all.

"How undignified." The voice was one that Elizabeth recognized but could not make her mind believe. She turned toward the doorway, and there stood Emma in a long, exquisitely tailored woolen coat, her hands buried in a fur muff. Behind her stood a grinning Phillipe, who removed his French-styled broad-brimmed chapeau.

"Emma," Elizabeth cried and ran to her daughter, who embraced her.

Elizabeth, still clinging to her daughter, craned her neck to look at her husband. His eyes betrayed all. She looked back and forth between her daughter and Darcy, finally settling her gaze upon him. "You knew of this."

Emma began to giggle. Darcy, who was smiling widely, raised his eyebrows. "We have been communicating secretly through Foster."

Emma kissed her mother on the cheek. "I wanted so to surprise you. You are surprised, are you not?"

Elizabeth opened her mouth to speak but was at a loss for words.

Benji came running down the stairs and stopped in front of his sister, his eyes wide. "Hullo, Emma." He made no move toward her but became suddenly bashful in her presence.

Emma, however, was not so restrained and hugged him to her. "My how you have grown."

That embrace seemed to break the spell. Benji then ran to Phillipe and extended his hand. "I am so glad you are here, Phillipe. Papa does not want to go out in the cold and get a Christmas tree."

This caused the entire company to laugh. Darcy extended his hand to Phillipe. "Welcome to Pemberley." He then turned to Benji, "Give the man a moment to collect himself before you drag him out into the snow."

When they had all settled in the drawing room and the tea was poured, Elizabeth finally looked her daughter over from head to toe. She settled on the small bump protruding from beneath her gown.

"You are expecting a child." It was a declaration, not a question.

Emma reached over to take her husband's hand. "We are."

"And you have come home." As soon as the words were out of her mouth, Elizabeth noticed that Emma and Philippe gave each other a look that she knew well. Bad news was coming, or at least not the good news for which she had hoped.

"We have come for a visit," Phillipe said finally. "A short one." Elizabeth watched him look from one of them to the other. Her heart fell.

"So, you are returning to New York, then," Darcy said.

"No, Mama, Papa. Paris. We are going to live in Paris," Emma squealed. This was a surprise.

Phillipe explained. "We were not really accepted in New York but were determined to try to make a good life together, even if we had only ourselves for company." He gave Darcy a rueful look. "But—"

"But," Emma interrupted, "Phillipe was offered a position with an engineer he knew from his student days at the *Ecole Polytechnique*. Unfortunately," Emma said, hardly able to contain her glee, "the position is in Paris." She clapped her hands together in delight.

"As I was saying," Phillipe looked over at Emma, "a friend from the *Polytechnique* reminded me of my student days there. I really was a free man in France. There was nowhere I could not go, no one to whom I could not speak, no salon or ballroom where I, and my wife," he glanced toward Emma, "would not be welcome. I do not know why I did not think of it sooner."

"Paris was really not safe before now," Darcy said wisely.

"That is true, *mon pere*."

Elizabeth could not help but smile. She wondered at how her Darcy felt about Phillipe calling him father.

"You will not be a gentleman of leisure, then?" Darcy asked. Elizabeth was well aware of the upper classes looking over their noses at those who were in any way employed.

Before she could formulate another thought, Philippe replied, "It is not my nature to take leisure, any more than it is yours, *monsieur*." There was a twinkle in his eye. "With your duties here at Pemberley, and your work in Parliament, are you really ever at leisure?"

Elizabeth hoped that her husband would not take offence at such a declaration, but her fears were assuaged as Darcy laughed. "I had not considered it before, but I do believe you are correct, *mon fils*."

Emma would not be left out of the conversation. "We will be much closer to you now, Mama. Will you come and help me when the baby's time is due?" She looked down at the small protrusion in her dress.

"Most certainly. There is nothing that could keep me away." As Elizabeth said those words, Benji jumped up and ran from the room. Elizabeth noticed that he had been listening intently.

A few moments later, he returned and put something in Emma's hand. She looked down at it. "It is my duck from Toby. It is my present for the baby."

Emma gazed down at the small wooden toy for a moment, and then looked up at her mother. Elizabeth could see by her expression she was much moved by her brother's gesture. "Oh, Benji, I could not possibly take it. It is too precious a gift."

Benji pushed the duck into Emma's hand. "No, I want you to have it for my new cousin."

Emma smiled. "The baby will not be your cousin, Benji, but your nephew. You will be an uncle."

Benji looked at his sister quizzically. "I will be an uncle, like my Uncle Charles?" Emma nodded. Benji sat up a little straighter and pinched his face into a haughty expression. "I will be an uncle. Uncle Benji." He stopped a moment and looked at his father. "No, I believe the baby must call me Uncle Bennet. It is more proper. I mean, once the baby can talk." He then turned to Phillipe. "Are you ready to find the tree yet? It will be dark soon."

Philippe nodded. "I am ready."

Darcy rose. "I believe I will join you. Foster will get the wagon and we will find a suitable tree."

Emma rose as well. "I will go and fetch Harriet. She and I will begin to cut ribbons for the decorations."

Within moments, Elizabeth stood alone in the drawing room. She could hear Benji's delighted exclamations and crossed the room to observe from the window out of which she had so recently gazed in sorrow. In a few unexpected moments, everything had changed, and she felt herself lit from within.

There in the thin winter light, she could see her Darcy trudging through the snow, deep in conversation with Emma's husband, Benji running ahead only to fall and roll in the snow. Emma's husband. Emma's husband who'd brought her back to them.

She must write to Jane at Netherfield immediately. They must bring her father and her sisters and their families to Pemberley for the new year.

Yes, they all must see this new and astonishing year in together.

Elizabeth left her post by the window and crossed to the secretary at the far end of the room.

There she began her letter to Jane.

ABOUT THE AUTHOR

Maggie has always been a romantic at heart. She has spent most of her life teaching music in public schools. Her travels have taken her all over Europe, and she has lived in Africa and Asia. She refined her writing penning screenplays. *Elizabeth in the New World* was her first novel.

<u>Get in touch with Maggie</u>:
Website: moohabooks.com
Facebook: Maggie Mooha's Book Group
Instagram: @mmooha5817
Twitter : @mmooha
LinkedIn: www.linkedin.com/in/maggie-mooha-120a6624

www.BOROUGHSPUBLISHINGGROUP.com

If you enjoyed this book, please write a review. Our authors appreciate the feedback, and it helps future readers find books they love. We welcome your comments and invite you to send them to info@boroughspublishinggroup.com. Follow us on Facebook, Twitter and Instagram, and be sure to sign up for our newsletter for surprises and new releases from your favorite authors.

Are you an aspiring writer? Check out www.boroughspublishinggroup.com/submit and see if we can help you make your dreams come true.

Made in the USA
San Bernardino, CA
17 January 2020